EMBRACING SKELETONS

Marston Moor – site of the Civil War battle – has been peaceful for centuries. Now violence has visited it again. The body of a child is found – part incinerated, half starved and worse. The detectives of York CID have seen some shocking deaths in their careers, but this murder is different.

For DC Carmen Pharoah, fresh from London and struggling to make her mark, this could offer an opportunity for some proper detective work – as long as she doesn't get sidelined by her boss Leif Vossian. Vossian himself has a personal stake in the case – it brings back an appalling tragedy from his own past. Then there is the police pathologist, Bill Hatch, saddled with a sulky teenage daughter, who remembers hearing about a similar killing in another part of the country years earlier – is it connected?

Disturbing undercurrents underly the investigation almost from the start. An eyewitness offers evidence as to who dumped the body, but other information points to the existence of a more widespread evil than the murder of a single child. A young burglar, a local landowner, the newcomers on a housing estate – all appear to be involved, but in what? Vossian and his team are faced with an almost impossible task, one given an added edge when the suspicion arises that there is a traitor in their midst.

EMBRACING
SKELETONS

Peter Turnbull

HarperCollins*Publishers*

Collins Crime
An imprint of HarperCollins*Publishers*
77–85 Fulham Palace Road, London W6 8JB

First published in Great Britain
in 1996 by Collins Crime

1 3 5 7 9 10 8 6 4 2

© Peter Turnbull 1996

The Author asserts the moral right to be
identified as the author of this work

This novel is a work of fiction. Any resemblance to real
people or events is purely coincidental.

A catalogue record for this book is
available from the British Library

ISBN 0 00 232615 9

Set in Meridien and Bodoni

Photoset by Rowland Phototypesetting Ltd
Bury St Edmunds, Suffolk
Printed in Great Britain by
Caledonian International Book Manufacturing Ltd, Glasgow

The author wishes to thank those professionals who have been involved in the investigation of Generational Sadistic Abuse, those professionals who have counselled and supported survivors of GSA and survivors themselves, without the assistance of whom this book could not have been written.

'. . . he'd been found in a cupboard, his teeth were impacted into his gum, he had head injuries, his eardrums were blown, faeces were dribbling because his anus was ripped. I could only tell him he had good blood pressure, it was the only positive thing I could find about him to feed to him and he left the surgery beaming from ear to ear because he had good blood pressure.'

Medical practitioner after examining
a nine-year-old victim of GSA,
Margate, Kent, 1987.

Five days in May

1

Monday, 3rd May, 14.30–22.00 hours

There are, it is said, ghosts on the moor. Not human forms which cast no shadows but rather sounds with no identifiable source, sounds of men shouting, of horses screaming, of the explosion of musket and cannon. It is also said that it does not do to stand where the White Guard stood as the battle surged about them who met their end by refusing to yield and so obliged the Parliamentarians to slaughter them. To stand where the White Guard stood is to feel a chill even on the warmest of days. Those rumours Richard Baldwin had heard, often, yet he had never heard any sound that he could not easily explain, and he had been visiting the moor near daily for some three years. Nor did he think the area merited the name 'moor'. There are moors in Yorkshire, high, rugged, hostile places, places to be treated with respect by dweller and visitor alike. But here, the gently undulating land, now under crops, would, he felt, even in the seventeenth century, be hard pressed to claim the title of 'moor'. Richard Baldwin had been drawn to the moor because of its historical significance, having become aware late in life of the influence of the English Civil War still had on Britain at the cusp of the millennium. He had read books about the war and had learned that almost no household had escaped unscathed. He had also noticed how the centres of Parliamentarianism roughly corresponded with present-day Labour Party strongholds, and how the centres of the Royalist cause roughly corresponded to present-day centres of Conservatism, but yet he could see no link, no reason why this should be, especially because so far as he understood there had been Agrarian and Industrial Revolutions in the nineteenth century which had changed the demography and the economic base of Great Britain. Richard Baldwin had left secondary modern in the summer that the Stars and Stripes had been planted on the moon, and he had left without qualifications. Now comfortably in his forties, he lived in a terraced house in Scarcroft; small, damp, but his, and he bought a dog from Animal Rescue for company and to provide something for him to care for, and at about the same time that he had bought Susie he realized that he was able to vote for his political leaders because some three hundred years earlier England had been plunged into a bitter Civil War. It had then become a pattern of Richard Baldwin's life that on the days he was on the morning shift he would return home, collect Susie and take her to the moor. She got her exercise and he felt that he was paying homage; touching history.

On Monday, 3rd May, mid-afternoon, Richard Baldwin drove to Marston Moor with Susie sitting excitedly in the rear seat. He parked his three-wheeler by the obelisk commemorating the battle and walked up the trackway between two fields of maize, ground which had at 7.00 p.m. on the 26th July 1644 been the location of the Parliamentarian lines, towards the clump of trees on the skyline which was still known locally as Cromwell's Plump. Richard Baldwin cleared the maize and walked up the slope of rough pasture with Susie ranging across the ground some distance behind him. He enjoyed the view from Cromwell's Plump, particularly looking eastward towards his adoptive city, a low grey mass in a fold of green. If the sun was at the right angle, the Minster, from this vantage point, would glow like a nugget of gold in a pan of silt.

He walked up the hill, striding for Cromwell's Plump and enjoyed the sense of strength he felt in his thighs. He had always appreciated possessing thick, muscular legs, 'a sportsman's legs', a woman had once told him. They were legs, he felt, that with good boots could carry him any distance and his ambition to walk the length of Britain was no idle fancy. Susie ran past him, towards the clump of trees, familiar with the walk, and had quickly learned to associate the small stand of trees with a chew of liquorice which Richard Baldwin always gave her when he joined her there. He watched his dog with pleasure, enjoying her happiness with her.

Then he saw Susie stop. She 'pointed' towards the trees. Richard Baldwin suddenly felt a hollowness in his stomach as he followed Susie's gaze and saw a small mound on the ground. He glanced around him. He and his dog seemed to be the only living things in the area. Even the lane on which he had parked his car was empty of traffic. In the distance he noticed the Minster glowing like a jewel, yet on this day he was unmoved by the vista. On this day he was concerned only with the small mound under the trees towards which Susie was advancing at a crouch. Richard Baldwin began to walk towards the trees.

So far as he could tell it was a male child, naked, badly burned about the legs to the point that the feet were little more than ash, below the feet was an area of charred ground as if the boy had managed to pull himself away from the flames before succumbing to his injuries. Richard Baldwin looked down at the boy, the open mouth, open eyes, the heavy bruising about the neck. About eight years old, he thought. He leaned forward and slipped the leash on to Susie's collar.

'Have to find a phone box.' He tugged the lead gently. 'Have to tell the law, Susie.'

Carmen Pharoah sat at her desk and glanced out of her office window at the Ouse moving sluggishly under Micklegate Bridge. She was alone in the room, which was not old by York standards, nor yet was it new. Red brick, abutting the Law Courts, it was nearing its first centenary, she thought, though she was by no means well versed in the municipal architecture of northern England. She curled her hand around the mug of freshly poured coffee, still too hot to drink, enjoying the warmth against her palm. Carmen Pharoah stood and walked to the filing cabinet, took her key and unlocked it. She pulled the drawer open and ran her slender fingers over the spines of the files and selected the one which she had remembered needed an item of recording adding. She was returning to her desk, carrying the file, when

11

she heard Vossian's thumping footfall in the corridor, bearing down on the DCs' room. She had come to know the footfall well.

'Just you, is there?' Vossian stood squarely in the doorway. Carmen Pharoah didn't reply, but held eye contact. She had rapidly formed the opinion that the man just didn't know how to smile and to date had seen nothing that might disabuse her of that notion.

'You'll have to do then, won't you?' Ice in his eye.

'For what, sir?'

'Body of a little lad has been found.'

'Oh?'

'Oh, indeed. Poor little snapper, he's only about eight, if that.'

'Do you wish me to attend the scene of crime then, sir . . . ?' She laid the file on her desk.

'No. I've got a squad of men doing that; I wish you to take your tail to the home of the man who reported the find. He phoned three nines, gave his details, told us what we'd find and where we'd find it and didn't hang around. But what he said we'd find was what we found and we found it right where he said we'd find it. He's a bloke called Baldwin, 197, Moss Street, Scarcroft. Pay a call, take a statement and then get your tail over to the York District, they're doing the PM there right now. I like the force to be represented at the postmortems. Shows interest, good practice; bring the result back here. Poor little snapper. And put that file away before you go.'

'Yes, sir,' said Carmen Pharoah to an empty doorway, as Vossian's thundering footfall faded in the corridor.

'We do the walk two or three times a week, especially in the summer and autumn.' Richard Baldwin patted Susie, who wagged her tail as she nestled beside him on the settee. 'We do it when I'm on the early turn, have half the afternoon to myself then. It's just me and her really, isn't it, Susie, pet? I don't find it too easy making friends, it's not easy being black in York.'

'So I'm discovering.' Carmen Pharoah found she relaxed

in this man's company. 'Try being black, a woman, and a police officer in this town.'

Baldwin smiled. 'Aye, I can imagine. I come from Leeds. I don't remember, but that's what's on my birth certificate. I'd be better off there, but I'm used to York. I have one or two mates, there's a working man's club close by that doesn't mind a black face, and I work at the railway station, just across the road really.' Baldwin shook his head. 'But York, you see, if you ask me, if you take away whatever it is that brings the tourists, and if you take away the university, you're left with a small town that's too isolated for its own good. That's why it's difficult to be different here.'

Carmen Pharoah nodded. It was, she thought, an astute observation for a man who appeared to her to have had little education, and who, by his house, read little, no books at all in the room in which they sat: a television, an ashtray overflowing with ash, football pools coupons, a copy of a tabloid newspaper and a print of the Queen on the wall above the clock. She opened her pad. 'So what can you tell me about what you found on the moor. Marston Moor, is that the name of the place?'

'Marston Moor. That's right. Well, nothing that I didn't tell the officer when I made the phone call. Susie found the little lad at Cromwell's Plump.'

'Cromwell's Plump?'

'Yes, love, a group of trees on the moor. When we go to the moor we walk up from the monument to the Plump. Susie gets her liquorice at the Plump. She makes for the Plump because she likes her liquorice.'

'Your call was received at 15.15 hours. So it was just prior to that that you found the body?'

'About fifteen minutes.' Baldwin nodded. 'It took a bit of time to walk to my car, then I drove to the next village and I looked for a call box. About fifteen minutes between finding the body and making the call, probably less, but most of that was taken up in walking from the Plump to my car, love.'

'I see.' Carmen Pharoah was becoming used to the strange use of the word 'love' by the people of this county and had once been amused to listen to its liberal use by two muscle-ripping navvies prior to their engaging in a murderous exchange of blows, something she recalled as being along the lines of 'this is what I think of thee, love' – *smack!* It was, she found, the way of it in this cold and windy town and she made no comment whenever she encountered it, although in the early days it had jolted her.

'I didn't run. No hurry. The little lad was dead. I didn't need to be a doctor to see that. Burned where he was left and the ground near him all burned, like. As if he'd pulled himself out of the flames but couldn't save himself. Do you know who he is? Who'd do that to a little lad?'

'No, I don't know.' Carmen Pharoah shook her head. 'But we'll find the answers, I'm still just getting to know my boss but he seems to have the bit between his teeth. He's an angry man, all right.'

'Well, I hope you get the animal what did this. His legs . . .'

'Yes, I heard. I presume that you didn't see anyone acting suspiciously?'

'I didn't see anyone at all, love. I rarely do. There's always the occasional car, always one or two folk stopping at the monument, but few walk over the battle site. A few people lay wreaths at the monument sometimes on the anniversary of the battle, sometimes on Armistice Day, but once you've the road behind you, you're on your own, love, and I didn't see no one, love, just me and Susie there. No, I didn't see no one.'

'Nothing out of place, no unusual activity?'

Richard Baldwin shook his head. 'The only thing out of place was that lad's body. That's the only thing I noticed, anyway. I mean I saw him, turned there and then, took off and phoned three nines from the first call box I came to, love. But I didn't bust a gut. Like I said, the little lad had gone to a better place.'

'How on earth do you know?'

'What could be worse than this? Nothing could be worse than this.'

'I don't know, I spent a day in Manchester once.'

Baldwin giggled.

Carmen Pharoah suppressed her own laughter. 'Have you

ever seen anything of a suspicious nature at all in that area, at any time?'

'Can't say I have, love. Me and Susie, we've been going there for some years now and that little lad has been the first bad news we've come across there.'

'You'll be going back, though?'

'Oh aye, I feel as though I've missed out if me and Susie don't go up the Plump a couple of times each week, when I'm on early turn, that is. When I'm on late turn Susie has to make do with a walk around the block.'

'Well, there'll be police lines there for the next few days. It's a scene of crime, not to be violated.' She closed her notepad.

'Aye, I've seen the like before.' He ruffled his dog's ear.

Carmen Pharoah stood. Tall, a good six feet, thought Richard Baldwin. She was a giant in his small living room. He asked what had brought her to York, saying he could tell by her accent that she wasn't local.

'A train.'

Carmen Pharoah stepped out of Richard Baldwin's living room and into Moss Street. She had never before encountered terraced housing of this type, just a door separating the main living area from the pavement. No small garden between the house and the pavement, no hallway in the house; one foot on the pavement, an open door, the other foot on the living room carpet. The door was closed behind her after a sensitively long pause. A man walking on the far pavement eyed her with hostility. She stood and returned his glare until he turned his eyes away, as if from experience he recognized the stamp of authority of an officer of the City of York Police. She got into the unmarked police car. She drove the short distance through the cramped and ancient city to the York District Hospital and parked in the 'staff only' car park. She placed a 'police' notice on the windscreen so as to prevent the vehicle being clamped. She walked towards the brick-built angular building, entered the main entrance and asked directions of a porter as to the location of the pathology department.

It was a small body, thin to the point of emaciation, very pale skinned, she thought, as if he had never in life been exposed to the sun. He lay face up, the top of the skull had been removed and the brain had been extracted. The arms were risen with rigor. The legs were blackened and charred by thermal injury, the feet totally incinerated. It was not the first postmortem that Carmen Pharoah had attended, not by any means, although she hadn't attended so many that she felt herself able to say, as the old sweats in the force have been heard to say, 'I've attended so many PMs that I think I could do one.' But she had attended sufficient PMs to sense a certain mood, a certain poignancy, a certain anger being present at this PM that she had never experienced before. An ambience of solemnity hung over the room. There seemed to be a coming together in spirit, a communion, between her and the pathologist as he snapped on the surgical gloves, and also with the mortuary attendant, who was clearly deeply moved by the sight of the young boy on the stainless-steel table. Each badly wanted to do something for him, but said little.

The pathologist was a short man, rotund, with stubby fingers, untidy hair below a largely bald head. Unusually for a member of the medical profession, especially a pathologist, he was a smoker. Carmen Pharoah had glimpsed nicotine stains on his fingers before they were plunged into surgical gloves, and even at the respectful distance she stood from him and despite the heavy odour of formaldehyde, she could smell the odour of stale tobacco smoke coming from the man. He had a certain 'working-class' appearance, despite the nature of his employment. He appeared to be the sort of man that might be seen upstairs on buses, engrossed in the evening paper. Carmen Pharoah warmed to him. The mortuary assistant was a small and slightly built man who, despite his distress at this particular PM still had warmth in his eyes which spoke of a personality of good humour and good nature. Carmen Pharoah liked him, also.

'Bill Hatch.' The pathologist smiled at Carmen Pharoah. 'We haven't met.'

'Carmen Pharoah. DC.'

'This is my assistant, John Fry.'

Carmen Pharoah and John Fry nodded to each other.

'So, a male infant.' The pathologist lifted a small silver tape recorder from the pocket of his smock and clipped the microphone to his lapel. 'Testing, testing, one, two, three . . .' He spoke softly. 'Oh, the moon shines down on Charlie Chaplin, his boots are cracking for want of lagging . . .' He played back the recording and then switched to 'record' again and said, 'Right, Juliette, this is for myself, Dr Hatch. The date is the third of May, time is 17.40 hours. The deceased is a child of the male sex, white European by race. Aged possibly six years, but there is a pale and emaciated pallor, which, even allowing for postmortem body changes, may indicate that he could have been eight or nine years at time of death. Rigor is established . . . He was found out of doors?' Bill Hatch glanced at Carmen Pharoah.

'Yes. And in an exposed position.'

'I see. Found out of doors and in an exposed position. I would estimate that death occurred between twenty-four and forty-eight hours ago. I note thermal injury to the legs, and the feet are incinerated, the skeletal integrity of the feet has disappeared. There is bruising to the neck on a massive scale, the eyes and mouth are open. The brain has been extracted for tests, but I'm confident that it will show signs of oxygen starvation.' He turned to Carmen Pharoah. 'I'm naturally reluctant to commit myself but I have every confidence that my findings will be that death was caused by strangulation.'

'Murder?'

'Oh, most definitely.' Hatch ran his hands over the left forearm of the deceased. 'Fracture,' he said, 'old, not set properly. This little boy has many cuts and scratches about him, but he also has a look of neglect. I'll arrange a full skeletal X-ray. There may be other old fractures.'

'We'll probably know him then.'

'You will?'

'I should think so, or the Social Services will. Neglected, fractures, he'll likely be on the city's Child Protection Register. He'll be easily traced if that's the case.'

'Only if he's from York. I did a PM once on a murdered woman whose body was found on our patch. Turned out her boyfriend had driven her from Bristol to dump the body.'

'Point taken.'

'Aye, reason I remember that is that it turned out he didn't bundle her body into the boot. He put her in the passenger seat, propped her up next to him, all the way from Bristol to York. Had to stop for petrol so he put a pillow under her head and it looked like she was asleep. Got away with it – the drive, that is. He's doing time right now.' Hatch leaned forward, as if noticing something. He peered into the mouth of the dead boy and, drawing back with a deeply furrowing forehead to a scalpel, he placed it gently inside the mouth. Carmen Pharoah watched as he slowly gave it a half turn and then withdrew it. He put the blade of the scalpel to his nose and sniffed. 'Smell's gone,' he said, 'as you would expect it to have done by now, but . . .' He inclined the blade towards Carmen. 'What do you make of that?'

Carmen Pharoah stepped forward. She noted a brown substance smeared on the blade of the scalpel. She caught her breath and looked up at Bill Hatch. She shook her head. 'Can't be . . .'

'It is.' Bill Hatch placed the scalpel in a tray of disinfectant. 'It's excrement.'

There was a silence in the room.

'An old fracture,' said Hatch, 'not properly set, strangulation, postmortem incineration . . .' Hatch rested his fleshy hands on the side of the dissecting table. 'Alarm bells . . .'

'I'm sorry?'

'Alarm bells,' he repeated. 'I don't know. I'm coming up to retirement. I've been cutting up bodies almost all of my working life and I tell you they talk to you, they really do, and this one is talking to me. Aren't you, young man? You know you are setting the alarm bells ringing, don't you, son? You know I'm frightened to do this because I know what I'm going to find, but . . .' Bill Hatch lifted the corpse reverentially and gently rotated it through its axis and laid it stomach down. Then he prised the legs apart. They cracked as he did so. 'That's rigor breaking,' he said.

18

Carmen Pharoah didn't hear him for the sound of herself catching her breath. Bill Hatch shook his head. 'I just knew it. I find visual evidence of anal rape, badly distended anus, torn flesh, blood on inner thighs.' He glanced at Carmen Pharoah. 'I can't help feeling that death must have come as a blessed relief for him.' Hatch once again rotated the corpse and laid it on its back and once again did so with a gentleness and reverence which impressed Pharoah. He took a second scalpel. 'Stomach is distended due to build up of gases. You may like to take a deep breath.' He drew the scalpel across the stomach. As the flesh parted the gases escaped with a sharp hiss. Hatch pulled his head back to avoid the smell. Then, leaned forwards ... 'Oh ...'

'Dr ... ?' Carmen Pharoah sensed Bill Hatch's distress.

'In all my years ...' Hatch shook his head ... 'I dare not believe this ... I've never seen anything like this ... but here it is ...' He placed the scalpel inside the stomach cavity and turned it gently just as he had done when he placed the scalpel inside the boy's mouth. He retracted it. It had a smear of what appeared to be excrement on the blade. Hatch wiped the blade and once again inserted the instrument into the stomach cavity, he withdrew it with a portion of beetle on the tip. The silence in the postmortem theatre was heavy as he laid the insect part beside the excrement. He dipped again and brought out a length of common earthworm. He laid the scalpel down. 'I can't go on,' he said. 'It's of little use, anyway, I can see it all from here. This lad's stomach is like a compost heap. No actual food can be identified. People will eat anything if they're hungry enough, even their own faeces, and it won't poison them.'

'It won't?'

Hatch shook his head. 'Not if it's done immediately before any bacteria can infest it. The same with urine; in fact, people who practise eastern religions often drink their own urine, not harmful at all if done immediately on discharge. Like I said, excrement and urine are not in themselves harmful, it's the bacteria they attract that poisons people. And insects are a good source of protein. Insects have kept people alive and kept them from being driven to eating their own faeces.

But this lad isn't emaciated enough to be driven to eating insects, let alone his own or anyone else's excrement. My guess is that he was starved of food for some twenty-four hours before he died, at the very least, and forced to ingest insects and excrement. He was then strangled, but not before he was raped. The dried blood on the inner thighs indicates gross sexual abuse at about the time of death. But the distended anus also indicates he was exposed to the long-term practice of this. There are numerous cuts and bruises of varying ages. I particularly note linear cuts, to the side of the head, to his groin, and also to his eyelids. Six in all, each about two inches long. Clearly deliberate and appear to have been carefully placed, as if with a ritualistic quality, and made so as to leave deliberate scarring. I think those cuts are quite old, months if not years.' He shook his head. 'In all my days . . . What has happened to this child?'

Carmen Pharoah could only shake her head and as she did so she noticed tears beginning in the eyes of the mortuary attendant.

'Well, whatever,' Hatch continued. 'There's more to this than a distraught single parent who's come to the end of her tether . . . the perpetrator, or perpetrators were male. I'll do a rectal swab. I'll be able to obtain traces of the semen deposits, semen is hardy stuff, it doesn't deteriorate easily, but I'm not at all confident that we can isolate the DNA signature, two or more perpetrators will have caused cross-contamination of the individual signatures. But I'll do it anyway.' Carmen Pharoah nodded. 'We'd appreciate it. If you don't mind, I'll leave now. I've really seen enough.'

'I quite understand.' Hatch smiled. 'Confess it's enough for me and Mr Fry, too. But we'll press on regardless. I'll have my report typed up and faxed to you a.s.a.p. I'll send it for the attention of DI Vossian as normal, shall I?'

'If you'd be so good.'

'Dare say you'll give him a preliminary verbal.'

'Dare say I will. Dare say he'll expect it.'

Carmen Pharoah walked away from York District Hospital. It was a warm evening in early May, a harbinger perhaps of a long, hot summer. A high blue sky. A wisp of cloud. But all she could do was shiver.

Bill Hatch listened to the recording he had made during the postmortem and then dictated a more detailed report which he delivered to Juliette. He returned to his study to await the transcription which would require his signature. He sat with his feet on his desk and glanced out of the window, out over Wiggington Road to the houses beyond. He felt agitated, deeply troubled. It was not simply that the postmortem had been the unfolding of a dreadful tale, rather it was more that he sensed an even more dreadful tale about to begin. The postmortem wasn't the end: it was the beginning. It was too early to panic, but a grim possibility had begun to gnaw at his mind. He returned his gaze to his study, the shelves, the books, the photographs of his family when they had enjoyed happier times and which stood alongside photographs of Wilfred and Wilfreda, then back to the papers on his desk. They would appear a discarded mass to an observer, but he knew where each was, and to which each pertained. It was the way his mind worked and had always worked, to the despair of his parents, especially an obsessively neat father, his teachers, spouse and colleagues. But he could not change, nor did he particularly want to change, and drew comfort and reassurance from the observation that a tidy desk is the sign of a sick mind. He glanced out of the window again to follow a green and cream Yorkshire Rider single-decker bus as it travelled smoothly down Wiggington Road towards the city centre. He was pleased that York had not reached for the sky as other towns and cities had, and had kept all the buildings down to the human scale. The Minster dominated the skyline as he felt it ought to. He left his chair and switched on the electric kettle, on the floor, under the window, where he kept it, together with the tray of coffee, milk and spare mugs. He made a mug of coffee, and had drunk only a third when there came a light and reverential tap on his door. 'Come in!' he called in a friendly manner, and smiled as a bespectacled young woman entered and handed him two sheets of paper.

21

'Upset you, Juliette?' Hatch took the report from Juliette's slender fingers.

'Did a bit, Dr Hatch.'

Hatch nodded. 'Did a lot, you mean. It upset me too, I confess. It wasn't the easiest PM I have conducted and it's one of the ones I'll remember.'

'So young.'

'No more than ten, probably some years younger, maybe just six or seven. I found the ageing difficult. I'll take a tooth tomorrow and cut it in a cross section, that'll give the lad's age, plus or minus a year.' Hatch indicated for her to take a seat while he read over the report. 'But this afternoon all we were seeking was the cause of death and indications as to identity.' He read the report and then fumbled for a pen and signed it.

'I'm glad you got some semen traces.' Juliette stood and took the report from Hatch.

'Couldn't really fail, he was full of the stuff. From a lot more than just one man, but it may be too mixed up to obtain genetic fingerprints. That'll be up to the boys who occupy the next box in the procedural system. But I'll send them off nonetheless. If you could fax that report to DI Vossian at Friargate Police Station.' He paused, then asked, 'How old are you, Juliette?'

'I'm sorry?' She was startled by the question but answered. 'Eighteen. Nineteen next month.'

Hatch nodded. 'I don't know how long you plan to stay in this job, Juliette, but I think that's about the most disturbing report you'll have to type, they don't really get worse than that, it's a bit like getting the worst over with, but if it's too much for you, I could easily arrange a transfer within the hospital.'

'No.' Juliette Lovesey shook her head with determination. 'No, it's not too much. You know I felt I wanted to do it, wanted to be careful not to make a mistake. I wanted to do that for him, whoever he was.'

Hatch smiled. 'Good for you, good for you. I'm pleased to have you with me.' He stood. 'Well, that's me for the day

. . . good gracious, I hadn't noticed the time . . . you've
worked late to type this.'

'I wanted to.'

'Again, thank you. Could you fax it before you go? I live
out towards Hambleton. Can I give you a lift?'

'Thanks, but I'll catch a bus. I live on the Trafford Estate.'

Bill Hatch left York on the Fulford Road. He followed it to
Selby, crawled in the traffic under Selby Abbey and drove
out of Selby towards Hambleton. He turned off the main
road just before reaching the village, and turned his Land
Rover into the drive which led to his smallholding some
thirty minutes after leaving York District Hospital, and parked
beside a blue Citroën 2CV. Both the Land Rover and the
smallholding had been his beloved possessions for over
twenty-five years. The Land Rover was a Series I, short wheel
base, rag top and was already very second-hand when he
had purchased it for the equivalent of two weeks' salary. But
it had just kept going and had always been green, except for
a brief period when Veronica, then aged about ten, had found
a can of red paint and another can of yellow paint, and
had thought, 'What a good idea if . . .' But ordinary Dulux
gloss-interior house paint had not stood the test of time on
a Land Rover used daily in all weathers, and the original
green had resurfaced. Eventually. The property had been
bought as a working smallholding, but Hatch had turned it
into a comfortable if modest bungalow, surrounded by a
generous garden, while letting a greater part of the land lie
fallow. The fallow didn't bother him; Bill Hatch often
reflected that the plans he had for the rest of the 'garden'
were what had kept him going over the years. He entered
the house, opening the front door, which had been 'rescued'
from a Victorian house that was being demolished and which
he had had to have hung on a specially built frame. Inside,
he picked up the mail on the table in the hall as Sam bounded
up to him. He knelt and patted the Labrador warmly.

He walked from the hall into the living room where his
daughter reclined on the settee. ' 'lo, Dad,' she said, without
taking her eyes out of *Cosmopolitan*.

'Veronica,' Hatch mumbled as he scanned the gas bill, 'I thought you were back home to study?' He walked through the lounge towards the kitchen.

'Am,' she sighed.

Bill Hatch pinned the gas bill to a cupboard door in the kitchen with a blob of Blu-Tack and walked back through the lounge and out of the French windows and stood on the patio. He was a man with grey hair and stabs of rheumatism, and he knew better than to argue with a nineteen-year-old, who, like all nineteen-year-olds, knew everything there was to know about absolutely anything. He stepped off the patio and on to the lawn, with Sam sniffing and wagging behind him, and walked to a dry stone wall which he himself had built and which enclosed an orchard of eating-apple trees of about half an acre. He picked up a bucket of swill and emptied it into a trough. Two Gloucester Old Spots came running out of the orchard and snuffled into the trough. He leaned over the wall and patted them. He enjoyed their good fortune: a clean sty, a half-acre of orchard to forage in, endless clean drinking water. He had bought them to raise and fatten for slaughter, but had learned that pigs are intelligent, clean beasts and can be bonded with as much as a dog can be bonded with. So, though over time he had sold their litters, Wilfred and Wilfreda had become part of the family, and at their end would be placed in deep graves, despite the reputed succulence of their meat.

Leif Vossian read the report which had been faxed from the pathology department of York District Hospital. It contained all the details that Carmen Pharoah had relayed to him in her verbal feedback. He looked across his desk at Ken Menninot, a well-built man in his mid-forties. 'Clean, you say?'

'As a new pin, boss.' Menninot raised his thick, black eyebrows. 'A little charred vegetation where the accelerant, I presume petrol, had spilled and burned. But, honestly, if an angel had flown down and laid the little lad there and torched him, it couldn't have been cleaner. It's been a little damp over the last few days, the dirt tracks are soft but the area

24

around Cromwell's Plump is thickly grassed. A lightly stepping person wouldn't leave footprints.'

'I see. Have you seen the report from Bill Hatch?'

'No. I know the contents. Carmen Pharoah told me. She was a bit shaken.'

'I can see why. What do you think of her?'

'Early days yet, boss, but I think she'll shape up.'

'I think you're right. She'll have some adjustments to make. But this is one serious murder, Ken.' He shook his head. 'I mean, I thought I'd seen it all before. Can you contact Missing Persons?'

'Carmen's already done that. No child of that age has been reported missing.'

'Just locally, though?'

'No, she asked for a national sweep.'

Vossian nodded. He was a man of chiselled features, lined with age and worry, golden hair swept back and curling up at his jacket collar, the hard blue eyes of a seasoned cop. 'Maybe she will shape up after all.'

'And she's faxed all the details to CATCHEM.'

'She has?'

'She has.'

'She's got the makings, then?'

'Well, she's hardly without experience, boss.'

'Aye. All right then. Can you prepare a press release, keep the details of the injuries down to strangulation, sexual assault and partial incineration.'

'Very good, boss.' Menninot stood and left Vossian's office.

'Oh, Ken?'

'Yes, boss?' Menninot turned on his heels.

'Thanks for staying on; I know you have a fair drive to Beverley and I know you were due to finish at two.'

Bill and Veronica Hatch sat in silence as the clock in the hall chimed eight.

'Not bad, really. I mean considering.' Veronica placed her fork centrally on her plate and Hatch reflected that if Nadine had done anything to their daughter it was to drum table manners into her head. Good manners, especially table manners, was something which had been held in high esteem by Nadine's family, each generation having impressed their importance on the successive generation. The valuing of good manners was believed to have come from Nadine's grand-mother who had entered service as an under-maid aged thir-teen and had clearly been influenced by the ways of her employers. Hatch nodded his thanks, knowing his daughter, he knew that she was offering high praise.

'Don't you eat anything other than casseroles?' She began to collect the used plates and dishes.

'Fish and chips from the chippie, grilled chop and a can of curry-flavoured beans, that sort of thing, quite sufficient to keep body and soul together,' he replied matter-of-factly, quite surprised by Veronica's question. Not because of the question itself but because she seemed to him now to speak only when spoken to. This was not because of any childhood conditioning, but rather he thought it was the mark of a young woman who had come to find her parents dull and no longer needed on the voyage: to be consigned to the hold, if not jettisoned completely. 'It's what is known as survival cooking and I survive well. Why, do you do any better?' But Veronica was already gliding towards the kitchen, dis-interested in conversation. Hatch stood, turned out of his chair and walked into the hallway. The resonance of the chimes was dying but still just perceptible as he picked up the phone, consulted his address book and then dialled a Leicestershire number. 'Hello . . . Bill Hatch here . . . that's right, fellow in the bar with the concertina . . . Yes, thank you, I am. Are you well? . . . Good . . . er, look, I'm sorry to phone you at home but something's troubling me and I'm sufficiently irritated by it that it just won't wait until the morning . . . thanks, I appreciate it. Tom, you recall that when we met at the conference in Aberdeen . . . whenever it was? Well, I certainly remember the weather. February, wasn't it? We had a chat over coffee and you spoke about a PM you had conducted on a grossly sexually abused girl of about ten years of age? That's it, found in a field . . . You mentioned that she had strange cuts to the hairline, eyelids and groin . . . Can I ask if the police ever found the reason

26

for those cuts? I see. What about her identity? No news there, either . . . ? It's just that I was obliged to perform a similar PM this afternoon . . . No, a male child, but the injuries were similar to the injuries you had encountered, gross sexual abuse, gross neglect, you name it, and he had the same sort of cuts you mentioned that you found on the girl . . . Yes, it does, it does take something from you. Well, thanks, hope I haven't depressed you. I'll let the police up here know about the girl in Leicestershire. There might be a connection, despite the time gap of eight years, is it . . . ten? I see. Ten years. Well, thank you again, Tom. Doubtless we'll bump into each other . . . Oh, certainly, anything I find out, anything and everything. 'Bye.'

Carmen Pharoah finished her shift at ten p.m. She walked home aggressively and let herself into her house and urgently, frantically, tore off her clothing as she strode towards the shower. She sank in the cubicle and crouched in the hot water and steam weeping for the young boy whose body she had seen lying on a metal table. She involuntarily pictured him not in death but in life, and not merely in life but his last hour of life, moments of pain and terror and a feeling of utter helplessness . . . the despair . . . things that no child should experience at all, yet all must have been compressed into his last hour of existence and he must have been feeling them as a pair of hands began to compress his throat. She pushed her head fully under the jet of water in a vain and desperate attempt to cleanse the image from her mind.

Bill Hatch turned his Land Rover into the gravel car park at the rear of the Altered Case in Selby. No one knew the origin of the name of the pub, but the ancient sign – now swinging gently in the evening wind – over the door showed a man in a nightshirt, quill in hand, studying a parchment by candlelight. Bill Hatch entered the Case and turned into the public bar. He nodded to a group of people who sat around the room, many nodded to him. Guitars occupied as many seats as did people. Sheet music was strewn over the table tops, together with loose leaf folders containing lyrics. He bought a pint at the bar and sat next to the door and lit a Players. He had arrived late, and as the remainder of the evening progressed a man with a lean face who kept a list of names on the table in front of him between his beer glasses said, 'Right, Bill? Right, big 'and for Bill 'atch.' Bill Hatch stood under the low oak beams and the nicotine-stained ceiling and squeezed two chords from his concertina. He said, 'Two sea shanties,' which he then duly sang, earning a ripple of applause. But he had performed better. He was 'off'. That night his mind was elsewhere.

2

Mirrium Devers sat back in a cushioned, but metal-and-wood, upright chair. She held a mug of coffee. Adjacent to her sat Derek Wyatt, a man of trim beard, clean spectacles, fastidiously tidy desk and posters of birds and of Kirkstall Abbey on his office wall. He drank coffee from a mug embossed with 'Social Work Today' in red on a black background. A neat pile of back issues of *Community Care* occupied an occasional table which stood against the wall beside the door to his office.

'I really don't know.' Devers pondered Wyatt's question. 'It's not like the staff at Trafford Park to overreact. In fact, I've always found them to be on the ball, this time they were spot on. It's bad news.'

Wyatt nodded. 'That's fair comment. Who was it that phoned you?'

'Mrs Goodenough, the head teacher.'

'I've sat in conferences with her before now, she's good, a bit prickly but she lives up to her name, professionally speaking.'

'Phoned me and I passed it to the police because it was sexual abuse that was suspected; I spoke to the Domestic Violence and Child Protection Unit. They did their checks, nothing known; we did ours, a little track, struggling single parent, but never any bad news re the kids. We had a strategy meeting, Tom sat in for you. The upshot is that myself and an officer from the Domestic Violence and Child Protection Unit did a joint visit, later that day, in fact. She's part of the Pyrrah family, incidentally. In care when younger.'

'So tell me about it.'

*　　　*　　　*

29

Claire Shapiro drummed her fingers on her desk and reached for the thin file in her in-tray. She pondered the low ceiling of the claustrophobic interior of Friargate Police Station, and here on the ground floor it was especially claustrophobic, so she thought, and she especially felt the cramped nature of her office following the reorganization of accommodation which involved much carrying of desks and filing cabinets about the building, and as part of which she and the other 'kiddie cops' had been allocated the smallest and dingiest of rooms. A window high in the wall allowed natural light into the room, but afforded no view save for the red bricks in the building across the narrow street from her office, the window ledges of which building were adorned with stone cats which she noted were a feature of the buildings in this part of the town. She glanced to her side at the Police Mutual calendar which hung on the wall, and then, in a moment of sudden determination, clutched the file and left the kiddie cops den and entered the bustle of the enquiry desk area of the police station. She opened a 'staff only' door and scuffed the soles of her feet against each stone step as she took the stairs to the CID corridor on the second floor, where she knew with some envy that the officers had rooms with a view over the Ouse between Bishopgate and Micklegate – those officers, that is, with accommodation at the rear of the building. Those officers with accommodation at the front could look down into Clifford Street, or across to Clifford's Tower where many, many Jews had been slaughtered in one dreadful incident four hundred years earlier. Claire Shapiro walked along the parquet floor of the narrow corridor to the office of Leif Vossian and tapped on the open door.

Vossian, sitting at his desk, paused and then turned towards the doorway of his office and eyed Shapiro with a steely gaze. He saw a young woman, blonde, in a cream suit with an ID badge pinned to her lapel. 'Yes?' he said.

'DC Shapiro, sir, from the Domestic Violence and Child Protection Unit, downstairs.'

'Ah yes, I've seen you in the building, of course, didn't know what department you were in.'

'Can I have a word, please?'

Vossian indicated the vacant chair in front of his desk. Shapiro strode into Vossian's office and sat as invited in the vacant chair and watched an open-topped double-decker tourist bus, with few passengers, move slowly across Micklegate Bridge. She turned to Vossian and noticed his eyes for the first time, she saw how cold they were, grey-blue, she saw the lines chiselled deep into his already chiselled features. At a distance Vossian would appear to be a young man, close up she realized that he looked older than his actual mid-forties. She had heard about 'Leif's tragedy' but didn't know what it had been, but here she suddenly found herself in the presence of a tortured soul. 'It's about the little boy found on the moor,' she said.

Vossian made no reply, but eyed Shapiro steadily.

'Well.' Shapiro felt nervous. 'I don't know if there is anything in it, but this' – she patted the file she had brought with her – 'this is the beginning of a possible sex-abuse investigation. I understand that the boy whose body was found on the moor had been sexually abused?'

'Chronically.' Vossian grimaced and raised his eyebrows. 'News travels fast in this nick. Confess other things never move as fast as I want them to move, but there's no stopping gossip. So what connection do you see?'

'None as yet, but I felt that you ought to know, at least ought to be aware of this investigation, in case there is a link.'

'Fair enough.' Vossian settled back in his chair. 'Tell me about it.'

'Well, it's early days yet, sir.' Shapiro opened the file to remind herself of the facts. 'Essentially, it concerns a family who live on the Trafford, a single mother and three children. Family by the name of Hampshire, not known to us but known to Social Services, but no real bad news about the kids. The mother, Mandy Hampshire, is a Pyrrah.'

'Oh no.' Vossian's hand went up to his forehead. 'Not the Pyrrahs.'

''Fraid so. She married when young, marriage didn't last, he left her with three children. She kept her married name but continued to live on the Trafford, and effectively never

31

left home, her parents, her brothers and sisters, her nieces and nephews all living within a few hundred yards of each other.'

'And that one family is responsible for at least half the petty crime on that estate . . .'

'Well, that's her background . . . but this is quite different, if there's anything in it, that is. What happened is that the school referred the family to the Social Services because of concerns and the Social Services referred it to us because the concerns indicated sexual abuse. The eight-year-old, Sadie Hampshire, had been observed to exhibit sexualized behaviour and have age-inappropriate knowledge.'

'DC Shapiro, I do so detect social workers' jargon.'

'She was observed inducing eight-year-old boys in her class to attempt to insert their penis in her vagina and to hold the boys to her saying, "This is how it's done." '

'I see.'

'We had a strategy meeting at the Social Services Department – myself, social workers and staff from the school, and the upshot was that a joint visit was made to the Hampshire household late last week.'

'Go on.'

'We spoke to Mrs Hampshire – myself and a social worker called Mirrium Devers. Single mother, like I said, father of the children is in Full Sutton doing seven years for armed robbery. That is significant; even though they are separated, the fact that the father has had no contact with the children for four years becomes significant. Anyway, we chatted to Mrs Hampshire, she's a frail, timid-looking soul and we asked her if she could explain her daughter's behaviour.'

'She couldn't, of course?'

'No, and so we obtained her permission to have her daughter medically examined.'

'And?'

'Chronic penile penetration of the vagina and anus.'

'Oh . . .'

'So of course we had a look at the other children, aged three and six.'

'Not the same?'

32

'I'm afraid so. The three-year-old is a boy, but otherwise the same. The boy Shane has a distended and scarred anus. All show signs of chronic sexual abuse extending over several years.'

'Hence the significance of the natural father being in the slammer for the last four years.'

'Yes. Mrs Hampshire conceived her son just days before the father was arrested. They decided to separate while he was inside.'

'So we are looking for another perpetrator?'

'That's it.'

'Where are the children now?'

'In foster care under Emergency Protection Orders. We'll have to apply for Interim Care Orders soon. So someone was coming to the house, or the children were visiting someone. We clearly have to know who that person is.'

'Or are.'

'Are?'

'The lad on Marston Moor, he had been multiply raped. Far too much semen for one man.'

'Jesus.'

'So you'll be returning to the mother, Mrs Hampshire, no doubt?'

'Yes, myself and DC de Larrabeitta, and speaking to the children, of course, but information of this nature has to be allowed to seep out. But that's why I came to see you, it may be coincidence, but it may not.'

'Thank you.' Vossian smiled briefly. 'I'm pleased you did.'

Shapiro stood. 'And still no one has reported a missing child?'

'Not yet . . . there's still time . . . but in my waters . . .'

'But surely someone, somewhere . . .'

'You'd think so, wouldn't you?' Vossian glanced sideways at the Ouse sliding silently below his office window, and above, to a high blue cloudless sky of early May. 'But it occurred to me last night that over the years, once in a while, once every three or four years, we have received bulletins from other forces, just like the bulletin we'll be putting out about the lad whose body was found on the moor . . . you

33

know, a child's body has been found, no child has been reported missing. Sometimes attempts have been made to dispose of the body. The posters go up on the internal notice boards and in the public area, they stay up until they get replaced by something else. Then they get consigned to the bin, but the fact remains that a child's body has been discovered and no one knows who he or she was, and that seems to happen every few years.'

'I've seen the bulletins.' Shapiro allowed her eyes to gaze over the vista provided by Vossian's office, square angular concrete buildings doing their best to blend with the medieval. 'You wonder about their history, but, as you say, sir, then the posters get taken down and other pressing matters clamour for attention.'

Vossian swept his hand through his golden hair. 'It seems to me that there's two things to ponder regarding those bulletins. The first is that they are bulletins in respect of children whose remains have been found. The question that begs, it often seems to me, is how many children's remains are not found, ever.'

Claire Shapiro caught her breath. 'That hadn't occurred to me.'

'Confess it came to me in a flash, but it did so late in the day. You know yon way, like a kick in the stomach. And the other implication that has to be drawn from this is that there are more children in the UK than we know about. But' – he slapped his desk top – 'we'll press on, one stage at a time, and we'll keep each other informed. It may well be there's a link between your case and mine but for the time being we'll pursue independent lines of enquiry. If they merge, they merge, and if they don't, they don't.'

Again Claire Shapiro found that she could only pity Mandy Hampshire, whom she saw as a pale, waif-like creature, who did not sit so much as retreat into the armchair, of timid and nervous, jerky movements, pathetic, she thought, in her willingness and eagerness to please. Mandy Hampshire's home on the Trafford Estate was sparsely furnished: plastic-covered three-piece suite, a carpet that stuck to the soles of the shoes as it was walked on, combustible rubbish piled in the fire grate, yet a top-of-the-range television and video cassette recorder proudly standing in the corner of the room. Shapiro sat on the settee; de Larrabeitta – more cautious of crawling things, chose a hard upright chair next to the wall – let Shapiro lead.

'Dunno,' Mandy Hampshire said flatly, shaking her head. 'Dunno who could've done that to our Sadie, and our Kimberley, Shane too.' De Larrabeitta, observing, found Mandy Hampshire's acceptance of the crime against her children unsettling. Mandy Hampshire's reply was probably truthful, he felt, but the lack of any evident anger puzzled him to the point that he found it unnerving. The implication of the crime did not seem to reach her.

'I mean, it couldn't have been Jack. Jack was well tucked up before our Shane was born. I mean, Jack gave the lasses some dreadful hidings, he'd knock them senseless, but he'd not do *that* to them.'

'So who do you think could have?' Shapiro's voice was low, calm, but determined. 'It's not a one-off, it's been going on for some time, so do you have a man friend? Does anybody call regularly? Do the children go anywhere regularly?'

Mandy Hampshire shook her head and smiled as if to say, 'Thanks for the compliment but what man would want me?' Then she said, 'There's only Mr McGuire, but he wouldn't do anything like that.'

'Mr McGuire?' Shapiro probed and out of the corner of her eye saw David de Larrabeitta open his notepad.

'He and his family, they live in Endon, it's that area beyond the quarry.'

'Their exact address, please?'

'I don't know it. I know the house, but not the address, but they're good people, Christians, people of God and that, they came to see me when Jack, me husband, was tucked up. Don't know how they found out about me being on my own sudden like, but they knocked on my door and asked me if I wanted some help. I was by myself, two kids, one on the way so I said yes. Mr McGuire's a teacher and he came to help my kids, particularly Kimberley, she's my youngest girl, she's slow at reading.'

'So Mr McGuire came to help her and Sadie?'

'Aye.'

'Did you ever leave him alone with the girls?'

'Aye. He said it was all right for me to go out for a while, and they used to go to his house too. I used to go with them, they can't go to Endon alone, not at night, no lighting on the road once you're past the quarry, so I took them.'

'You just visited.'

'In the beginning. Later, when Shane was here, and out of nappies, the children spent overnights with Mr and Mrs McGuire so I could have a night on the town and that.'

De Larrabeitta groaned.

'I can't see what's wrong with that,' Mandy Hampshire whimpered. 'Mr and Mrs McGuire wouldn't do stuff to my children. Anyway, when can I see my children?'

'You'll have to talk to the Social Services about that.'

'But they won't tell me where my children are. I can see them twice a week in the Social Services Department, but I don't know where they are . . . my kids . . .'

'That's to protect them until we get to the root of this. They have to stay where we know they'll be safe.'

Mandy Hampshire began to whimper.

'What can I tell you about Endon?' Sam Meadows pondered the question as he curled his slender fingers round the plastic beaker of coffee. Behind him two constables who had unclipped their ties thudded darts into a cork board in the corner below the wall-mounted television set, two female constables spoke and listened to each other in hushed intent tones, at the bar the steward laughed with a sergeant and told the joke about the market trader on *Mastermind* whose specialist subject was plastic macks from ten ninety-nine to fourteen ninety-nine. 'It's a strange place, can't put my finger on why though, and it's got stranger in the last few years with the newcomers.'

'Where is it?' David de Larrabeitta asked. 'Exactly.'

'East of York itself,' said Meadows. 'You know the Trafford, off the Scarborough Road.'

'We've just come from there,' said Shapiro.

'Right, well, you've got the Trafford Estate, that's rough, the houses that aren't burnt all have satellite dishes . . . then there's the quarry, not a dangerous place, shallow sided, water gets a bit deep in the winter, but in the summer time it's a safe place for the kids to play. Better rival gangs fighting for possession of the quarry than playing chicken on the railway lines.'

'Damn right.'

'Well, after the quarry you've got a low-lying area, like a huge hollow in the ground, flat but lower than the rest of the Vale, about one mile from east to west, two miles from north to south, that's Endon.'

'Your patch?'

'Part of. Community constable in a rural area, I've got a lot of turf to cover, just me and my bike. Endon's only part of it, but I don't mind telling you I don't like going into Endon. Funny old place, is Endon.' He sipped his coffee. 'There's a church and a lot of houses surrounded by small-holdings, but no village as such. The area doesn't have a focus, no pub, no shop. The new families moved in, all came over the last five years, one lot from the south of England, another team from South Africa and such places, and a new minister, fellow called Seers, the Reverend Seers. He's some weirdo, he and all the newcomers seem to know each other quite well and don't have anything to do with the native population. It's as if they all knew each other before they came to Endon, yet they claim to have settled from, well, all corners of the earth. I asked them why they settled in Endon and I got the same reply, about wanting to get away from the rat race and you get a reasonable amount of land for your money in the Vale. So here we are.'

'What are they like?'

'The newcomers?' Meadows stroked his chin. ' "Alterna-tive" is I think the word they'd use. Grow their own food, flip-flop sandals, lots of cats and dogs, each family has children, each child swears like a trooper. Keep seeing a huge

37

green Mercedes Benz floating around Endon. See it in the drive of the newcomers' houses, never in the driveways of the older established residents.'

'If you see it again will you note the registration?' Shapiro asked. De Larrabeitta glanced at her. She explained that it might be relevant and then she asked Sam Meadows to go back a step and explain what he meant about the Reverend Seers being weird.

'He seems to be a very aggressive character, pushing his way into the lives of his parishioners to the point that the old flock have deserted the church in Endon and have gone to the neighbouring churches. Only the newcomers seem to have anything to do with him.' Meadows drained his beaker of coffee. 'I called on him once, he was in the church hall and he wasn't keen for me to be there, so of course I hung around, being a copper and all.'

Shapiro and de Larrabeitta smiled and nodded.

'Don't know, didn't add up.' Sam Meadows gazed into the middle distance. He was a constable in his mid-forties, not, it appeared, at all keen on promotion, nor, it seemed to those who knew him, to be drawn to the cutting edge of police work such as the Serious Crime Squad or the Drug Squad, but inordinately happy to have a job which involved cycling his patch in the Vale, forging links with the local community, but always professional enough to remember that at the end of the day he was a police officer, as when he called on the Reverend Seers. 'There was a coffin in there.'

'A coffin?'

'A coffin. He said it was for a play they were putting on in which someone had to get out of the coffin. I mean, this was a church hall in the Vale of York, not some offbeat drama group in a basement in London, and he was a man of the cloth, wore a cape, too, speaking of cloth, didn't dress like a normal vicar in his cassock, favoured a cape. He cut a strange figure of a man. He had lots of masks, too, I remember – he said they were for a nativity play but they didn't look benign, they had a frightening quality about them, but more than that they were adult-sized. Too big for children, too heavy as well, made of alloy and painted black. They were not masks for a nativity play, not a nativity play that I would want to see my kids taking part in.'

'As you say,' de Larrabeitta echoed, 'doesn't add up.'

'I asked if I could use the toilet,' Meadows continued. 'Didn't need the toilet, but I wanted to see as much as I could. There was a figure on the toilet wall, ironwork, about six inches in height, it was of two skeletons embracing.' Meadows shrugged. 'I clocked it all for future reference, but no crime was being committed so I left him with his coffin and nativity masks, about twenty masks in all, incidentally. Why the interest?'

Claire Shapiro told him about Mandy Hampshire's children and the McGuires.

Meadows nodded. 'I see. Well, the McGuires are one of the newcomers, been here in the Vale for about four years. They were among the first to arrive, in fact, and their house is about twenty minutes' walk from the nearest point of the Trafford. Are you going to call on them?'

'We'll have to.'

'Proceed with caution. I'll keep my eyes open now I know what might be going on. I mean, that might explain the behaviour of the newcomers' children. Foul-mouthed, aggressive little devils.'

Claire Shapiro's heart sank. David de Larrabeitta felt sick. More children to be concerned about.

The McGuire household proved to be a solid, square, stone-built whitewashed house with outbuildings in about six acres of land. It was untidy to Shapiro's eyes, unkempt gardens and vegetable plots, components of motor cars on the front lane. The pathway and the adjacent driveway were of house bricks laid on soil and had been pounded over the years into some measure of consolidation. Weeds grew from between the bricks and long grass stood between the pathway and the driveway. A car and trailer stood on the driveway. De Larrabeitta reached up and knocked on the door.

It was opened suddenly and both cops had the impression, the impression which was never to leave them, that they had been expected and their approach to the house closely monitored. It was the manner in which the door was snatched open and the man's face thrust out, as if disembodied from the chest. The face was bearded, hair tied back in a pigtail, round spectacles, a check-patterned shirt and overall-style jeans, ending in Indian moccasins on his feet.

Shapiro and de Larrabeitta showed their ID. 'City of York Police, Domestic Violence and Child Protection Unit.' Shapiro spoke. 'We'd like to ask you a few questions.'

'There's nothing the matter with our children.'

'Can we come inside?'

A woman came up behind the man. She had a small face and close-cropped hair. She laid a hand comfortingly and questioningly on her husband's forearm. She had piercing eyes and a hostile glare which made her husband's smile false and superficial, but he said yes, they could enter the house.

The interior of the McGuire household seemed to Shapiro and de Larrabeitta to be relaxed as they read the room, akin to a house shared by students, not particularly unclean, but untidy, and with the smell of incense in the air, as if the McGuires had been hippies in their teens and now, in their forties, were still hippies. 'Please,' said Mr McGuire, 'do take a seat.'

Shapiro and de Larrabeitta sat side by side on a double futon. Mr McGuire sat in an armchair. Mrs McGuire remained standing indignantly by the fire, at present unlit. The house seemed to both officers to have a certain chill about it which was not wholly explained by the absence of a source of heat.

'Mr McGuire.' De Larrabeitta spoke. 'Can I ask you if you are acquainted with the Hampshire family?'

'Yes,' he replied, smiling with his eyes, but it was a false smile, Shapiro saw that, de Larrabeitta saw that: false, false, false.

'In what capacity?'

'Why?'

'Just answer the questions, please, Mr McGuire.'

'All right. As a neighbour, as a helping hand since her

40

husband – her partner – is in prison and as a tutor to her children.'

'You're a teacher?'

'Yes.'

'Not in a post at present? I mean, it is term time at the moment.'

'I don't teach in the mainstream. I don't care for the formal approach. I'm better at individual one-to-one tutoring.'

'I see.' De Larrabeitta nodded.

'So you're a home tutor?' Shapiro pressed for clarification.

'Yes.'

'Other children beside the Hampshires?'

'Yes.'

A pause.

'Mr McGuire, you may be aware that the Hampshire children are in the care of the local authority.'

'Yes. Poor woman.'

'Do you know why?'

'No, no, I don't. She seemed to be managing with what help could be given.'

'In fact, it's more serious than that, Mr McGuire. The fact is that the children have been grossly sexually abused.'

A second, longer, pause.

'Oh, I'm sorry to hear that,' Mr McGuire said softly, but Mrs McGuire suddenly snarled, 'We had nothing to do with that!' Her face flushed. 'I think I'd like you to leave my house, accusing us . . .'

'I don't think we accused anybody, Mrs McGuire,' Shapiro addressed her. She found the woman's reaction very interesting, very interesting indeed. 'But since you make the claim, Mrs McGuire, we would like to point out that the only male believed to have had access to the Hampshire children is Mr McGuire here.'

'What are you saying?' Mr McGuire hissed the words.

'We'd like to put it to Mr McGuire' – de Larrabeitta spoke – 'that Mr Hampshire having been in gaol for the last three or four years, the only man known to have regular frequent access to the Hampshire children is yourself.'

'No comment.' Mr McGuire sat back in the armchair and

looked less friendly than hitherto. Standing beside the fire-place, Mrs McGuire flushed with anger.

'But you appreciate our concern?'

'Of course, but I know that I'm not responsible, my wife knows that I am not responsible, and you have an awful long way to go before proving that I am responsible.'

'So you're saying that you deny perpetrating any sexual act of any kind with any or all of the Hampshire children?'

'Yes. Emphatically.'

'I see.' Shapiro eyed him intently. 'You appreciate why we have to put this to you?'

'Yes, I can understand why, but my answer remains the same.'

'You're new to the area?' de Larrabeitta asked suddenly.

'Yes. Been here about four years, but in this part of England we'll still be considered new after forty years. Came from the south, Dorset way.'

'Why?'

'Why what?'

'Why did you come north? Why settle in Endon?'

McGuire shrugged. 'Fancied a change,' he offered. 'No other reason. New horizon, new start, you get more for your money here in the Vale than you'd get in Dorset, and the reputation the north has for being cold is a myth. The east wind's a biter in the winter, but the summers here are as warm as in the south.'

'We understand from our community constable that a number of newcomers have arrived in Endon over the last few years and have bought smallholdings. New minister, too.'

'That's the case,' McGuire agreed. 'The property was being sold, it was attractive to people wanting to start afresh.'

'Known to each other?'

'Sorry?'

'The incomers. The new families and the new minister. Our community constable . . .'

'He's the officer with the mountain bike?'

'Yes. PC Meadows. He has the impression that the incomers all know each other, that they socialize together.'

42

'That's probably true to a point, if only because we have the same thing in common, being incomers, and the locals don't seem so keen to want to know us. So, yes, we talk with each other.'

'I see.' Shapiro paused and then asked how many children the McGuires had.

'Two. They're at school at the moment. We send them to the primary and the secondary school on the Trafford. It's not an impossible walk, but in winter we drive them there.'

'You don't teach in the mainstream but you send your children to a mainstream school?'

McGuire answered simply, 'Yes.'

'Well.' Shapiro stood. De Larrabeitta followed her cue and stood also. 'Thank you for seeing us, you appreciate we'll have to get to the root of this. It's likely we'll have to call back, but thanks for your cooperation.'

'There's no need to call back at any time!' Mrs McGuire turned away from the cops and stormed out of the room.

Outside, Shapiro and de Larrabeitta walked down the path, beside the car and trailer to the pasty-grey road. They walked in silence to where they had parked their car; about them flat fields, the occasional house, a church, a church hall.

'Thought you stopped the interview a trifle early.' De Larrabeitta watched a pair of magpies glide over a green field of unripened wheat.

'I know' – Shapiro looked down as she walked – 'but I suddenly felt as though we were on thin ice. I just felt that . . .' She shook her head. 'I don't know, woman's intuition, a cop's intuition, the combination of both, but it's just what Sam Meadows said, there's something odd here, something I couldn't put my finger on. He'd have just kept denying it anyway and soon we would be just going round in circles. I think we'll want to see him again, but I think we need to be on much surer footing. I felt as though we were floundering. I don't know, David, something's going down here.'

'Next step?'

'Talk to the Hampshire kids. Lord knows, that'll take time, but eventually they might tell us something. But right now, you know the rule; if in doubt, do nowt, let things pan out, then you'll know what to do.'

It was Tuesday, 4th May, 14.00 hours.

Claire Shapiro wrote up the visits to the Hampshire and the McGuire households in the steadily thickening Hampshire file and then drove home to Wetherby. She let herself into her home, a modest narrow-fronted but deep terraced house, and knelt to acknowledge the purring welcome of Pablo and Vincent. She had chosen to live outside York, the nature of her work being what it was, it did not do, she felt, to live where she might bump into people whose lives she had been obliged to put under the minutest scrutiny, often exposing more of their lives, their sexual preferences, their sexual history, than is often exposed in the more conventional criminal enquiry and often not getting a result in terms of a conviction. And she lived alone: she preferred it that way. She was a child of a warring family and a survivor of a stressed marriage, and the peace of a house to herself and her cats was to her of passing bliss. She went upstairs, showered, changed into casual clothes and returned to the living room where she sat cross-legged on the floor and enjoyed quality time with Pablo and Vincent.

David de Larrabeitta too returned home to a warm welcome from his son, soon to commence school, and an icy-cold nonreaction from his wife, who tended to glance at him once each time he returned from work and then forgot him until he returned from work the following day, whereupon she would glance at him once and then forget him again. David de Larrabeitta was puzzled and agitated by this because there had been no row, no falling out, and he had given in to all her demands; he had agreed to live in the city, whereas, like most police officers at Friargate, he would have preferred to live out of the city. But Carla would not move more than a few hundred yards from her mother. He had even agreed to turn convention on its head and upon their marriage he had taken her name rather than vice versa, despite the distress this caused to his father, who was proud of the Sant lineage, having traced his line back to the Crusades. It had especially

44

distressed de Larrabeitta's father because David had been the last of the Sants and needed a son, if not sons, to carry on the name. But David Sant had been a young man who was deeply in love, his mind had been set, and the Sant line had come to an abrupt end in a modest Roman Catholic chapel. Again, hard for his Protestant father to accept.

He didn't know how to cope with a wife who wouldn't even speak to him and he knew deep within him that Carla would leave him, and for no reason that he could identify. If their home had been large enough she would have slept each night in the guest room, but they had no guest room, so each night they slept side by side, warm flesh and blood, yet a sheet of steel had fallen between them. It was only Christopher's joyful chuckling upon his arrival home each day that offered any warmth in his household, but he knew in his heart of hearts that his wife would leave him. He knew it. And she'd take Christopher with her. He knew that too.

Tuesday, 4th May, 14.30 hours
Ken Menninot pressed the phone to his ear. There was a silence on the line, a little nervous-sounding breathing, but otherwise silence. Then the voice spoke again. 'No . . . no, I won't give my name. You know me.'

'We do?' Menninot doodled with his pen underneath the part of his notepad upon which he'd written 'young, male, local accent'. He stopped doodling and wrote 'known'.

'Aye . . . I've been banged up.'

Menninot wrote 'served time'.

'So I'm not giving my name, because the only reason I was out there at that time was because I was up to naughties.'

'Naughties? So you and your lady friend saw it? Bit cold for naughties, though; I mean, the height of summer . . . even at night, but it's still cold at the moment.'

'Not those sort of naughties. I was checking a gaff, I was on a mission.'

'I see, sighting up a farmhouse?'

'No. Can't ever do a farmhouse, always got dogs. No, I was sighting up a house in Long Marston. It was when I was on the way back I saw headlights coming up between the fields, so I hit the deck and rubbed soil on my face.'

The voice was familiar. The owner was not just known to the police, he was known personally to Detective Sergeant Kenneth Menninot of the City of York Police. 'Go on.'

'I had a camouflage jacket, trousers, dark trainers, so I reckoned he wouldn't see me, but I know how a white face can shine in the dark, so I smeared dirt on it. This Range Rover came up to the group of trees on the moor.'

Rob 'Roy' McGregor. Had to be. Menninot grinned. 'Colour?'

'Yellow. Yellow Range Rover.'

'Then . . . ?'

'Well, it turned a circle and halted beside the trees and this bloke got out and opened the rear door and pulled this body off the back seat and carried it under his arm and dumped it near the trees. I mean, I'm just a few feet away, I watched it, I was scared . . .'

'A body?'

'A little lad. No clothes.'

'Did the arms and legs hang loose or were they stiff?'

'Loose, dangled, the head 'n' all.'

Menninot scribbled. 'Go on.'

'Then the bloke, he went back to the car, got a jerry can and sprinkled petrol over the lad, tossed a match, and went back to the car. He put the can in the back and got in the driver's seat, and he said, "That'll do, give the foxes a roast dinner," and took off.'

'That'll do? So there was someone else in the vehicle?'

'Suppose. I didn't see them.'

'That's what I was going to ask you.'

'Anyway, he drove back down the road and drove off, to the left, away from the city.'

'I see, this man, would you recognize him again, Robert?'

'Maybe . . .' Then silence. 'Oh. Who's that?'

'Mr Menninot.' Ken Menninot smiled. 'Robert, do you ever learn? You're not six weeks out of Doncaster nick, and here you are sighting up gaffs for another mission.'

'How did you know it was me?'

46

'Come on, you know that I've interviewed you more times than you've had birthdays and Christmases put together. You're a known bandit, a regular customer. We get to know our customers' voices.'

'Oh. And it was you put me in Doncaster.'

'You put yourself there, Robert. How was it?'

'A teddy bears' picnic. Private gaol, see. And I knew a lot of the lags. I was in the riot. South Yorkshire boys thought it was their nick, so Leeds boys had to put 'em right, and I pitched in with the Leeds boys. So after the riot it was OK. Wouldn't mind going back.'

'Just as well, eh? I mean the way you're going. Where are you phoning from?'

'Phone box on the estate.'

'So, do you want us to pick you up, or do you want to call in and finish this.'

'Finish?'

'Aye, remember we're at the bit where he's just poured petrol on the lad and driven away. I want to hear the rest of the story.'

A pause.

'I'll come in, my mum will go spare if she thinks I'm getting pulled again. She's always on at me to go straight.'

'Sensible woman.'

'You'll not be charging me?'

'No. I mean, with your form and your confession to being on the moor having looked at a house in Long Marston, the beaks would send you down, loitering with intent. Especially if you had a jemmy.'

'No jemmy, I wasn't carrying, just sighting up a gaff.'

Leif Vossian sat opposite Bill Hatch. He said he hoped that he wasn't interrupting anything.

'As you see.' Bill Hatch leaned back in his chair and indicated his desk. It was a shifting sand of papers and medical journals. 'Tidying up. There is a theory that desk tops are made of wood but I've got to dig down a lot further before I'm able to prove or disprove it. Coffee?'

'No, thanks just the same.' Vossian glanced at the wall

47

above Hatch's desk, at two framed photographs, one of an attractive blonde-haired young girl in a rugby shirt at that point in life where womanhood begins to blossom, and the second of two pigs. 'Pigs?'

Hatch smiled. 'Not just any pigs, let me tell you. They're Gloucester Old Spots. It's a rare breed but not endangered as such, plenty of breeding pairs up and down the country, and those particular two, they're my babies.'

'Your babies?'

'Wilfred and Wilfreda. I bought them four years ago. My wife and daughter had left me some years earlier. I dare say I needed a family.'

Vossian winced inwardly but showed no emotion.

'She was five at the time, my daughter, I mean. My wife reckoned I preferred the bottle to my family. She said if I couldn't make the choice, she'd make it for me. I dare say she was right. I've knocked it on the head now, just an occasional pint of brown and mild, as in last night at the Folk Club. That'll do me for a few days. But Nadine won't come back, we've lived apart for too long to enable us to pick up the pieces, she says, and I dare say she's right about that too. She's living in Staffordshire now, discovering her roots, or so she has told Veronica.'

'It's not a county I know.'

'Me neither. Anyway, I heard about the Orchard Pig, which is another name for the Gloucester Old Spots, and as I had just laid out an orchard, I bought a breeding pair. Frankly, I had intended to slaughter them, by which I mean sell them for slaughter and have a few chops for myself. A butcher in the village was going to do the actual business, the pork they produce is sweet and succulent. But not now.' He glanced at the photograph with affection. 'Now they'll live out their natural as perhaps the most fortunate pigs in Old England. And when they die they'll be laid in a deep grave which I'll dig myself. And if I go first I've arranged with Veronica to attend them.'

'So you haven't lost touch with your daughter?'

'Not at all. Nadine won custody, my drinking saw to that, but I was given access, usually school holidays because

Nadine initially went to London and settled Veronica in a school down there. It meant that I didn't get alternate weekends, which would have been the case if she had remained in the locality. Anyway, now she's nineteen she makes her own arrangements. In fact, she's living with me at the moment, studying for her first-year exams. She's at Lancaster.'

'Medicine?'

'Politics or *Cosmopolitan*. I confess I can't decide. She says she's reading politics but all I ever see is her with her nose in a fashion magazine. Heavens, I worry about her, I really do, and with not a small amount of guilt mixed in. You see, she was a late child, an only child, her parents separated which means only one thing; she was spoiled rotten. And that's her father speaking. Anyway, she does what she wants, gets her own way almost all the time, it seems to me, and to compound the felony she's quite attractive, as you see.'

Vossian glanced again at the photograph of a beaming Veronica Hatch, fetchingly athletic and healthy looking. He envied Hatch his worry and his guilt.

'I can't help but see a great fall just around the corner for little Miss Hatch. And that's still her father speaking. You know, I would have liked to see her go into medicine, if only because of the discipline required to obtain a medical degree. But she said she'd heard about the rate of alcoholism in the profession and the divorce rate in the profession and that was quite enough to put her off. She also pointed to my wife and me as proof – which we couldn't very well argue with. So politics it was. But you're not here to listen to me talk about daughters and pigs.'

'No, that's true enough, Dr Hatch. What I really wanted to talk about were the findings of the PM you performed on that lad. I don't know what it is, but I feel I can't quite take it on board from the report alone. I think I need to hear it for myself.'

'I can understand that. I can let you view the corpse if you wish.' Vossian pulled his head back. 'Not at present, thanks all the same.'

'Still, I know what you mean. All I can say is that it is as I described in the report.'

'Eating faeces and insects?'

Hatch nodded. 'The stomach was otherwise empty.'

'Sodomized?'

Hatch nodded. 'Over many years, I should think.' Hatch paused. 'There is one thing I didn't put in the report. It's not strictly relevant to the PM, but I would have told you anyway, had to do some checking first.'

'Oh?'

'Yes. Last winter, I mean two winters ago, January or February last year, I attended a conference of forensic pathologists in Aberdeen. Aberdeen in winter ... Oh my ... Anyway, I was having a beer at the hotel bar on the first evening, chatting to a bloke from Leicestershire, and he told me that he had conducted a PM on a girl of about ten years of age whose body had been found in a field, just dumped by all accounts. Definitely murdered elsewhere and dumped. We're going back ten years or so, not a recent case.'

'OK.' Vossian listened with interest.

'But this PM stayed with him; there's always one or two which stick out in your mind. This was his. I felt at the time he needed to talk about it. You know yon way?'

'Aye.' Vossian nodded. 'I know yon way.'

'Well, that young lassie had been anally and vaginally raped, again over time given the degree of distending. But she also had the same cuts I observed on the lad. Two on the hairline, one on each eyelid, and two about her genital area. Deliberately and carefully placed. Nobody could offer an explanation. She wasn't identified. The Leicestershire Constabulary had a whip round and purchased a single plot for her rather than see her put in a common plot with a couple of down and outs. But she didn't get a headstone, nobody ever knew her name and she was kept refrigerated for two years before being buried.' Hatch shook his head. 'She had been strangled, too, incidentally. I mention it only in case you may feel that from a police perspective there is . . .'

'A link.' Vossian anticipated Hatch. 'It's a possibility that looks as if it's well worth exploring.'

'I hope I don't have to do another PM like that again in a hurry. At all, in fact.'

'I hope you don't have to, either.'

'Aye.' Hatch glanced at Vossian. 'Aye. You know, I was impressed by your officer.'

'I would have sent a male officer, but she was all I could spare.'

'Listen, she stood up to it better than many a man would have. You know, you wouldn't believe the number of full-back types that crash to the floor the moment that I reach for the scalpel.'

'Oh I would, I assure you.' Vossian smiled and Hatch saw a glimmer of warmth in the man's eyes. 'I've done that myself, and I used to enjoy a game of rugby.'

'Well, she didn't flinch. She just left when she'd had enough, but not before she had absorbed the gist of the findings and so had something to report. I can respect that.'

'Reassuring, I suppose.'

'I take it you don't like women in the CID?'

'I don't. But that's just within these four walls.'

'Of course.' Hatch leaned forwards and rested his forearms on his desk. 'My father didn't like women in the police force at all, in or out of uniform.'

'He was in the force?' Vossian looked with interest at Bill Hatch.

'Sergeant in the Derbyshire Constabulary when he retired. I was the token ex-grammar-school boy at the Manchester University Department of Medicine. Just me among all those ex-public-school types who delighted in insulting with innu-endo. No defence against it, at least that I was able to find. Then I attended a forensic postmortem and knew immediately what I wanted to do.' He patted the papers on his desk. 'Made it.'

'Lucky you, eh? I always wanted to drive steam loco-motives.'

'What are you going to do about the lad?'

'Try to find out who he is. That's the first step.' Vossian stood.

'Hope you have more luck than the Leicestershire boys.'

*　　*　　*

Leif Vossian left Hatch's office and drove out of the hospital grounds. On a whim, and knowing he had the time to spare, he drove to Fulford cemetery. He reversed his car into the small car park at the cemetery gates, catching sight of the swings and slides and climbing frames on the grassy play area on the far side of the narrow road, opposite the cemetery gates. Always painful for him. After his chat with Bill Hatch they were now poignant, too. He walked into the cemetery, which, save for a cluster of council houses to his right, wasn't overshadowed by building or hillside. In front of him a distant church spire gleamed like a spike of marble against the foliage. He walked to the far corner of the cemetery, enjoying the singing of an unseen blackbird as he did so. In the area of the recently turned graves he stopped and knelt beside a black headstone. 'Don't know about this one, Meg,' he said softly, picking at the weeds. 'It's not like anything we've had before. Maybe something in Leicestershire once, about ten years ago, but apart from that, nothing . . . I've no expertise to draw on, you see . . . I've got bad feelings about this one. I've had bad feelings before and I've always been right. And you, dear heart, are you and the kids looking down on us fumbling and groping about in the dark? Because that's what it feels like, Meg. This case feels like that. I know now what it means to look through a glass darkly. There's nothing but darkness now, even on a day like today. Nothing but darkness.'

Ken Menninot placed the plastic beaker on the table in front of Robert McGregor. 'There you are, Robert. Coffee as promised. See, lad, that's the way of it: you look after us, we look after you. You go on a mission, we tuck you up.'

Robert McGregor shrugged. He was slightly built, but had a certain appeal to his features, which Ken Menninot believed went a long way to explaining the easy time he'd had in Doncaster gaol. There was no doubting Rob 'Roy' McGregor's popularity, though little in his personality or actions could account for it, not that Menninot could observe. But that was the way of it inside youth gaols: small and good-looking boys get adopted as mascots by the gorillas.

'You know you should leave it out, Robert.' Ken Menninot sat opposite Robert McGregor and offered him a Dunhill.

'You don't smoke yourself, Mr Menninot?' Robert McGregor took a cigarette from the packet.

'No. As you may recall. This is a courtesy pack.' He lit the cigarette with a disposable lighter. 'I buy them to offer folk as and when.'

'I remember now.' McGregor inhaled deeply.

'There's no future in it.'

'What? Smoking? If smoking doesn't kill me, something else will. We've all got to go some way, some how.'

'You're too young to be talking like that, but I meant missions. There's no future in it.'

Again McGregor shrugged. 'What else is there? And don't say work. There's no jobs. I know guys in their thirties, never had a job, never at all in their life. I'm nineteen. No bits of paper. I've got track for burglary. I mean, who's going to give me a start, I mean who? See' – he drew on the cigarette – 'see the way it is is that I get tucked up. I don't have a hard time, I get remission for good behaviour, but I've learned some new dodges, got some new contacts. I get back on the Trafford, promise me old mum no more missions because she don't want me turning out like me old dad.'

'I can see why. Where is he now, your dad?'

'Armley. It's the worst nick in the region. Screws are all right, it's the facilities. Hasn't been modernized since it was built a hundred and fifty years ago. That's what my dad says, anyway. So I promise the old lady no more missions, but the Income Support doesn't go a long way and you get bored, bored, bored. After a few weeks . . .'

'A few, like two or three in your case?'

A shrug of the shoulders. '. . . after a bit you start thinking of a successful mission, a good haul and no heat. The idea sort of takes hold and once you start thinking of a successful mission . . .'

'You wander on the moor, to do a recce?'

'Aye. There's a shorter way to get at the back of the houses at Long Marston, but I like to know what's behind me. So I

53

came at them from over the moor. Worked down on them for about half an hour. Helps me plan my escape.'

'So you sighted up a few gaffs?'

'One in particular.'

'Which one, in particular?'

Robert McGregor smiled and shook his head.

'No matter. You know that if one of the houses at Long Marston gets turned over, then we'll be quizzing you?'

'But not now? There's to be no charge for loitering with intent, that was the deal.'

'That's the deal. This time you're a member of the public giving information. But if you're seen on the moor again it can only be because you are loitering with intent.'

'OK, OK.' McGregor took another deep drag on his cigarette. He sipped the coffee.

'So, we've got to the bit where you've flattened yourself against mother earth because a pair of headlights are coming across the moor in your direction. Time?'

'About two o'clock in the morning. It took me an hour to cycle home – I got home at three.'

'I remember your cycle. Huge panniers over the rear wheels.'

'I'm not interested in hi-fi stuff, I go for jewellery, stuff like that.'

'I remember that as well.'

'So I was coming back. I was over the hump moving downhill near some trees, rough ground. I watched headlights come along the road.'

'Which direction?'

'Towards York.'

'OK.'

'Then they slowed. They turned up the track between the fields, I hit the deck. Came right at me, then the beam passed over me as the car turned. I rubbed dirt on my face and looked up. It was a yellow Range Rover, it would have to be. I mean a Range Rover, or something like it, to move over that ground.'

'All right.' Menninot wrote on his pad.

'So then this guy got out. Pulled this body from the back

54

seat. Dumped it near the trees, went back for a can of petrol, doused the body then the grass round the body and tossed a match. I was scared he'd see me 'cos the place lit up a bit. There wasn't much flame really. He didn't exactly soak the body with petrol. Most was on his feet and legs. Then he went back to the Range Rover, and he said, "That'll do, the foxes can have a roast dinner," or something like that.'

'So there was someone else in the car?'

'Or he was talking to himself. I didn't see anybody. I mean, I've cycled away from a mission talking to myself. It's the excitement. I'd say things like, "I did all right there, just got to get home now." That bloke must have been excited . . . nervous like . . .'

Menninot smiled. 'You get a Brownie point for that.'

Robert McGregor looked pleased with himself.

'Now.' Menninot tapped his pad with his ballpoint. 'Some details. Tell me about the man. What did he look like?'

'Tall.' McGregor crushed the remains of his cigarette in the ashtray. 'Light-coloured hair. Wax jacket. Checked trousers. Shiny shoes.'

'Not dressed for walking, then?'

McGregor shook his head. 'No.'

'Would you recognize him again, do you think?'

'I don't think so. Most of the time my head was turned away. Especially when he set the petrol on fire. I was scared that the glow might reflect on my eyes, so I turned away. That's when I really could have clocked him, it lit up as light as day, but then I was so close . . .'

'Fair enough.' Menninot stroked his chin. 'Now, tell me about his voice. Was he local? Did he have an accent?'

'He was posh.'

'Posh?'

'Aye. He reminded me of one of the AGs at Doncaster. He was talking to us one day in the sports hall. Told us he'd just left the Air Force. Another lad said his brother was in the RAF regiment and had just got his first stripe up and the AG said very good, but he didn't know this lad's brother. He'd been in the RAF Intelligence, and besides he'd been an officer. The bloke who said the foxes can have a roast dinner spoke like the assistant governor who just left the RAF.'

'I know the type. So then this guy drove off?'

'Aye, but slowly, in a wide circle, as if he was scared of chewing up the grass and leaving tracks. It looked that way to me, at least.'

Again Menninot smiled. 'Robert, you are pulling down Brownie points like there's no tomorrow. You're doing really well.'

'I am?'

'You are. So then . . . ?'

'Well, then I went to the body, it was a little lad, and got his arms and pulled him away out of the flames. I took my jacket and put out the flames on his legs but I could see his ankles were gone, I mean gone. I left the grass burning 'cos I reckoned the guy would be clocking his rear-view mirror and he'd smell a rat if he didn't see no flames.'

'Good lad. Good thinking.'

'Then the bloke got to the road and took off the way he'd come. Fast.'

'Fast?'

'Flying! Anyway, I could see the lad was dead. I reckon I panicked a bit, ran off the moor, ran to where I'd stashed my bike near that monument thing. Then I cycled home.'

'Didn't think to call us, let us know what you'd seen?' Menninot picked up the phone on the desk and tapped out a four-figure internal number. 'Scene of Crimes?' he said before McGregor could offer an answer. 'DS Menninot here, reference the Marston Moor murder . . . Aye. The little lad . . . Can you get a team up there again, as soon as . . . We're looking for tyre tracks left by a Range Rover. It turned in a wide circle near Cromwell's Plump and remained stationary for a minute or two. There might be something that you could take a plaster cast or a photograph of. Thanks . . .' He replaced the handset, gently, and then picked it up again and tapped out a second four-figure internal number. As it rang out he winked at Robert McGregor. 'See how the police force works, Robert? A lot of people doing different jobs, sort of fitting their own piece into the big jigsaw puzzle . . . Hello, Traffic? DS Menninot, reference the murder on Marston

56

Moor . . . who hasn't heard about it? We have a witness who has given information and we now believe a yellow Range Rover was involved. Left the moor at about two a.m. on the third of May, yesterday, travelling in a westerly direction. Could you enquire if any of your patrols saw the vehicle? Any information at this stage would be gold dust. Thanks.' Menninot replaced the phone and said, 'So what prompted you to contact us?'

McGregor shrugged in the manner that Menninot noticed that he had. Menninot didn't press him. 'Right, Rob, another coffee then we'll get all of this down in the form of a statement.'

It was Tuesday, 4th May, 15.15 hours.

3

Wednesday, 5th May, 13.00 hours–17.00 hours
Tessie Cahill had started to drink at 10.00 a.m. She had a
bottle of Crabbies that had been gathering cobwebs in her
larder for some weeks. Each day that she had been able to
leave the bottle untouched was an achievement. For her it
was one day at a time. But today, today, all logic and reason
left her and she had started with the Crabbies, and had done
so on an empty stomach. She had had no breakfast and not
much of a supper the previous night: just a 'heat and serve'
from a plastic packet. It was how she survived. When she
had finished the Crabbies she went outside and had walked
down the concrete pathway which cut through her overgrown garden and walked to the bus stop, as if on autopilot.
She had received the trigger that had caused her to reach
for the bottle, and to finish the bottle, and now, with the
taste of alcohol in her mouth, she was, lemming-like, bent
on her own destruction. She was able to muster just enough
self-control to walk past the Swan with Two Necks. She knew
herself well enough to know that if she went into the Swan
she'd remain in until she was thrown out and scratched for
life. She knew that she needed her local and so was able to
walk past it and on to the bus stop. The Crabbies felt good
inside her. She felt mellow, a pleasant dulling of reality. For
Tessie Cahill, alcohol was an anaesthetic which she needed
from time to time. Her purse was a comforting weight in her
coat pocket, metal mostly, but she also had a ten-pound note.
It would be enough, especially on her empty stomach, and
with the helping start of the bottle of Crabbies. Yes, it was
more than enough. She jumped a hopper into the city and
got off at the railway station and walked up the rising curve
of Queen Street beneath the ancient walls to the Windmill

at the corner of Queen and Blossom. She ordered a glass of Crabbies. Then another. And another. She began to sing and was asked to leave.

She stepped out into the chill shade of the early May air, underneath a crisp, blue sky. Tessie Cahill knew she should be feeling cold when not in the sun. But she didn't. The ancient wall at Micklegate Bar began to sway and blur. She looked along Nunnery Lane, long and lonely. She knew that there were more pubs down Micklegate. She focused on the traffic lights and crossed Blossom Street when the green man shone. She called at the Punchbowl Hotel where she had another glass of Crabbies, leaving before she was asked to leave.

Tessie Cahill swayed towards the city centre. She didn't notice people avoiding her. She stopped and turned into the doorway of a vacant shop unit. She could no longer withstand the pressure on her bladder so she spread her legs and held her skirt out in front of her and let go. With her back towards Micklegate, she didn't see the mother grab the gaping boy and bundle him roughly along the pavement.

Shivering after the discharge of urine, she continued along Micklegate until she saw another pub. She stumbled in, attracted by the promise of warmth and brushed up against a table. The landlord held up his hand in her direction and shook his head. Tessie Cahill turned obediently, unquestioningly and faltered back outside. She staggered into the road. A car braked to avoid her. A woman screamed as Tessie fell against the car.

She fell on to all fours.

She vomited in the gutter.

She was arrested.

'Sadie.' Claire Shapiro spoke softly. 'My name's Claire. I'm a lady police officer, and you know that that means you and I are friends.'

Sadie Hampshire nodded and then glanced at her foster mother for reassurance. Then she nodded again.

'You're happy here with Mrs Fee?'

A quick nod of the head.

'It's a nice house, isn't it?' Claire Shapiro looked about her. She saw a neat, ordered house, but a house that was a home where children were allowed to 'be': their toys were on the floor, their paintings Blu-Tacked to the wall.

'Yes.' Sadie Hampshire nodded.

'Have you seen your mummy since you've come to live with Mrs Fee?'

No reaction.

'Twice-weekly contact at the Social Services building.' Mirrium Devers sat adjacent to Claire Shapiro.

'I see. You like seeing your mummy, I'll bet?'

'Yes.'

'I bet you do, love. I bet you want to be home as soon as you can.'

'Yes.'

'Well, listen, Sadie, me and your social worker here, we both want the same, we both want you home as soon as it's safe for you to go home, but do you know why you and your little sister and brother are here with Mrs Fee?'

Sadie Hampshire looked uncomfortable, her eyes narrowed.

'It's all right, Sadie, you're with friends. No one's going to hurt you and you can take as much time as you like, there's no hurry. So do you know why you're here with Mrs Fee?'

Sadie Hampshire threw a quick, nervous glance towards Mirrium Devers, who smiled and said, 'That's all right, Sadie, you can talk to Claire and you won't be getting your mummy into any trouble.'

Claire Shapiro looked at Devers. The promise Devers had just made was, she thought, ethically fraught, and it was not a promise that she as a police officer could guarantee. Shapiro was not without experience and she knew that the Hampshire children had been chronically sexually abused over several years, and even if the mother had not been the perpetrator, she had clearly failed to protect them as the law demands, she may even have been an accomplice. Such had been known: offer the man the children to stop him from leaving. It was just such a statement that made her find joint working with social workers difficult.

'It's about bad things.' Sadie Hampshire sat rigid in the chair. Claire Shapiro returned her gaze to the girl, and smiled and nodded knowingly and approvingly. She held eye contact with her, not wanting any further help from the social worker. 'Would you like to tell us about the bad things, Sadie?'

Sadie Hampshire remained silent.

A clock ticked.

'Well,' Mirrium Devers began, and Shapiro tensed with dread anticipation of further lures and empty promises. 'Don't tell us for yourself, tell us for your brother and sister, because you remember what it was that you asked me about them? You remember you asked me if Kimberley and Shane were going home. Remember that?'

Sadie Hampshire nodded her head.

'And I said why? And you said that you didn't want them to go home, do you remember? This was about a week ago when we were driving to Mrs Fee's house for the first time. I said why don't you want them to go home? And you said that it wouldn't be nice for them at home. Can you tell Claire why you want to go back to your mummy but you don't want Kimberley and Shane to go back?'

'Bad things.'

Shapiro felt she had to hand it to Devers, she'd got over the first obstacle. The beginning of the disclosure was always the most difficult part and she'd done it without leading the little girl. She had quoted something the girl had said and that, in her book, didn't amount to suggestion. Shapiro knew that interviewing children is the most difficult of all interviews. It's almost impossible to do it without leading the child in some way, yet once that has been done the interview has been compromised, and any disclosure has been ruined from an evidential point of view. But so far, so far there had been no leading, as the spools on the twin audio deck spun silently, and strong evidence was so, so important because here, sitting rigidly in a chair in a modest but proud council house in Dringhouses, was a little girl who looked like any eight-year-old girl, clean and smart in a floral-pattern dress, her hair in a ponytail, buttoned-up shoes and white ankle socks, and who was as dilated as a married woman.

'Do you want to tell us about the bad things, Sadie?'

'He hurts me with his willy.'

'Hurts?' Shapiro continued to hold eye contact. 'Where does he hurt you, Sadie?'

Sadie Hampshire placed her hand briefly and lightly between her legs and then indicated her bottom, also quickly and lightly.

'Good girl.' Shapiro smiled. 'Between your legs at the top, at the front and back.' Said more for the benefit of the tape, but very obligingly Sadie Hampshire said, 'Yes.'

'Who does this to you, and to your brother and sister?'

Sadie Hampshire remained silent. She held eye contact with Shapiro but said nothing. Shapiro searched for something to say, knowing the importance of maintaining the dialogue in such circumstances.

'How many children does this happen to?' Again it was the social worker who sprang to the rescue.

Sadie Hampshire looked steadily at Devers but remained silent.

'Well, shall we say more than ten or less than ten?'

Claire Shapiro once again looked at Devers. More than ten? There were only three children in the family who were known to visit and be visited by a man whom she herself found odd, but ten . . . ?

'More than,' said Sadie Hampshire suddenly.

Claire Shapiro's mouth opened a little. She found her attitude changing towards Devers, who she saw as a do-gooding young woman with short black hair, black spectacles, clad in denim and carrying a leather shoulder bag. She still saw all those things but was also beginning to see a social worker who knew her stuff. She turned to Sadie Hampshire and said gently, 'Who are the other children?'

Sadie Hampshire remained silent.

'Sadie.' Devers spoke softly. 'Would it be a good idea if the other children came to live with Mrs Fee, or someone like her?'

Sadie Hampshire nodded.

'So shall we go and get them?'

Another nod of the head.

'But we can't go and get them and bring them to Mrs Fee, or someone like Mrs Fee, unless we know who they are.'

'Tom and Harry.'

Devers nodded. 'I know Tom and Harry Pyrrah. Min and Joan too.'

'Yes, Min and Joan and Irene and Sydney. Robert and Susan and Jane and Anne.'

Mirrium Devers smiled and said, 'Don't worry, Sadie, we'll go and make sure they're safe from the bad things. Where do the bad things happen?'

'In houses, in a hole in the ground.'

'Can you take us to the hole in the ground?'

Sadie Hampshire shook her head. 'Go in Meakey's car.'

'Or to the houses?'

She remained still. The implication of this for Devers and Shapiro was that she knew which house, or houses. Then Sadie Hampshire said, 'Ben's house.'

Devers smiled. 'Ben's house,' she repeated. 'And other houses too?' The girl nodded.

'Which houses, Sadie?' Shapiro pressed.

But Sadie Hampshire turned and looked at her foster mother for the first time since the interview began.

Devers settled back in her chair and addressed Shapiro. 'I think that's it for today,' she said.

Shapiro said, 'Yes, thank you, Sadie. Would you like to go now?'

Sadie Hampshire made no reply, but slid off the chair and ran out of the room.

There was a silence between the three women, broken when Shapiro stood and said, 'The time is 15.00 hours, Sadie Hampshire has left the room. The interview is concluded.' She switched the tape recorder off. 'Ten, more than ten, less than ten?' She addressed Devers. 'I thought we were only dealing with three children? Although having said that, myself and a colleague did ponder the implications of the McGuires having children. He's a guy who lives in Endon that the Hampshires are known to visit and vice versa.'

'I see, but to answer your question, frankly I had what the Yanks would call a hunch, and I did do a bit of digging around and asking colleagues for information before I came here.'

'And?'

'In a nutshell, Mrs Hampshire – Sadie's mum – was in care herself when a young girl. She bounced in and out, her dad was a drunk, kept knocking the children about. I looked out her file, her and her siblings were noted to display sexualized behaviour, but it wasn't picked up on; in fact, the children were reprimanded for it. Social work has come a long way since Mandy Hampshire was a child. I visited Mandy and asked her about it and she admitted that she and her siblings, boys and girls, had been sexually abused by their father. I know him – Ben Pyrrah. He's not the brightest of creatures and frankly I don't think he realizes what he did wrong, he just saw his children as legitimate sexual playthings, probably because his father had had that attitude and that family's learned behaviour reaches back to the Dark Ages. Anyway, Mandy's upset about speaking out against her father, but she sees it, rightly, as the first step to getting her children returned. We'll have to see some demonstration of her condemnation of the practice, then we can ask for a Supervision Order, get the children back with her but keep a close eye on the situation, possibly negotiate a housing transfer, give her a fresh start. That's how I'd see this case panning out, but it's early days yet, we'll see what we find.'

'Indeed. So it's likely to be the children's grandfather? That teacher we visited yesterday, McGuire, he's probably not responsible at all. No wonder his wife was angry . . . Mind you, Mrs Hampshire said that was the only other home the children visited.'

'She probably didn't consider her relatives houses as other houses.' Devers shrugged her shoulders. 'If you like, I'll show you a genogram I worked out for the Pyrrah family, it's back at the office, but the gist of it is that the Hampshire house is not an isolated family. It's part of an extended family, all of whom live on the Trafford. About eight addresses in all and the centre of the web is old Ben Pyrrah, the children's grandfather, and his children are now abusing their children, or in the case of Mandy Hampshire née Pyrrah, are allowing their children to be abused because they think it's normal. The family live in and out of each other's houses, spend overnights in each other's houses. We first realized something was amiss when we kept finding the wrong children in the houses we visited, not just calling round, but settling in for the evening. The Pyrrahs just have no concept of what a nuclear family is, they see themselves as one family living at eight addresses, and I'm now quite convinced that the children are all known to the adults, particularly the male adults, in the network, and by that I mean known in the biblical sense.'

'Oh my God!' Shapiro gasped.

Mrs Fee paled but remained speechless.

Devers continued. 'All the children have a wary look about them. I'm not sure if they know who their fathers really are, but a husband or partner's name will go down on the birth certificate for the form's sake. And as I said, the top spider in the web is Ben Pyrrah, pot bellied, hot breathed, white whiskered and who wears a permanent grin, but then if you had been enjoying not just your wife, but your children and your grandchildren, wouldn't you have plenty to grin about, especially if you saw nothing wrong with the practice?'

'I dare not believe this.' Shapiro shook her head.

'I had difficulty taking it on board' – Devers spoke matter-of-factly – 'but the fact remains that if you call on any household in the extended Pyrrah family you won't be able to guarantee which children you'll find there. Mrs Hampshire's spilled the beans about her father. I asked her if she'd make a statement to the police and she said she would. That's what I meant about not getting Sadie's mum into trouble.'

'I see.'

'She'll give a statement which will be strong enough for you to take action, and until now she didn't fully understand that doing that to children was wrong. She's a woman of limited responsibility.'

'Fair statement then, I suppose,' Shapiro conceded. 'Still, I'd rather you didn't pre-empt police action. Strains relationships.'

Devers inclined her head, sideways.

'We'll have to visit Mrs Hampshire – I want to hear this from the horse's mouth. I mean, incest and sexual abuse of children. Stories like that come from bog Ireland or the Forest of Dean, but not a York housing estate. How will Mrs Hampshire react to me, do you think, the family are well known to us, very anti the police?'

'If she sees you as a step towards getting her children back she'll cooperate. We can go and see her right now if you've got the time.'

'I've got the time. God in heaven, for this I'll make the time.'

'Good, but before we go there's something else.'

'There's more?'

'Regrettably.' Mirrium Devers turned to Mrs Fee. 'I'm sorry, Mrs Fee, you've been left out of this, but would you care to tell DC Shapiro what you've been telling me, and do you have those drawings to hand?'

Mrs Fee stood. She was a round, motherly woman, a flat face and a page-boy haircut that reminded Shapiro of a figure from a medieval tapestry. She moved quickly, as if responding to the urgency of the situation. Crossing the floor, she opened the bottom drawer in a piece of furniture and extracted a folder which she handed to Devers. 'You're better at explaining things than me,' she said, resuming her seat.

'Very well, there's something more going on here.' Devers opened the folder and handed two drawings, clearly produced by children, to Shapiro. One drawing showed a figure in a cloak, with what appeared to be an erect penis protruding from the cloak. The figure held a shepherd's crook-handled staff. The second drawing also showed the figure in a cloak, on a smaller scale, but with the additional smaller figures, hand in hand, forming a circle around the cloaked figure. 'There's one or two similar drawings in the office,' Devers explained. 'I've never seen anything like them.'

'Sadie says the figure in the cloak is called "the master",' Mrs Fee offered. 'But I haven't asked her about the drawings, like you advised me.'

'I've asked Mrs Fee not to react to anything the children

66

draw,' Devers said by means of explanation, 'but to listen to what they say and to ensure that they have ample supply of crayons and paper, and let them draw what they want to draw and not question them or admonish them if the drawings appear offensive.'

'Good idea.' Shapiro looked at the drawings. They were, she felt, indeed strange drawings for children to have produced.

'It seems to me,' Devers continued, 'that the children are drawing something out of themselves, purging themselves of something but I don't know what. Mrs Fee has agreed to keep everything they draw safe and hand them to me. How do you find the children, Mrs Fee?'

'They're strange, strange children.' Mrs Fee shuffled in her seat and considered the room about her as if searching for a beginning to her delivery. 'Behaved strangely. I've only had them for a week or so now, nervous at first, on edge, but once they began to relax . . . well, I have had three wet beds every morning since they came, not one of them has had a dry night. I mean, you expect the occasional wet bed, but every morning, from all three . . .'

'Mandy Hampshire told me the children didn't wet the bed at home,' Devers explained. 'I thought it might link with the drawings, which they didn't do at home either. It's as though it's part of a release, some kind of emotional discharge once they realized that they were in a safe environment. But I'll let Mrs Fee explain . . .'

'Aye,' Mrs Fee continued. 'You see, it's not just the one thing, it's all together, it's a build up, the accumulation, that's the word . . . they said they didn't like snakes and after what Miss Devers told me had happened to them, I thought snakes were, well, like a man's private parts . . . but my husband was spending some time with them one day and they didn't show any fear of him, didn't show any fear of men, but they were looking at a wildlife book and they came to a section on reptiles and they became terrified when my husband turned the page and got to the pictures of snakes. Snakes held a real terror for them, insects too. Just yesterday I caught a spider that had got into the house to put outside; Sadie watched me and she just blurted out, "I'm not going to eat it." I mean, as if I was going to make her eat a spider.'

Claire Shapiro shook her head slowly in disbelief and in wonder.

'So I'm now logging everything as Miss Devers asked me to, every strange thing that they do, everything they show fear of, time and day, everything gets recorded, and I'm keeping all the drawings.'

'There's something I can't fathom.' Devers addressed Shapiro. 'You see, one of Sadie's drawings back at the office shows a car crammed with people pulling a trailer which appears to be full of gadgets, one of which may be hi-fi speakers, and she apparently told Mrs Fee that it was a drawing of them going to the quarry.'

'She also has described the quarry as the "hole in the ground",' Mrs Fee added. 'The "hole in the ground" and the "quarry" are one and the same place, at least that's the impression I have.'

'Right,' Devers continued, 'but the Pyrrahs are as poor as church mice, they eke out a miserable existence on Income Support, except for Ben Pyrrah, who's lived long enough to draw his state pension.'

'So what you're saying is that there is no car in the Pyrrah family.'

'That's it, no trailer, no expensive hi-fi equipment either, just rented TVs and VCRs. You see, large-scale sexual abuse and incest in an extended but socially isolated family is one thing, but that, bad enough as it is, doesn't explain a terror of snakes, a refusal to eat spiders, getting into a car to go to a hole in the ground and a man in a cloak called "the master". I can't fathom it.'

'You know the McGuires, the teacher that has contact with the Hampshires?'

'Lives in Endon.'

'That's him. He seems to wander in and out of the frame of suspicion. A moment ago I thought he was out and that all the bad news was down to the Pyrrahs, but now I wonder about him again. You see, he's got a car and a trailer. I just throw it in. It may be of significance.'

'I'm learning not to dismiss anything.' Devers stood. 'Thank you, Mrs Fee. Shall we call on Mandy Hampshire?'

Carmen Pharoah savoured the lunch of chilli and baked potato which she had prepared. She sat on the floor of her living room, soothed by the calm, unhurried voice of the Radio Three commentator. Classical concerts broadcast live were, she felt, far more satisfying than the clinical perfection of the CDs played on Classic FM, and the jokey good humour of the Classic FM 'hosts' did not seem to her to sit well with the music they played. So Radio Three it was. At one p.m. she slipped out of her tracksuit and changed into her work clothes – conservative grey suit and sensible shoes, a light full-length raincoat – and set off to walk to work. She walked down Buckingham Street, turned left into Skeldergate opposite the Sea Cadet Headquarters, across the Ouse Bridge and into Friargate, reaching the rear 'staff only' entrance at the police station just fifteen minutes after leaving her flat. She had quickly found that her walk to work was one of the advantages of living in York, especially as she had bought 'within the walls', as she had found the local expression had it. The long, tedious commute across London twice a day was so unpleasant a memory that in her mind it seemed time distanced in years rather than weeks. She signed in, walked up the stairs and into the detective constables' room and slumped into her chair.

'Afternoon.' Simon Markova looked up at her and nodded.

Carmen Pharoah tore a page from her desk calendar. 'Are you coming or going?'

'You and I are on the afternoon turn. Pretty quiet at the moment, for the CID, anyway.'

'You shouldn't say that.' Carmen Pharoah smiled at Markova. 'Tempting fate. Any developments on the little boy?'

'In fact, yes.' Markova leaned back in his chair. He was a man in his late thirties, and who Carmen Pharoah found handsome in a rugged, uncompromising way. 'Ken Menninot's found a witness.'

'A witness!'

'Indeed. I don't know the result of that, he's still writing it up. Leif went to see the pathologist, that was yesterday. Can't think why, it's all in the report. Suppose he might have wanted to hear it for himself. Anyway, he came back scowling. This case has got to him.'

'I'm not surprised. It's got to us all.'

'In fact . . . ssh.' Simon Markova held up a finger to his lips. 'What do I hear?'

A heavy footfall echoed in the corridor.

'Tramp, tramp, tramp, the boys are marching,' Markova quipped. 'It's you or me . . .'

Leif Vossian suddenly loomed in the doorway, staring coldly at Carmen Pharoah. She held his gaze.

'DC Pharoah.'

'DI Vossian.'

A pause. Tension in the room.

'There's a woman in the cells. We know her well. She's a regular customer. Not a bandit. Nutty as a fruitcake. Totally unhinged, no furniture at home at all. Name's Tessie Cahill.'

'Not Tessie again.' Markova leaned back in his chair and grinned, hoping to ease the tension in the room.

'Aye. Tessie again. And in fine form. She was brought in legless, after she'd pissed and puked her way along Micklegate. We won't be charging her, we rarely do because she's not responsible in the eyes of the law. She's sobering up pretty fast. When she's fit I'd like you to arrange to have her run up to the Foss. They'll keep her in, fill her full of drugs and protein. Let her out again and she'll be OK for a few months and then she'll go on the batter again.'

'The Foss?' Carmen Pharoah raised an eyebrow.

'Foss Dyke Hospital. It's the local funny farm, though in these days of, what's that phrase, political correctness, is it . . . ? Aye, that. I suppose I should call it the local psychiatric health facility.'

'I wish you would.' Carmen Pharoah looked steadily at Leif Vossian, who was unable to prevent a glare of anger at her rebuke flashing across his eyes.

'Go and talk to her. She's rambling on about Marston Moor. It's got to be total fantasy coming from her, but I don't want to leave any stone unturned. Not on this one. Go and take a statement.' Vossian turned smartly on his heels and marched away towards his office.

'Go and take a statement, *please*,' said Carmen Pharoah as Vossian's footfall died away. 'Honestly! Does he think the cost of politeness comes out of his pocket?' She looked at Markova. 'See, that's my lot, the token woman and the token black on his squad and what work do I get? Go talk to the drunken lunatics. I mean, there's men out there who rape and strangle ten-year-old boys and so what job do I get to do? Take a statement from a known psychiatrically ill woman then ship her off to . . . What's that place?'

'The Foss.'

'The Foss,' she sighed, and shook her head. 'And the manner of that man . . .'

'Don't read too much into it. I don't think there's an officer in York who hasn't written Tessie's name in his notebook at some point.' Markova stood. 'Come on, I'll go with you, so you can't say it's all down to racism and sexism. Let's go and hear her story.'

Tessie Cahill sat shivering in an interview room at the end of the cell corridor. She clutched a beaker of black coffee. She looked up as Pharoah and Markova entered the room.

'Wotcher, Tessie.' Markova sat opposite her. Pharoah sat beside him. 'Had a little refreshment, I hear?'

'Not met you before have I, pet?' Tessie Cahill beamed at Carmen Pharoah.

'Detective Constable Pharoah.' She smiled at Tessie, taking in her image, a big-boned woman, matted black hair, shabby clothing.

'Pharoah? Like in Egypt?'

'Not spelled the same. So no, nothing to do with them.'

'Seen you before, mate.' Tessie Cahill looked at Markova.

'DC Markova.'

Tessie Cahill nodded. 'I remember your face, forgot your name. You don't sound local, big man.'

'Cheshire born and Cheshire bred,' said Markova. 'That's me. Strong in the arm and weak in the head. So what made you take a drink, Tessie? Things getting on top of you again? Ready for another spell in the Foss?'

71

Tessie Cahill fell silent. She had the hum of an unwashed body, and the searing hot breath of an alcoholic.

'Have not seen you for some time, Tessie.' Simon Markova smiled as he pressed her. Carmen Pharoah enjoyed the approval and acceptance which Markova extended to Tessie Cahill, and she liked the sensitivity of his manner. She thought him a man with a good heart. Tessie Cahill looked at the floor and then at Simon Markova and smiled. But she said nothing. Outside, a cell door opened with a rattle of keys and clanged shut.

'Tessie,' Markova pressed gently. 'Tessie, my boss, Mr Vossian, he told me and Miss Pharoah here that you wanted to talk to someone. What's wrong, Tessie, somebody been harassing you? Kids on the estate noising you up?'

Tessie Cahill remained silent. She seemed to Carmen Pharoah to be away, or blanked off, as she understood the expression to be.

A few seconds of silence passed. Carmen Pharoah found herself becoming irritated with Tessie Cahill, but at the same time increasingly impressed by the patience that Simon Markova was displaying.

'We can't help you if you won't speak to us, Tessie.' Markova broke the silence, softly, gently.

Tessie Cahill's head moved a fraction of an inch to one side and as it did so Carmen Pharoah observed a look of alertness enter the woman's eyes, as if she had returned from wherever it was that her mind had taken her. 'Aye,' she said, speaking with a strong local accent. 'Aye, I've been doing right well, off the bottle, taking the pills . . . I get agitated this time of year.'

'Tell us.' Markova's attitude seemed to Carmen Pharoah one of genuine concern. She found herself being moved by the man.

'I just do, love, but I get through it. I have to.'

'So tell us, Tessie. What is it about this time of year that upsets you?'

Tessie Cahill looked at Simon Markova and then at Carmen Pharoah and then at Simon Markova again. 'I don't know whether to say anything,' she said.

'If you're worried about something, Tessie, or if you have information to give . . .'

'It's not that.' Tessie Cahill shook her head. Her eyes once again began to appear vacant.

'No. Tessie.' Markova put his hand on her arm. 'Don't go off again. Stay with us.'

Tessie Cahill's head gave a slight, almost imperceptible jerk and her eyes became alert again. She smiled. 'You've met me before.'

'A couple of times.' Markova smiled. 'Where do you go when you do that?'

'Just away from here. Different places.' Tessie Cahill smiled.

'So tell us, Tessie, why did you take a drink when you were doing so well? You've not been lifted for months now.'

'Nearly a year, love.'

'So what's happened to undo all the good and put you back on the skids?'

'I don't know whether I can tell you. I don't know who you are.'

'We've told you. I'm DC Markova. This lady is DC Pharoah.'

'Aye, but who *are* you? Who do you work for? Who's your boss? What's that big word? Loyalty. That's it. Where does your loyalty lie?'

'To the police force,' Markova replied. 'To the upkeep of law and order, to the citizens of the City of York.'

'Mind you, you would say that, wouldn't you? You're not going to admit being part of it, even if you were.'

Markova raised his eyebrows. 'If you've got something to tell us, Tessie . . .'

Tessie Cahill turned to Carmen Pharoah. 'I'm schizophrenic, pet.'

'I'm sorry.' Pharoah smiled.

'At least, that's the label I've been given. But it doesn't mean I don't know things.'

'Of course not.'

'I know about that lad.'

A silence descended on the room.

'I know about that lad they found on the moor. The one in the newspapers and on the television. I know about him, love.'

Markova nodded. Pharoah remained impassive.

'I'll tell you. I'll tell you because there's two of you and I'll tell you because they're not scared of me because I'm a headcase, that's why they leave old Tessie alone. Nobody believes her anyway, not old Tessie. But still, you never know who you're talking to.'

'Please don't talk in riddles, Tessie,' Markova said softly, but authoritatively.

'I'm not, I'm not talking in riddles. Lots don't exist but they do really, I've seen them, underground, kept in cages, shivering, lots of children.'

'Tessie, that'll do.' Carmen Pharoah laid her hand comfortingly on Tessie Cahill's wrist. 'I think we'd better get the police surgeon. Ask him to have a look at you.'

'Unless you'll go to the Foss voluntarily, Tessie,' Markova prompted. 'You know the form as well as we do.'

'Aye, back to the Foss, Redcar ward. Old Tessie's home from home.' Tessie Cahill began to rock backwards and forwards and as she did so she began to sing 'Home Sweet Home'. Then she stopped suddenly and eyed Carmen Pharoah intently. 'But before I go, I can help you, pet. There's two of you. I can do something to help you. I want you to phone Mr John . . .'

'Mr John?'

'He'll tell you. You'll listen to him. You'll not listen to me, there's no reason why you should. I'm cracked, I am a nutter, I'm a schizophrenic and an alcoholic, why should you listen to me? You don't need to get forms signed, I'll go to the Foss and they'll take me in . . . I think I want to go in . . . if you can get me there.'

'We'll get you there, Tessie.' Markova smiled. 'Unmarked car, so you won't be seen by the citizens in the back of a police car.'

'So tell me about Mr John?'

Tessie Cahill leaned forward. 'He's the man that's got the knowledge.'

74

'So you say. Who is he?'

'I've got his phone number. He knows about the little boy. I've got his number.'

'Where?'

Tessie Cahill tapped the side of her head. 'In here, love.'

'So what is it?'

'It's Wetherby 6734267.'

'6734267,' Carmen Pharoah repeated, and wrote it on her pad.

'He lives in Wetherby, he told me, but I haven't been to his house but he told me he lives in Wetherby. I've talked to him in my house and at the Foss. He gave me his number and he said I should phone him if I got into bother because of this.'

'This?'

'This business. Mr John will tell you, love. Mr John will probably tell you things that you won't really want to hear, Mr John will.'

Carmen Pharoah smiled. 'We'll phone him, Tessie. We'll let him know where you are. Just wait here, we'll get a car organized and come back in a minute or two.'

Walking down the corridor, Simon Markova asked, 'Are you going to phone the number?'

'Can't do any harm.'

'How old do you think she is?'

'Tessie? Fifty, fifty-five.'

'She's thirty-four.'

'I can't be doing with this.' The man was elderly, agitated.

'Indeed, sir.' The traffic patrol officer avoided eye contact, remained calm and wrote in his notebook.

'I mean, I'm running this car out of benefits, I'm on long-term sick. I just can't be doing with damage such as this. This is a quiet village. You'd think the car would be safe, but someone's caught it.'

'So I see. Wrecked the wing. You're running it out of welfare benefits, you say?'

'I am. I've only got third-party insurance. He's got to pay for it.'

'Do you think you can afford it, sir?'

'Of course I can't. But I can't do without a car.'

'I see, sir. Your tyres are down to the wear bars, and your tax is up for renewal at the end of this month. I confess, I find it difficult to run a car on a salary. I can't see how you can do it on benefit. And the damage makes this vehicle unroadworthy. And it's on the public highway.'

'I have to park it here. I don't have a drive.'

'Well, you're committing a road traffic offence.'

'How do you work that out?'

'By having an unroadworthy vehicle on the public highway.'

'But that's not my fault. You'll have to catch the bandit that did this. He'll have to pay. See, it was a yellow car, that's a start for you.'

'Yellow?' The police officer knelt down. 'So it was. I hadn't noticed that. That's very interesting. When did this happen, sir?'

'Night before last. One of my neighbours heard the crash in the middle of the night, so she said. I only noticed it an hour ago.'

'So we're talking the early hours of two nights ago. The third of May?'

'I think so. Does that help you?'

'Probably. Can I ask you not to touch the damage? Not to dislodge these flecks of yellow paint?'

'Taking it seriously at last. Good. Very good of you.'

The police officer nodded. 'Oh yes, Mr Halliday. I think we'll be taking this very seriously.' He reached up to the radio attached to his collar and pressed the send button.

Mandy Hampshire sat hunched in her chair, clasping her hands together in her lap and looked to Shapiro and Devers a pathetic, pale, lost and frightened woman. Once again the top-of-the-range television and video recorder sat oddly among the spartan and the threadbare, among the make do and the mend.

'I just never knew it was wrong,' she whimpered. 'Not

76

until now, not until my kids were taken off me. Not until Mirrium told me. Will I get them back?'

'There'll have to be guarantees about their safety first, Mandy.' Mirrium Devers spoke softly, yet her voice had the unmistakable note of authority.

Shapiro's eyes wandered briefly to the window and the rear garden, overgrown, with a single garment – a vest – hanging on a clothes line and which was occasionally ruffled by the breeze.

'You see,' continued Devers, bringing Shapiro's attention back to Mandy Hampshire, 'they've been raped, whichever way you look at it they've been raped. I know that you didn't do it, but equally you didn't protect them.'

'I didn't think it was wrong,' Mandy Hampshire pleaded. 'That's just how it was.'

'As you've said, Mandy,' Devers continued with a soft-spoken but a determined and directed voice. 'But if we go to the judge in the County Court and ask for a Care Order so that they can be returned to you with Social Services' supervision, you'll help yourself if you can indicate who it was that did it, and demonstrate some determination on your part to ensure it won't happen again, and listen, believe me, I want your children back with you as much as you want them back.'

'Honest?'

'Honest.'

'Well, it was me dad what done it.'

'Your father,' Shapiro clarified. 'Ben Pyrrah?'

'Aye . . .' Mandy Hampshire nodded meekly. 'And me brothers, I expect.'

'And your brothers!'

Mandy Hampshire nodded. 'It was done to us, my dad did it to me when I was about eight or nine.'

'And your mother, where was she?'

'She held my hand the first time . . . after that she just stayed downstairs each time.'

Shapiro felt sick, but she continued. 'Your children don't always sleep here, do they?'

Mandy Hampshire shook her head.

'They sleep over at other people's houses?'

'Aye.'

'Your relatives' houses? Your brothers, your parents?'

'Just my father now.'

'I'm sorry. Anybody else?'

Mandy Hampshire shrugged her shoulders.

'Come on, Mandy,' Devers pressed, 'this is not helping you, you're not protecting your children by shielding someone.'

'Them folk in Endon. The McGuires.'

'I see.' Shapiro wrote in her notepad. 'And they also spend nights with your father and your brothers?'

'Aye . . . they go to school from their houses.'

'And your nephews and nieces, does the same thing that happened to your children happen to them?'

'I suppose . . . they spend nights in relatives' houses, and them folk in Endon too, spend nights with me dad, go to see him on Saturday and Sunday afternoon if he asks them to call. It's just how it is. I thought all families were the same. Now I know they're not. It's better the other way – this way, Mirrium's way.'

'You've said you'll make a statement, you'll find that's the easy part, but would you be prepared to give evidence in court against your father and brothers if it came to it?'

'It'll help me get my children back?'

'It'll more or less guarantee it.' Devers smiled. 'But don't see that as a bribe, it's not meant to be. I'm prepared to work to help you get them back with or without your giving evidence or even making a statement to the police. But what would help is not simply for you to make the statement about what went on with respect to your children being wrong and promising you'll protect them in future, but for you to translate that change of attitude into some form of action, some demonstration of your sincerity, and speaking out in court would be, well, pretty well ideal.'

'It's not up to you?'

'Not me personally. These days social work decisions are taken by a committee called a case conference, to which you'll be invited, and ultimately the decision about the return of the children and any Care Order will be made by a judge.'

'Do I need a solicitor?'

Devers nodded. 'I'd engage one if I were you. You'll get Legal Aid for this, so it won't cost you a penny.'

Derek Wyatt drove out of Leeds on the York Road. He'd enjoyed the meeting. Transferring a child protection case from one authority to another is best done with personal contact if distance allows. Had the family decided to relocate to Cornwall then the transfer would have had to be done by Royal Mail, fax and telephone, but York to Leeds is no distance, no distance at all, and it provided Wyatt with the opportunity to look up old colleagues in Leeds Social Services, all of whom wanted to know what York was like to work for. Wyatt would say, 'Same frying pan, different fat.' Driving out of Leeds on the New York Road he noticed the sign to Halton Moor. He glanced at his watch: he had the time to spare. He turned into the estate. It was more run down than he remembered, more burnt-out houses, more burnt-out cars, more overgrown gardens, more houses with satellite dishes. He looked wistfully at certain houses, glanced with a sense of loss down certain streets and as he did so felt the poignancy of lapsed time. But he'd been told it would be like this, if he stayed long enough, if he lived long enough: just as old postmen return and walk their rounds, and retired policemen return to their first beat, so a social worker will eventually return to his or her first patch. It's where the emotional investment was at its greatest, and most profoundly felt. Twenty years on he still remembered his first clients, subsequently to be referred to as agency users, he remembered what their homes smelled like, the names of their pets, names of their relatives, all still fresh in his mind, all from the first few weeks when he was insensitive and ill-advised enough to walk around an area of multiple social deprivation swaggering, with a briefcase and with a university scarf round his neck: he had quickly learned the art of blending with denim and duffle coats and a canvas knapsack. His managers hadn't thought the image professional, but they hadn't had to survive in those streets; especially at night. Wyatt drove off the estate, rejoined the New York Road and settled down to enjoy the return drive to York, enjoying the flat, lush fields of plenty on either side of the road underneath a wide blue sky. He thought a good summer was promised.

He parked his car in a multi-storey and walked to the Social Services Department offices on St Leonard's in the graceful terrace of buildings occupied by various local authority departments. He signed in and said hi to the telephonist, disabled and confined to a wheelchair, but prompt and professional, keen to play his part in the greater scheme of things, and walked up the angled stone staircase to his office. He entered his office, its walls decorated with posters of birds, his all-consuming passion, and a poster showing the ruins of Kirkstall Abbey. He sat at his desk, peeled a yellow self-adhesive label from his phone and read the handwritten note: *Your wife phoned, can you phone her – nothing to worry about. Steve.*

There was a gentle tap on his door, he looked up, Mirrium Devers stood there, dark and serious, if not – in his mind – severe looking, as ever. Behind her was DC Claire Shapiro with whom he had crossed swords on many occasions during case conferences. 'Boss,' Devers said. 'Boss, we've got a problem.'

'You'd better come in.' Wyatt indicated the vacant chairs, one adjacent to his desk, the other against the wall, underneath the poster of Kirkstall Abbey.

'Claire's going to report to her senior officer directly.' Devers sat adjacent to Wyatt's desk. 'But she agreed to sit in with me to make sure I got the details right, if that's agreeable to you?'

'Of course.' Wyatt smiled at Shapiro as she sat in the chair beneath the poster. 'More than welcome.' Then he fell silent and remained silent, growing aghast at the implications as Devers slowly and methodically related the account of the practices within the Pyrrah family, and the genogram which showed Ben Pyrrah at the centre, and of the yet to be explained drawings and the possible link with the family, if not families, in Endon.

'So in effect,' she said, 'we've got – apparently we've got

80

– an extended family that's organized itself into a child sex
ring and they don't seem to see anything wrong with it, but
also a possible link with the incoming families who've settled
in Endon and the weird minister, coffins in the church hall
and malignant-looking nativity masks. It just doesn't add up,
there's something rotten in the state of Denmark.'

'I'll say.' Wyatt nodded.

'These are two of the drawings, Mrs Fee has two more. As
you see, one appears to show a figure tied to a tree or a stake
with red stuff running down his arms, legs and chest, and
the other a cloaked figure with horns on his head.'

Wyatt looked at the drawings. 'What do you make of them,
Claire?' Shapiro shook her head. 'They fox me,' she said,
'but you can't dismiss them as children's fantasy. But we've
now got a further fifteen children to worry about. It's going
to be one of those dreadful dawn raids that you read about.
I've been hoping against hope that I wouldn't have to be
involved in one.'

'Let's let the power of the authority of a case conference
decide the game plan.' Devers' cynicism was undisguised.
'But I will be arguing for grabbing the kids at school if it
comes to that. They're all of school age, apart from Shane;
it's term time, we'll invite the school to the conference, do
it with their prior knowledge and approval. I'd see it happening like that.'

'Neater.'

'Apart from anything else, we won't know which children
are in which house, but we know all except Shane will be
at school.'

'We'd better get a conference organized a.s.a.p.,' said
Wyatt. 'I'll start convening that now.'

'I'll go and feed back to my senior officer.' Shapiro stood.
'He can decide whether to execute the warrant to arrest Ben
Pyrrah before or after the conference. Probably before, if I
know Mr Vossian. With Mandy Hampshire's statement we've
got enough to arrest and hold him for a long time.'

'I'll phone the Fostering Desk,' Devers said, 'give them the
breakdown of the families. Fifteen places, they're going to
have a fit. Can you record all that before you leave for the

day? I think we'd better ensure that this file is up to date at all times.'

'Of course.'

Mirrium Devers noticed the bottle-green Mercedes saloon as she drove out of the multi-storey car park. It had appeared to come as if from nowhere. She thought she was the only car on the exit ramp and then, after pausing at the public highway, she glanced in her rear-view mirror and saw the huge car sitting close up behind her. It seemed to follow her, and then she lost it in traffic and drove out to Bishopsgate to a pleasant semi-detached house with a generous garden. She sat in the comfortably appointed living room of the house and addressed a frail, silver-haired lady: 'You don't have to commit yourself, Mrs Lane' – Devers turned the page of a Community Care Assessment form – 'we'll take you to see one of our homes, perhaps spend a day there.'

Mrs Lane smiled briefly. 'It's come to it, can't manage on my own.'

'Not with you taking falls like you've had in recent weeks, Mum,' said a man who was himself clearly of retiring age. But this, Devers had found, was not an unusual situation with Britain's ageing population. 'Lucky I called when I did yesterday,' continued the man, 'you could have been lying there for days.'

'Could I ask you to read over the form, please, Mr Lane.' Devers handed the form to the frail lady's son. 'If you agree with the boxes I've ticked, based wholly on the answers you or Mrs Lane gave as I asked the questions, perhaps you'd ask Mrs Lane to sign, or you can sign on her behalf if you wish. I think we will be able to offer a place in an aged persons home very quickly, but it's Mrs Lane's decision, and we must respect that. If Mrs Lane wants to soldier on alone in her home we respect that as well and do what we can to assist.'

'Of course.' Mr Lane nodded.

'No, I'll go in,' Mrs Lane said softly. 'I don't like it but I know in myself the time's come.' She sighed. 'Time's well past, in fact. I'll sign the form if Tom says it's all right. I've got my marbles but I can't see so well. My body's gone but my brain's all right. Give me that form.'

'It's all right to sign, Mum.' Tom Lane handed the form to his mother and placed a ballpoint pen in her hand. 'Just there on the line.' He turned to Devers. 'What'll happen to the house?'

'It's Mrs Lane's property. I'm afraid it'll have to be sold to pay towards the cost of her keep.'

'I was afraid of that.'

'If it's any compensation, I was recently in your situation. Many, many families have this experience these days.'

'Any road round it?'

'None that I was able to find.' Devers stood. 'If they have to go into care and if they've got the money, they pay.'

She left the Lane household and walked on to Montague Road where she'd parked her car. She enjoyed work like Mrs Lane's elderly assessment, it was always a welcome change to visit houses where social workers are seen as an ally rather than an enemy.

She drove home to Wistow, and turned into the drive of the house she and Sandy were renting. Her neighbour, tending his garden, scowled at her as she got out of her car. So what? she thought, so she and Sandy weren't liked, didn't fit in in the little village where people work hard to be the same as each other. She entered the house and saw a note pinned to the fridge door: *Back late tonight, parent/teacher meeting – love, Sandy.* Devers tore up the note and tossed it into the wastebin and walked into the front room and looked out over the pasture-like front lawn and saw a bottle-green Mercedes saloon with tinted windows glide past the house.

It was Wednesday, 5th May, 17.30 hours.

4

Wednesday, 5th May, 16.00 hours – Thursday, 6th May,
01.30 hours

John Sorenson was a slender man in his mid-thirties. His
warm eyes smiled from behind steel-rimmed spectacles as
he sat on a futon and beamed across the varnished
floorboards and sheepskin rug at Pharoah and Markova, who
both sat in armchairs of hide suspended on stainless-steel
frames. Modern classical music played softly in the background. A squash racquet leaning against the bookcase indicated to Pharoah that Sorenson worked hard to retain his
waistline. 'So what can I tell you?' he asked.

'Well.' Carmen Pharoah laid her mug of coffee on the low
table which stood between her chair and Simon Markova's
and drew her notepad from her handbag. 'Anything you can,
Mr Sorenson. Anything you'd like to tell us. We're particularly interested in the link between the murdered boy, Tessie
Cahill and yourself.'

'There is a link, I dare say.' Sorenson glanced sideways
out of the window towards the green expanse of Wetherby
racecourse. 'Though it's not what you might think. Nor can
I give any specific information about the murder.'

Carmen Pharoah took a deep breath. 'You're losing me
already.'

'Well, I'll put you in the picture. I am a freelance journalist
and aspiring writer of popular nonfiction. I've published one
book, about the cholera epidemics in the urban north in the
nineteenth century. It was well received by the critics but
nobody's buying it.' Sorenson allowed himself a brief smile.

'For one thing, I wouldn't dismiss Tessie Cahill as an alcoholic schizophrenic. Well, alcoholic perhaps. But schizophrenic, no. She's sane. God only knows how she's been

able to keep sane, but she has. Or if she does have a condition, it's not schizophrenia.'

'I'm sorry, Mr Sorenson, but she's a known schizophrenic. She was admitted to the Foss less than an hour ago. The demand for NHS beds is legendary. They wouldn't admit her if she wasn't insane.'

'How wrong you are, Ms Pharoah, how wrong you are. They believed she was mad, and they still do.'

'A misdiagnosis?' Simon Markova offered.

Sorenson nodded.

'Go on.' Carmen Pharoah allowed a hint of irritation to creep into her voice.

'Did the murdered boy have more serious injuries than were described in the press release? I mean, worse than partially burned and strangled, which is all the press release said. Quite grisly enough, I know, but was there more?'

Pharoah and Markova glanced at each other. 'Such as what?' asked Pharoah.

'Such as damage caused by sexual abuse.'

'Yes,' said Markova. 'Yes, there was that sort of injury.'

'Cuts and bruises?'

'Fair wear and tear or something more deliberate?' asked Markova. 'We have to ask you to be more specific.'

'Well, linear cuts to the eyes, hairline and groin?'

Carmen Pharoah drew a deep breath and nodded. 'Cuts of that description were noted. But we must ask you to keep that to yourself, if it leaks it could prejudice the enquiry.'

'It'll do more than that, Ms Pharoah. It'll send the City of York Social Services Department into a mouth-foaming mass panic. The police as well, I dare say. I assume that the boy hasn't been identified?'

'Not yet.'

'Nor will he be. Chances are that his birth was never registered.'

'Oh . . .' Pharoah gasped.

'You perhaps heard of that girl found in the Brecon Beacons?' Sorenson spoke softly, knowing he had caught Carmen Pharoah's fullest attention. He addressed her, sensing that Markova would remain sceptical. 'About eight years of age, similar sort of injuries. She was never identified. Or the two-year-old boy found on a refuse tip at Millom. He too was partly burned. All that was known about him was that he was local. They could tell that because he had higher than normal radioactivity in his bones, which is symptomatic of Cumbrian children. He too was never identified.'

'I've heard of that incident,' said Markova, nodding. 'I remember the posters going up in police stations across the north, and into Scotland, I believe.'

Again Carmen Pharoah said, 'Go on.'

'Does the day on which the boy's body was found hold any significance for you? I take it that he was murdered shortly before he was found?'

'Yes. Twenty-four hours, possibly a little more.'

'So, his body hadn't been lying there for weeks?'

'No. No.'

'Then the date is significant. He was murdered on the night of the first or second of May. His body kept hidden and then dumped on the moor in the very early morning of the third of May.'

'We assume that to be the timetable. Why?'

'That is the date of the feast of Beltane.'

Simon Markova laughed nervously. 'You can't mean witchcraft?'

Sorenson shook his head. 'Would that it were, you wouldn't have half the problem, but we wouldn't do such a thing anyway.'

'We? Are you . . . ?'

'A witch? Yes, I dare say I am. Bit of a clumsy term. I don't have a broomstick but I keep a black cat, she's out mousing somewhere. Here's where I put my cards on the table and explain my motivation. I am a follower of Wicca. I am a follower of the right-hand path. Wicca is a religion wherein cosmic power is harnessed for doing good. Our creed is "Lest ye harm none, do what you will." Witches value freedom and harmlessness. We believe in a basic love of nature, we love natural foods, we care for the environment and show compassion to others and to animals. We also believe that the effect of working magic will be returned threefold. Quite a formidable prevention to the working of evil. No. What you have got on your hands here is the work of people who are dedicated to the left-hand path. This is Satanism.'

'Oh no.' Carmen Pharoah put her hand to her forehead.

'I'm afraid that what you have here is a child sacrifice during the feast of Beltane, which is one of the major dates in the Satanic calendar and on which a human sacrifice is made. It's a major date in the Wicca calendar too, but following the right-hand path as we do there is no sacrifice of any description.'

Pharoah and Markova remained silent.

'The boy would have been sodomized many times during his life, but during the ceremony itself he would have been raped by two or three men in the inner circle of the coven before being strangled by the High Priest, or Priestess. He may also have been forced to eat noxious substances before he was murdered.'

'He was,' Carmen Pharoah said softly. 'And yes, there were indications of multiple rape.'

'But all this could still be a paedophile sex-ring murder. What points to Satanism is the fact that the lad hasn't been reported as missing, and he won't be because Satanists breed children and keep them for sacrificial purposes, whereas paedophiles will abduct children. And the other thing that points to Satanism is the linear cuts. I've heard reference made to such cuts before, and in fact I know someone who has such cuts on her body. As do you.'

'We do?'

'Tessie Cahill, no less, who was just this afternoon admitted to Foss Dyke Hospital, apparently suffering a relapse of her chronic illness. In fact, she always gets agitated about this time of year, at Beltane and other Sabbats, and takes to drink. If I know Tessie, what would have tipped her over the edge was the news story about the boy on Marston Moor.'

'She was upset about him,' Carmen Pharoah conceded.

'You see, she would have seen the significance. But Tessie also has such cuts, I've seen them, at least the ones on her hairline and eyelids. She told me they were made when she was eight and are as they appear: ceremonial. She was

87

dedicated to Diana, the Satanic deity of sex, and the cuts supposedly allowed Diana to enter her body and control thought, sight and lust.'

Simon Markova sat back in his chair causing the leather to squeak as he moved. 'You'll forgive me if I say that I find this a little far-fetched?'

'Of course I would.' Sorenson smiled. 'In fact, I would expect it. It took me eighteen months of research before I could accept it, but people who are not known to each other, and who live in all corners of this right little, tight little island, have reported the same rituals, the same practices . . . They're all survivors, people who counsel survivors, people who have investigated referrals of Satanistic abuse.'

'And they talk to you quite freely?'

'No. Not really freely. They've all been very cautious. There is an anti-Antichrist network in the UK, and it's shot through with paranoia. Discretion isn't the word to describe it. But once I had convinced one person I was on the level, I was recommended on to another and eventually met people who don't know the first couple of people I spoke to. And not all by any means would speak to me, even then.'

'But all had similar tales?'

Sorenson nodded. 'And with evident distress and fear.'

Simon Markova shook his head. 'I'm still not sure.'

'I fully expect you to be sceptical.' Sorenson paused. 'You see, the extreme nature of the abuse, children bred for lust and eventual sacrifice, children of three being raped, being forced to skin animals alive, and by that I mean that if the child is to pass the test and be assumed further into the group the animal must be alive *sans* skin.' He held up his hand. 'I know what you're going to say, but yes, it is possible – I have checked it with a vet. A strong dog will live up to an hour without its skin before succumbing to the shock. A cat will live for about half an hour in the same condition.

'It's my conviction that this barrage of examples of grossly degenerative behaviour, this ritualized cruelty, is Satanism's first line of defence. And isn't it effective? Few people get beyond it, the great majority of people just can't take it on board and dismiss it as too extreme to be possible. It took me a long time to accept it but I'm powerfully driven, one of my motives is to do something, publish something, that shows the clear separation between the right-hand and the left-hand paths as my contribution to Wicca. Satanists give witchcraft a bad name. The two are completely separate. Having said that, I believe that Satanists have recruited from witchcraft, but to leave the right-hand path for the left is akin to deserting to the enemy in wartime.'

'I still can't take it in.' Markova sighed. 'Children skinning animals. Alive. It's just not possible.'

'Isn't that what people said when the first stories of the camps began to filter out of Nazi-occupied territory? I wasn't around at the time, but I believe that the individuals who risked their lives to bring news of the camps to Allied ears met only disbelief and scepticism. I can imagine their dismay.'

'I can believe it,' Carmen Pharoah said quietly. 'They still practise voodoo and santaria in the West Indies. I went to a convent school and the nuns were terrified of voodoo.'

'Oh, there's voodoo in the UK.' Sorenson spoke matter-of-factly. 'And juju from Black Africa. Both came with the immigrants. And they link with each other. I spoke to one woman, she had spent some time in South Africa when she was a girl. Her parents were Satanists and she remembers a coven of Satanists meeting with a group of juju folk in the bush for a twenty-four-hour long ceremony. Black and white people joining together to worship an evil deity, and that was the days when apartheid was at its height. By day those whites would have been virulent defenders of apartheid. But colour didn't matter when they put on their robes and passed the cup of blood around. The climax of that particular ceremony apparently involved the impaling of a black girl on a spear which was kept propped upright while she died on the end of it. Didn't make a sound, I'm told. Must have been in a state of deep shock. More coffee?'

Pharoah and Markova declined.

'You don't mind if I do?'

When Sorenson returned, padding into the room in Indian buffalo-hide sandals and curling and sinking on to the futon,

Carmen Pharoah asked him about his connection with Tessie Cahill.

'Goes back eighteen months,' he said. 'Maybe nearer two years. Heavens, have I really been at it that long? Anyway, it was Tessie who started it all for me. I did a piece about Yorkshire ghosts. Nothing original, just a jog around the well-known apparitions in the county. Sold it to the *Evening Post* and paid the gas bill. That's how I scratch out a living.'

'You don't seem to be doing so badly.'

Sorenson shrugged. 'Articles for newspapers, articles for magazines. I can eat and fund my research. The house is still heavily mortgaged. I'm thirty-six, I should have paid most of it by now. Missed some payments of recent months, but . . .' He waved a hand dismissively. 'It's the pattern, lean periods occur. Well, I wrote the article about local ghosts, the squad of Roman soldiers marching through York, the sound of a horse galloping along the road from Selby to Snaith, you know the sort of thing, and I received a letter from Tessie, me care of the *Post*. I've still got it somewhere, if you'd like to see it. That letter started everything, you see. Scrawly, spidery writing, in black ink with wavy red lines round the edge of the paper. A real fruitcake, I thought. But the letter asked me if I wanted information about "more than ghosts"? I confess that intrigued me. If she had said "more ghosts" I wouldn't have followed it up, but "more *than* ghosts", well that aroused my curiosity.'

'Yes,' Carmen Pharoah said. 'I can see how it would.'

'I thought she was a crank. Then I got to know her and now I think she may be one of the cleverest and strongest people I know. Anyway, I was in a lull. No work coming in, hence the piece about ghosts. You can always tell when there's no real news about, because then the newspapers will start printing articles about ghosts and the paranormal, anything to fill those column inches. So I thought I'd follow up the letter. I thought that if there was nothing in the "more than ghosts" bit then I might still be able to do a case study of the letter writer. She was probably chronically mentally sick, and so a piece about what community care means in practice might come out of it. So I made arrangements to call on Tessie in her untidy council house. I asked a mate to come along to wait in the car so that if I yelled, or broke a window, he could come to my assistance.'

'Sensible,' Markova acknowledged grudgingly. He continued to eye Sorenson coldly.

'Well, you've seen the estate that Tessie lives on, and you'll know better than me that a little old lady can slot a marine if she's able to slide the blade in at the correct angle. Can't be too careful. Confess, I realize now that I'd met her only after she'd done an awful lot of sorting out inside her head and was at that stage where she wanted to tell someone. You know that way, not to put upon someone, or dump all your bad news, but just to tell someone. I've heard of people talking to inanimate objects, or telling the bush in the garden. I think it's called disclosing. So she disclosed to me, and like you, Mr Markova, I was deeply sceptical at first, but my commitment to Wicca helped and there was also something about the calm, dispassionate matter-of-fact way in which she spoke which I found compelling.'

Ken Menninot and Leif Vossian sat in Vossian's office. Vossian leaned forward and peered at the road atlas.

'I see what you mean.' Vossian followed a minor road with his fingertip. 'So, he was seen to turn left towards Tockwith? Then his vehicle was apparently in collision with a parked vehicle here in Little Ribston. After Little Ribston is Knaresborough, Harrogate and the Dales. We've got a sample of the yellow paint found on the parked vehicle off to the forensic science lab, I hope?'

'Certainly have, boss. They're just waiting for a vehicle to match it with. The owner of the parked car is impressed by the length the police are going to to trace the owner of the vehicle that rammed him so he can claim against him for the damage.' Menninot thought and hoped his quip might raise just a quiver of a smile on Vossian's lips. It didn't.

'I take your point that this indicates a local villain. As you say, choosing Marston Moor as a place to dump the body implies coincidence or local knowledge. And if he did ram the parked vehicle in Little Ribston it meant he had crossed the A1. If he was a foreigner he'd have got out of the area on the A1, and fled north or south. But he didn't, he drove on minor roads towards Knaresborough. Yes, I think you're right, he's local.' Vossian closed the road atlas. 'Ken, I want you to give this your undivided. I don't like unsolved crimes, as you know. I like even less unsolved murders, and even less than that do I like unsolved sex murders of children. There's a nasty turkey going gobble, gobble, gobble out there, Ken, and I want him in the coop.'

Menninot stood and picked up the road atlas. 'Well, you're not alone there, sir. I can't remember when a crime has generated so much anger in Friargate, and I've been here since the dawn of time, seems like it, anyway.'

'So there's a bit of telephone work at present, tedious, but it gets results. You anxious to get off?'

'Well . . .' Menninot glanced at his watch. 'My shift did finish half an hour ago, but a case like this . . .'

'Do what you can as far as you can. Then hand over to Markova and Pharoah. Where are they, by the way?'

'Interviewing a member of the public who offered information.'

'Both of them?'

'Yes, boss, both of them.'

'Just you and me in CID in the building?'

'That's about the size of it. They can be called up on the vodaphone if needed.'

'Aye, suppose I still don't like spreading my jam any thinner than necessary. I don't like two people doing a one-man job, and receiving information is not a two-hander. In my experience, if you send two people out on a one-man job, only one of them does the work anyway, the other has a nice time as a fly on the wall. But I'll talk to them when they get back. So, how are you going to proceed, do you think?'

'Well, I'm fully aware that once beyond the walls, this is North Yorkshire, land of milk and honey and green wellies, hunting pink and many, many Range Rovers, but so far, as I have observed, not many yellow Range Rovers. It sounds like a respray or a one-off special order to me, so I'll phone the concessionaires in the area. They'll take used Range

Rovers as trade-ins against a new model and knock them out again and take them back again a few years later, and they get to know the vehicles in their area. I would have thought a yellow one would shine like gold in their field of knowledge.'

Vossian said, 'Yes, I like the logic.'

'The other end of the rainbow may well be a panel-beating business; the man that Robert McGregor described didn't sound to me like a do-it-yourself merchant, and his damaged vehicle would have to be repaired. Just a lot of phoning around, as you say.'

Ken Menninot forced a smile and left Vossian's office and walked down the corridor to his room. He had promised to take his son out for the afternoon upon his return from work; he was now obliged to work overtime. He sat beside his desk and adjusted the photograph of his wife and children, picked up the phone and dialled a Beverley number. 'Guess what?' he said when a female voice answered the call.

'Late work?' The thin voice didn't hide the disappointment therein.

'The lad they found on Marston Moor. Just a few calls to make. I'll be home when I can, but I won't be taking Thomas out.'

'He'll be disappointed.' Said with the suggestion of threat, of consequences.

'I know it's not the first time I've disappointed him like this.'

'I know that, too.'

'And it won't be the last. He'll just have to get used to being a police officer's son. Anyway, I did think that doing the things we'd planned in less than half a day was pushing it a bit, you know how I like to do things justice, and . . .'

'Want to give an example of being thorough in all things. Yes, I know, but it'll mean me dealing with the disappointment and him and Sara squabbling . . .'

'Well, he is still supposed to be sick.'

'The doctor said he could go out now, but to keep him off school a bit longer.'

'Anyway, point one, I'll compensate him in the next day

or two, and point two, he's alive – the lad on Marston Moor isn't. And they're about the same age. I'll be home when I can.' He put the handset down with finality. He picked up the phone again and phoned the police stations in Knaresborough and Harrogate, both constables who took his call were polite and helpful. They personally had no knowledge of a yellow Range Rover, but would place his request on 'Notices' and pass it to Traffic for special attention. Menninot replaced the phone and reached behind him and took the Yellow Pages for Harrogate and Knaresborough off the windowsill.

John Sorenson also replaced his phone and smiled at Pharoah and Markova. 'She's sleeping now, on Redcar Ward which is where she was last time she was in the Foss, and the time before that if memory serves.' He returned to the futon. 'By sleep I dare say they mean they've filled her up with chlopromazine or some other knock-out drops for so-called schizophrenics.'

'You don't appear to have much faith in the medical profession, Mr Sorenson?' Carmen Pharoah looked intently at Sorenson.

Sorenson held up his hand. 'Please don't misunderstand me. If I lose my marbles you can bang me up in the Foss any time. I have found the staff excellent, but only if I lose my marbles, and there's the rub, because they seem to see schizophrenia where it doesn't exist. If you ask me, it's a convenient cover-all label to stick on people who exhibit behaviour that can't be immediately explained.'

'So what *is* Tessie's condition if not schizophrenia? In your opinion?' Carmen Pharoah glanced over Sorenson's shoulder, out of the window and to the middle distance. Two horses were being cantered on Wetherby gallops, two specs of brown, on green under blue.

'I don't see the point of this,' growled Markova. But Carmen Pharoah laid her hand on his forearm. He glanced at her.

'Well, Tessie isn't schizophrenic . . . she has MPD,' Sorenson continued as he observed something between Pharoah and Markova, something either established or growing, her gentle hand on his arm.

'MPD?'

'Multiple Personality Disorder. It's a clinically recognized condition and not at all uncommon among survivors of extreme child abuse. I have figures somewhere and a pamphlet about it, but if again memory serves . . . if a child suffers extreme abuse, aged birth to four years, he or she will almost certainly develop MPD. If a child suffers extreme abuse aged four to eight years, there is a fifty per cent chance that that child will develop MPD and should extreme abuse occur aged eight and over, MPD will not develop because the personality is integrated by then and it will not disintegrate. It may change if the life should be dogged by tragedy, a happy child may grow into a sour adult because of a series of tragedies but the personality will not disintegrate as such.'

'You speak with a certain degree of authority on this subject,' Markova growled, 'for a journalist.'

'A combination of research and a first-class honours degree in psychology, plus postgraduate study.' Sorenson shrugged. 'Good enough?'

'Good enough,' Markova conceded with a sigh. 'You didn't continue in that field?'

'I started out but began to step to a different drummer, if you know what I mean. But to return to Tessie, so far as I can tell she has five independent personalities, I dare say you'll meet them. Anyway, Tessie, God bless her, realized that the more she spoke about her experiences and the more she revealed of her personalities, the more she was working herself into the bricks of the Foss. So she began to keep quiet, became docile, and cooperated so that the medics thought they'd found the right medication, and the occupational-therapy staff taught her survival skills, basic cooking, use of money, use of a launderette, and Tessie went along with it. In other words, she worked her ticket. She was helped by the introduction of community care legislation, which as you know encourages community-based care. Eventually she was discharged and the medics patted themselves on the back and chalked her up as a success. They gave her a drug regime of three pills a day, and each day she takes three pills and flushes them down the tubes so that when the nurse calls he finds the right amount of pills in the bottle and finds a stable-minded Tessie and he cycles away happy. Anyway, Tessie's been in the community now for about five years but occasionally she gets drunk and is known to yourselves, and she occasionally gets taken back into the Foss, as now, in fact.'

'She's cured,' Markova said quietly, 'it's as simple as that.'

'She was never mad, Mr Markova.' Sorenson spoke softly, holding eye contact. 'But when she was in her early twenties she couldn't cope with the guilt, her life fell apart, she began to talk of arguing with herself and speaking in different voices and was diagnosed as a schizophrenic. But she was never mad. The core personality, the Tessie you have met, is sane.'

'You mentioned guilt,' Carmen Pharoah probed.

'She murdered children . . . and she did other things.'

'Such as?'

'It may be better if she told you.'

'I suggest you tell us,' Markova said, icily. 'If you're holding information about crimes like murder. I suggest that you tell us all you know. Withholding such information is a serious matter.'

Sorenson smiled. 'I'm in possession of no details, only that which Tessie has told me.' Sorenson paused. 'I can only repeat that I am not in possession of any information about any murder at any time, anything I can say is only hearsay. And what Tessie can tell you is only background infor-mation.'

'That's not a great deal to bring us out here for, Mr Soren-son,' Markova said coldly.

'Not at the moment. But if I was to take one of you to meet Tessie at the Foss, I'm sure she'd talk to you, then you would get to know what went on behind the scenes in respect of the boy whose murdered body was found on Marston Moor. She'll be drugged for the next few weeks, but once she's eased off the medication, once she's reached the stage of self-medication, which means she flushes it down the tubes, then we'll go and speak to her.'

*   *   *

96

Ken Menninot drew a line through the fifth telephone number on his list and dialled the sixth. One more, he thought, one more and I'll break for coffee. He felt he needed a caffeine fix.

'Well, there's one here right now.' The voice cheery and helpful and spoken in reply to Menninot's query.

Ken Menninot's heart missed a beat. 'What?'

'There's a yellow Range Rover here right now. It's got a dent in the front offside wing. A small dent but the owner wants it looked at and then the whole vehicle resprayed.'

'Have you started work on it?'

'Not yet, love.'

'Can we ask you not to? Just leave it exactly as it is.'

'Aye, you can ask. I'll have to let the owner know.'

'You can leave that to us. Who is the owner?'

'Local big nob called Nigel Harrby. The Honourable Sir Nigel Harrby, local worthy, landowner, magistrate, councillor, failed Tory MP.'

'I've heard of him. He contested a safe Tory seat in the last election and lost it to the Liberal Democrats.'

'That's the lad. Toffee-nosed bugger but he pays his garage bills so I mustn't grumble.'

'What address do you have for him?'

A pause. 'This is the police I'm talking to?'

'City of York Police, not the Knaresborough Police.'

'Only I shouldn't be so free with this sort of information, it could cost me custom.'

'Well, you could phone me back, but since you've given us a name and a pretty unique name at that . . .'

'Aye . . . Well, it's Scythe Farm, out on the Northallerton Road.'

'I see.' Menninot scribbled on his pad.

The garage owner related the registration number. 'Almost brand new and he wants it resprayed. He had it resprayed from the original green, now he wants it green again. Fella doesn't know his own mind. He's got money to burn. So who am I to complain? Mind you, I shouldn't run the guy down, I could do with more customers like him.'

'Thanks for this. But don't mention this to Mr Harrby.'

'Very well. I'm not likely to see him, though. He doesn't pester me once he leaves me with a job. Really could do with more like him.'

'Thanks again.' Ken Menninot replaced the phone. 'Bingo!' He smiled and clasped his hands behind his head, then leaned forward and picked up the phone and tapped a four-figure internal number. 'Collator? Menninot here. I've got a vehicle registration number here, can you run it through your magic box and tell me who it's registered to?' He gave the information and then replaced the phone. 'Time for coffee,' he said, standing and walking across to where the coffee and mugs and kettle stood. He felt pleased, a sense of satisfaction. Getting a result is always worth overtime. It was overtime with no result that got to him. He poured boiling water on to coffee granules. He felt in his waters that the enquiry into the Marston Moor murder would start to move now, really start to move. His phone rang. He walked back to his desk and picked it up and listened as the collator told him that the registration number he'd been given was that of a Range Rover, yellow, registered to one Nigel Harrby, of Scythe Farm, Knaresborough. Menninot thanked the collator, added the information to the file, then left Friargate Police Station. Time, he thought, time to hit the ten seventy-nine. He had a home, and a family, to go to.

He drove down the A1079 leisurely, his wasn't, he knew, an unreasonable drive to and from work, a black surfaced road, mainly two lanes but dual carriageway in parts, driving almost straight across flat or gently undulating countryside, and even when still some miles out affording a welcoming glimpse of the thin Gothic towers of Beverley Minster to the homecoming motorist. He entered the town on trailing throttle, driving past the racecourse and turned left at the lights on North Bar Within, and moments later turned right into Molescroft Park. He drove along the road of proud, neatly tended gardens, of Volvos on brick-laid drives, of neat grass verges and turned left into the driveway of number 131.

He drank a mug of tea offered grudgingly by Mrs Menninot, who he felt had never and would never grasp that police

98

officers can't be guaranteed to get home on time. Ever.

Later, after listening to Sara's account of her school day and helping Thomas build a model aeroplane, he strolled into Beverley, just for the walk more than anything. He enjoyed living in Beverley, its ancient buildings, narrow pedestrianized streets, its strong identity which has prevented it from becoming a fashionable suburb of Hull. He settled here because his wife refused to leave, and in the early days felt he would miss the big-city bustle of his native Leeds. But he had settled, much to his surprise. He walked into Toll Gavel, the cobblestoned marketplace, the white telephone kiosks of Hull Telecommunications, the ribbon of shops and houses all kept to the human scale. He fetched up at the Monk's Walk in Highgate in the shadow of the Minster and enjoyed a pint or two.

Carmen Pharoah and Simon Markova sat in front of Leif Vossian's desk. Vossian sat motionless, eyed Pharoah, then Markova. He said, 'I'm astounded.'

The two detective constables remained silent.

'It was a waste of time for both of you to go. DS Menninot had to put in overtime because you two went off on what was a single-hander . . .'

'That was my fault . . .' Markova started.

'I don't care whose fault it was. It costs money to run a police station, and all you've got from him is that the infamous Tessie Cahill isn't a schizophrenic but has some other illness. And that she might be worth chatting to when she comes off the drugs. You did advise this man, what's his name . . . ?'

'Sorenson.'

'You did advise him of the consequences of wasting police time?'

'Well . . .'

'All right, carry on. You've still got a shift to finish.'

Leif Vossian drove home to his semi-detached house in Easingwold. He ate a supper of fish and chips while watching television and filled the evening by reading further from the biography of Captain James Cook who, like him, was a native of Cleveland. Leif Vossian had possessed the book for many years, promising himself that he would start it 'when he had the time'. Now he had the time, though not as he had planned, and still less than he would have liked. From time to time, as he read, he would look up from the pages and gaze wistfully at the framed photograph of a woman and two children which hung proudly, prominently above the fireplace.

At the end of the shift Carmen Pharoah accepted Simon Markova's offer of a drink. They had two. She said yes to coffee at his place.

Later, when they lay side by side and as the beam of the headlights of a passing car swept across the ceiling, Carmen Pharoah said, 'I used you, Simon.'

He turned to her.

'I'm sorry, but I really needed to be with someone tonight. And not in my house, I'm still living out of bin liners and cardboard boxes. I didn't want to go home and I didn't want to be alone.'

Markova remained silent.

'What I'm saying is that it doesn't mean anything. It doesn't mean it's leading anywhere. It doesn't mean it's going to happen again.'

It was Thursday, 6th May, 01.30 hours.

5

'Yes' – the tall thin man nodded as he looked down on Menninot with undisguised imperiousness – 'I own a Range Rover.'

'A yellow one?'

The man nodded. He wasn't giving anything away and Menninot knew he was going to have to work uphill. He also knew that he was going to have to box clever. This man would make any mistake of his a costly mistake. 'Why?'

Ken Menninot had driven across the rich countryside between York and Knaresborough with the intention of calling on Harrby, not to interview him, not to lean on him, but to let him know that he had been identified as a suspect. Menninot wanted to agitate him, sow a seed of fear, put him off his stroke. Scythe Farmhouse revealed itself to be a four-square and solid stone-built building, white painted, surrounded by a neatly kept lawn. Beyond were the farm buildings, a silo, twin John Deeres neatly parked. Nearer at hand was a bottle-green Mercedes Benz and a small pink Fiat: a conventional 'his and hers' image. Menninot pulled up on the gravel, where the Mercedes Benz and the Fiat were parked, between the house and lawn. He got out of his car and slammed the door behind him. He wished to make no secret of his arrival. It was about ten a.m. He noted this for his report as he approached the front door; and the weather had the makings of a fine day, especially for early May. The front door of the house was heavy, wooden, gloss black paint, a brass knocker. He rapped on it and the door was opened instantly by a maid, a middle-aged woman, starched black dress and stern faced. Menninot had the impression that she had heard his arrival and had stood behind the door

101

waiting for him to knock. He identified himself and asked to speak to Nigel Harrby. The door was then closed firmly in his face without a further word being spoken. Moments later the door was opened a second time, this time by a tall slender man in his sixties, light-coloured hair, brown jacket and plus fours. He smiled approvingly at Menninot. Menninot for his part sensed with the experienced intuition of a seasoned police officer that he was in the presence of a very dangerous man; the glint of gold in his smile, below icy eyes, the every-thing-in-its-place perfection of Scythe Farm. Caution. Danger.

'Why?' Harrby asked when Menninot had followed him as bidden into the drawing room, first door on the right off a wide wood-panelled hallway which smelled heavily of polish. 'Why are you interested in my Range Rover?'

'It's in connection with a serious incident.' Menninot read the room which, he noted, enjoyed the morning sun. Solid, expensive-looking furniture, brass ornaments, paintings of hunting scenes. 'You may have read about it, the body of a young boy found on Marston Moor?'

'Oh, yes. Yes. It's not often that I take an interest in local news but I did read that story. I imagine some single parent under stress, an episode of mental illness, not guilty of mur-der by reason of diminished responsibility, that sort of thing. Happens all the time.'

'So you know it was murder?'

'It said in the paper that he had been strangled, the rest is conjecture.'

'Could be dangerous, Mr Harrby.'

'Sir Nigel.'

'I'm sorry.'

'My title is the Honourable Sir Nigel Harrby. I like to observe it, it's hereditary, you see. I observe it out of respect to my ancestors.'

'Sir Nigel,' Menninot nodded, 'the reason I am here is that a Range Rover, a yellow Range Rover, was seen in the vicin-ity of Marston Moor on the night of the murder.'

'I see.' Harrby wasn't giving anything away. 'The night of the murder being . . .'

'Three nights ago. The night of second and third of May. Can you tell me where you were?'

'Well, here, I suppose.'

'You suppose?'

'Unless I'm given to sleepwalking. I haven't been out that late for . . . oh . . . many months. I've been shown the yellow card by my GP. Got to cut down on the alcohol and the late nights . . . and I've largely kept to that policy, but it's difficult to break the habits of a lifetime, and I like a tipple.'

'Your wife?'

'The Lady Cynthia?'

'The Lady Cynthia,' Menninot echoed, and thought that a man such as this just *had* to have a wife called Cynthia. 'I suppose she would be able to corroborate your alibi?'

'I should think so. We would have retired for the night at about eleven thirty and would have woken at about seven thirty, that is our routine and I can't recall the last time it was disrupted.'

'I see. I didn't see your Range Rover outside?'

'It's being resprayed. I had it resprayed yellow because I wanted it to be distinctive, but it's too loud, just doesn't blend at hunt meetings and I can't take it on shoots because the colour scares the game away.'

'I see, Mr . . . I'm sorry, Sir Nigel. Could I pick your brains about a matter.' Menninot allowed his body posture to relax. 'I know that you said you take little interest in local news, but being a farmer, a councillor, and a magistrate . . .'

'You have been doing your homework. Yes, I am all those, but principally a farmer. Five hundred acres of arable, it's pretty well all under rape seed at the moment. I don't like turning England into a yellow and pleasant land, but the EEC want it, produces margarine and lubricating oil and both reduce dependency on non-European imports.'

'Rape?' said Menninot, stiffening again.

'Sorry?'

'That yellow stuff is called rape? I didn't know that. I'm a city lad, and don't know much about what happens in the fields. Rape, you say?'

'That's it.'

'You know, when I was a lad farmers seemed to drive green Land Rovers and the fields were green. Now they drive yellow Range Rovers and the fields are yellow and full of rape. Funny that.'

'You were going to pick my brains about a matter?' Harrby spoke testily.

'Yes, I wonder if you believe that you have a finger on the pulse of this area, what makes the area tick?'

'Try me.' Harrby raised an eyebrow as if mollified by the implicit compliment.

'Really, it's just that Range Rovers being owned by the people they are owned by, they often know each other. I mean you wouldn't know off hand of any other yellow Range Rover in the area? It's not a common Range Rover colour.'

'No, off hand or any other way, I know of no other yellow Range Rover in the area.' He pressed a button on the wall. A bell rang in the hall, the door of the room opened instantly and the maid entered. Again, Menninot had the impression that she had been waiting just outside the door. 'Dolly will see you out. I've work to do.' He turned and stood facing the window. His back towards Menninot.

'Thanks for your time, anyway.' Menninot turned towards the door. He knew when not to push it. 'I'll go back to York, have another chat with our witness. Perhaps it wasn't a yellow Range Rover he saw.'

'You've got a witness?' Said hurriedly, as Harrby spun to face Menninot.

'Yes, in fact we have, a lad that's known to us – he was walking across the moor after sighting up a house to turn over in Long Marston – was near the trees when the head-lights approached so he hit the deck and rubbed soil on his face. He was wearing camouflage gear, ex-army stuff, so he wasn't noticed by the driver of the Range Rover, but he was close enough to see what was happening. He dragged the body out of the flames and put it out, but left the vegetation burning, in case the driver of the Range Rover was clocking his rear-view mirror and would turn back if the flames seemed to die down too quickly. He's a clever-thinking lad, but as I said, he probably mistook the make and colour of the vehicle, being night and all, but the flames . . .'

'Who is he?' Colour drained from Harrby's face.

Menninot paused. 'Why would you want to know that, Sir Nigel?'

'Well . . . I'm impressed, that's all. No other reason, Mr Menninot.'

'Detective Sergeant.'

'Sorry.'

'I'm Detective Sergeant Menninot. I like titles too, you see. But I'll go and have another chat with the lad. He didn't offer a very clear physical description of the driver of the Range Rover, but what he gave us could match you, and he did hear him speak, said he had a posh-sounding voice.'

'Posh?'

'As perhaps yourself, Sir Nigel; perhaps you would be seen as "posh" by some folk.'

In the hall Dolly bustled Menninot to the door and slammed it behind him. He enjoyed the heat from the sun as he walked across the gravel to his car. Scythe Farmhouse had had a chill about it. He drove back to York, feeling that it had been a successful visit. He had done what he had intended to do.

'I unnerved him, boss. Got well under his skin, rattled his cage, all right.'

Leif Vossian said, 'Tell me about him.'

Menninot sipped his coffee. 'Where to start . . . ? Well, your typical country squire, that's for sure. He's on the Knaresborough bench and I can just see him banging up poachers who nick a duck or a rabbit to feed their families and giving a token fine to a neighbouring landowner for a firearms offence. You know the attitude – "These things happen, we'll say ten quid", but the poacher from the council estate goes down for three months, such is shire-county culture.'

'I take it you're a labour voter, Ken?'

'Member of the Party,' Menninot said with no small amount of pride.

'Really?'

'Really. I attend branch meetings, pay my subscriptions, but I don't canvass or leaflet, not proper for a serving police officer to do that.'

'No. So back to the Right Honourable . . .'

'Well, he's got money, all right. Scythe Farm is a nice parcel of land. Mercedes Benz, two John Deeres that I saw . . .'

'Different world.'

'I'll say, but he was agitated when I told him about Robert McGregor, not by name, of course.'

'You think he's our man?'

'I would think so, boss, but right now we're still a touch short of E for evidence. Even a half-baked defence barrister could blow McGregor's evidence out of the water, a known felon, dead of night . . . I can't even see the CPS moving on it.'

'I think you're right.' Vossian handed Menninot a series of black-and-white photographs. 'Tyre tracks taken around the scene of the crime, identified as probably Range Rover tracks, but nothing to set them apart, no uneven tyre wear, for example, ordinary tyres. I've asked Scene of Crime to take a trip out to Knaresborough to photograph the tyres of the Range Rover in question, just for form's sake, and I'm sure they'll match, but without a "fingerprint" of uneven wear, or a unique tread, we're still no further down the road.'

'I think we should pull the vehicle, let the forensic science lab at Wetherby go over it with a fine-toothed comb.'

'We'll need a warrant.'

'We could get one.' Menninot raised an eyebrow. 'McGregor's eyewitness account, our suspicions. In fact, you know, I'd be inclined to charge Harrby with murder and that would force the hand of the CPS – they'd have to run with what we've got.'

Vossian nodded. 'Or else they'd have to go to the Magistrates' Court and ask that the case be dropped and the magistrates on hearing the evidence may insist they proceed, especially when the prime suspect is a magistrate – they wouldn't allow themselves to be seen to be giving a fellow magistrate preferential treatment.'

'Might be worth a shot, but it would still hinge on McGregor's evidence unless we can break Harrby's alibi.'

'If the paint on the damaged car in Little Ribston matches the paint on Harrby's Range Rover, then that's the alibi badly dented. Trouble is, there is no witness as to the exact time of the impact.'

Menninot shook his head. 'Pity, but let's not give up. We're getting there, inching forwards.'

Vossian paused. He consulted the view from the window, then the carpet on his office floor. Then he said, 'Look, Ken, I think we go for it. Take some uniforms and go back and fondle his collar. Bring him in and lean on him, but mind your manners, he won't be coughing to anything and he'll have his brief with him at all times.'

Menninot glanced at his watch. 'Midday.'

'You'll be working overtime again.'

'For this I don't mind. But that's not what I was thinking. We can hold him for twenty-four hours without charging him. How soon can we get a result on the paint match?'

'Probably not within twenty-four hours. But we can try and obtain a priority treatment, but other forces will be doing the same.'

Menninot stood. 'Right, I'll grab some lunch and then the warrants.'

Carmen Pharoah had woken in Simon Markova's bed. She had slipped out from under the duvet without waking him, had scooped her clothing from the floor and had stolen into the bathroom where she washed and dressed. She hustled a cup of coffee in his kitchen, a typically single man's kitchen, she thought, cluttered, not so much unclean as very untidy, and with the telltale permanent pile of unwashed dishes in the sink. She sat at the breakfast bar and leafed through Air India brochures about holidays in Goa as she sipped the coffee. She rinsed the mug and then slipped out of the house into South Bank Avenue, terraced houses on one side, playing fields on the other. She walked back to her house by way of Blossom Street. There were probably more direct routes, but she kept to the few roads she knew.

She let herself into her house and picked up her mail. Bills, a letter from the solicitors about the house purchase, glossy colourful circulars. She kicked the door shut behind her and stepped between the cardboard boxes and plastic bin liners as she made her way down the hallway. She showered and changed into clean clothing and only then did she notice the light flashing insistently on her answering machine. She strode across the room and pressed the play button.

'Hello . . .' Carmen Pharoah caught her breath. She listened to the message. 'It's seven thirty in the evening . . . didn't know what turn you're on . . . I just phoned to say hello . . . it's Wesley . . .'

Carmen Pharoah sank against the wall. She felt a pain in her chest, she wanted the pain, she didn't want it. She felt torn, she felt the urge to return the call, but to do so seemed akin to opening an old wound which she felt had already bled sufficiently.

Simon Markova opened his eyes at the sound of the gentle click of the closing of his front door. He felt a pang of disappointment, the bed seemed suddenly very empty. But she'd been upfront about it. She said that it hadn't meant anything, but he could not help the hope that it might, just might, be leading somewhere.

He had thought he'd made a good adjustment to the single life, a quiet house was far better than a house wherein children cowered while their parents snarled and spat insults at each other. Yet there was also an emptiness. He lay in the bed and savoured Carmen Pharoah's musk. He gazed up at the ceiling and allowed his eyes to follow a superficial crack in the plaster, which ran in a crazy zigzag from the light fitting and he thought about his situation. A silent house, he had found, was preferable to a warring house, but yet he found the sense of loss to be insidious, like an apple being devoured from within by a maggot.

Simon Markova rolled out of bed and clawed on his dressing gown. Went downstairs to his kitchen, made a pot of tea which he allowed to infuse before pouring it into a huge clay mug. He returned upstairs and drew a bath, as hot as he could bear, and immersed himself in it, mug of tea in hands. A light lunch, a short drive to work. But mainly his thoughts dwelt upon the lithe and long-limbed Carmen Pharoah.

Leif Vossian walked into Ken Menninot's office. It was empty. He glanced at the clock on the wall. Of course, Ken had said, 'lunch then the warrants', and if he knew Ken Menninot, the man would be eating outside, not at all partial to a steak-and-kidney pie in the subsidized canteen. Ken kept a neat office, even by police standards, it was never less than Bristol fashion. Except, Vossian noticed with dismay, on this occasion. On this occasion, in a blatant flouting of Home Office rules and utterly out of character for DS Menninot, a case file lay open on his desk. Vossian picked it up and reached for Ken Menninot's filing cabinet. It was locked. He'd got that bit right, but leaving a file open on his desk was inexcusable. And the Marston Moor murder file, no less. He wrote a brief note and left it on Menninot's desk. *Marston Moor murder file with me. Don't leave files on desks. LV.* He carried the file back to his office.

Rob 'Roy' McGregor rose from the plastic-covered settee and switched off the hissing gas fire. He slid into his camouflaged combat jacket and took the five-pound note from under the clock. Fish and chips again. By himself during the day, no work, not for him. His mother was at work in the kitchen of the hospital bringing in a penny and his father was doing three years in Armley. And he was disinclined to cook, so it was fish and chips again. He left the house by the side door and walked down the pitted and pocked concrete path and recalled how big these houses looked when he was small, and then suddenly they had looked small as if they had shrunk, though by then he'd seen other folks' houses, from within as well as from without. He turned left and walked down the road, passing identical house after identical house. Some had tended gardens, others less so; some had turned their front gardens into paved areas on which a car or a motorbike might stand, the cars in a state of being done up prior to sale; the bikes with massive padlock and chain holding them in place. This was council land. Some folk in work, some staying out of trouble, some out crooking, a land of teenage pregnancies and crack cocaine. Two boys of school age tried the door of a car, saw him approach and ran away. Robert McGregor smiled. He remembered doing that himself, until he had found he had housebreaking skills, the ability to move over dried leaves without making a sound, and he could slither his entire body through a six-inch gap.

He turned the corner and walked down the main road that ran through the estate. Here the houses are on a bus route and always kept in better repair than the houses in the side streets. And it's here that the tenants have taken the option to buy their property and advertised the fact by engaging builders to build Georgian bay windows on to the house. He knew he couldn't make it on the right side of the law. Who'd give him a start? But he could earn a living as a housebreaker, like father like son, and he had a code of conduct, he didn't mess up people's houses, didn't spray paint on the walls or defecate in the drawers. Only raided rich folks who could afford to lose a bit and had insurance anyway, and that, he felt, was what Mr Menninot didn't realize: it was a job, it was a skill, something to take a pride in. So you get banged up once in a while, you can survive that, it's a form of taxation, and you always leave the slammer with one or two more contacts, one or two more useful tips.

He crossed the main road and stood in the queue in the fish-and-chip shop. 'Fish and chips once, love, plenty of salt, plenty of vinegar. Come on, pet, let it swim. It's a fish, it won't drown.' He left the shop and retraced his steps, holding the fish and chips in the paper inside his jacket.

So now there's going to be a bit of a quiet period. Got to let this die down, this little snapper on the moor business, he would wait a couple of months, because that house in Long Marston was a peach, oh, talk about ripe, and no dogs and no alarm . . . he had to do it before anyone else did, and until then there was always the university. He could wander on to the campus, get taken for a student, never challenged.

He'd never yet walked off the campus empty handed, a good coat or jacket here, a pair of boots from the changing room, a purse on a shelf in the library, a mountain bike propped against the wall for thirty seconds, those students are all going to be doctors or lawyers, they'll make up the loss easily enough. He stepped into the road. They can afford to lose a bit, so that's the sketch, university, and the tourists as well, a little bit here and there, just to keep going until June or Ju –

Nigel Harrby replaced the phone and glanced across the deep-pile carpet to where his wife sat, ashen faced. Behind her, Dolly, the maid, stood equally ashen faced. 'It's the end.' He spoke softly, eventually breaking the silence. 'For me, anyway. One way or the other, it's the end. I have a few weeks, but that's all I have.'

Ken Menninot returned to his desk, satisfied after a full lunch. He picked up Leif Vossian's note, smiled and in an instant began to frown. He walked to Vossian's office with urgency in his step and stood in the doorway of his office and held up the note. 'What's this?'

'Look, Ken' – Vossian put his pen down – 'I'm not going to make a federal case out of it, but of all the coppers in this building, with your service you should know not to leave files on desks. The files remain in the cabinet, the cabinet remains locked. Home Office procedure.'

'I didn't.' Menninot remained calm. 'I didn't leave it lying about. I came back from Harrby's, wrote up my visit, then I locked the file away. Then I came to have that chat with you. Then I went out for lunch. I came to see you about midday. The last thing I did was to lock it away.'

'I found it on your desk at twelve thirty. I wanted to check a point with you, then I remembered you said you were going to lunch. It was then that I found it.' Vossian's face drained of blood. 'Somebody in this building accessed the file while you and I were chatting. What's in there that could damage us?'

'Name and address of our witness for one. I'd better take

111

a nip out to the Trafford, advise him to watch himself. We might have to offer protection, boss.'

'Offer it, but this might be enough to put the frighteners on him, if that's so, that's the case shot. Harrby can wait for another hour or two.'

Menninot drove out of York on the Scarborough Road and at the edge of urban sprawl turned right into the Trafford Estate. He parked outside the McGregor household and walked up the pathway between the shrubs and knocked on the door at the side of the McGregor home. He knew it was preferred by the family as the main exit/entry to the front door, and the practice was not uncommon on the Trafford. Special guests enter and leave by the front door, stepping on, or off, the hall carpet. Family and frequent visitors enter and leave by the side door opposite the coal shed, stepping on or off the kitchenette linoleum. He knocked twice. He received no answer and returned to Friargate. Two hours later he listened, stunned, as the constable from the Traffic section stood in his office, consulting his notebook as he spoke.

'Well, yes, sir, we do have a witness, but not a good one. She's an elderly lady who just happened to have been glancing out of her window, through net curtains, and saw the whole thing. All she could say was that it was a large car, not the sort of car that is normally seen on the Trafford, travelling at speed and she said it seemed to drive at the youth. She said that it seemed to swerve slightly just before the impact, not to miss him, but more to make sure it hit him. So it seemed to the witness.'

'Any skid marks?'

'None.'

'So no attempt to slow down, either?'

'It wouldn't seem so, Mr Menninot. Knocked him into a garden, knocked him about twenty feet from the likely point of impact. Did the checks when we came back, found he had a bit of previous and was known to you, sir.'

'He was. I wanted him as a witness rather than a suspect.'

'I see, sir.'

'He was dead on arrival, I take it?'

'Yes, sir. Broken neck and fractured skull. He was identified by his mother. She is actually employed as a cook in the hospital, brought her from the kitchens to Accident and Emergency and she howled like a wounded animal. Jeanie McGregor, by name. A WPC went home with her. Iffy, don't you think?'

'Very iffy.'

It was Thursday, 6th May, 15.00 hours.

6

Thursday, 6th May, 15.30 hours—Friday, 7th May, 01.30 hours
Ken Menninot tore the cellophane from the audio cassettes
and slid both cassettes into the tape recorder. There was a
tension in the room, but a tension which seemed to all present to be contained and controlled by the solemn observation
of the Police and Criminal Evidence Act. Menninot started
the machine and the red recording light glowed softly. He
said, 'The time is fifteen thirty hours on the sixth of May.
The location is Friargate Police Station in the City of York. I
am Detective Sergeant Menninot and I am now going to ask
the other people in the room to identify themselves.'

'Leif Vossian, Detective Inspector with the City of York
Police.'

'The Right Honourable Sir Nigel Harrby.'

'Emanual Cohen, of Cohen and Company, Harrogate.'

'Sir Nigel' – Menninot consulted notes which he had prepared prior to the interview – 'you have been cautioned in
connection with the murder of a young person, a child of
the male sex, whose body was discovered on Marston Moor
on the afternoon of the third of May, about seventy-two
hours ago.'

Harrby said nothing. Cohen, a man of short stature and
hooked nose similarly said nothing, but listened intently.

'The reasons that we have of suspecting your involvement
with this crime are that a witness has described to us seeing
a man who matches your appearance taking the corpse from
a yellow Range Rover and carrying it to a stand of trees
known locally as Cromwell's Plump, where it was discovered
some hours later by a member of the public who was there
for the purpose of exercising his dog. You have a yellow
Range Rover.'

'Is that the sum of evidence you have against my client? Are you proposing that my client owns the only yellow Range Rover in the United Kingdom?' Cohen peered intently at Menninot.

'Yellow is not a particularly usual colour for a Range Rover,' Menninot said calmly. 'And so far as we believe it's the only one in this locality.'

'I see.' Cohen sniffed. 'And your witness to this incident, where was he standing?'

Leif Vossian leaned forward. 'Mr Cohen, may I point out that the purpose of this interview is not for you to defend your client, it is for the police to interview your client under the procedures and conditions laid down by the Police and Criminal Evidence Act, and it is your purpose to ensure that those conditions are met. Namely, that your client understands the questions, he is not distressed or fatigued, or under the influence of some substance that affects his level of awareness, that he is offered refreshment and allowed access to facilities.'

'Accepted.' Cohen inclined his head, sullenly.

'Sir Nigel.' Menninot spoke. 'Do you have any knowledge of the murder, or the disposal of the corpse in question?'

'I do not.'

'Where were you on the night of the second and third of May?'

'At home. I retired about eleven thirty p.m. I rose at seven thirty a.m. About.'

'About. So at two a.m. you were at home sleeping?'

'I was.'

'Is there anybody who could corroborate your claim?'

'My wife, our maid, though I presume they were both sleeping as well.'

'But do you own a yellow Range Rover?'

'I do. It's in a local garage being resprayed.'

'Why?'

'Why what?'

'Why is it being resprayed?'

'I told you this morning, yellow is a bad colour for rural use.'

'It has nothing to do with the fact that your vehicle collided with a parked car in the village of Little Ribston in the early hours of the third of May?'

'No.'

'But your vehicle is slightly damaged?'

'A scratch.'

'How did that happen?'

'I really don't have a clue.'

'Can you tell us when you first noticed it?'

'When I was walking towards the vehicle when it was parked in Knaresborough in the square. That was last week.'

'Last week? Wednesday, Thursday?'

'Wednesday. It would have been Wednesday that I first noticed it.'

'I see, Sir Nigel. I must now caution you and advise you that we have a witness deposition which states he saw a yellow Range Rover being driven from the scene of the crime, at great speed, in the direction of Harrogate and Knaresborough. This was about two a.m. on the third of May. On that same night, in the early hours of the morning in the village of Little Ribston, a motor vehicle which was parked at the roadside, on the main road, was struck a glancing blow by another motor vehicle. This incident was heard but not witnessed as such.'

Harrby smiled smugly.

Menninot continued. 'Sir Nigel, our accident investigators tell us that the vehicle which struck the parked car was travelling towards Knaresborough, away from Marston Moor. If we were to glance at the map we would see that the most direct route from Marston Moor to your home would involve driving through the village of Little Ribston.'

'I dare say it would.'

'We have received verbal confirmation, to be followed by a report, from the forensic science laboratory in Wetherby which concludes that the flecks of yellow paint found on the damaged motor vehicle match exactly a sample of paint taken from your Range Rover, and that the damage done to your vehicle marries exactly with the damage done to the parked vehicle. Now that, Sir Nigel, proves, and I mean proves, that your car did the damage, and witnesses inform us that that incident occurred in the night of second and third of May. Now, are you still saying that the damage to your vehicle was first noticed by you on Wednesday of last week, which would have been . . .'

'April the twenty-ninth,' Vossian offered.

'We will have to have a copy of that report,' Cohen said flatly, perfunctorily.

'Your client will be provided with a copy, Mr Cohen.' Menninot returned his attention to Harrby. 'Sir Nigel, can I ask how you think that your vehicle might be involved in the accident while you were at home sleeping? Did you perhaps lend it to someone?' Cast in the hope that Harrby would begin to lie himself into the dock by lunging at the fly and saying, 'Yes, yes, that's right, I loaned it to someone . . .'

Harrby remained silent and then disappointed Menninot and Vossian by saying, 'No, I can't explain it, and I won't explain it. I let the burden of proof rest with you gentlemen, you have to prove that I was driving my car at the time. I do not have to prove I wasn't.'

'You're inviting suspicion on yourself.'

'I can live with that.'

'Were you alone in the Range Rover that night?' Said suddenly by Vossian.

But again Harrby paused before answering, 'I wasn't in the Range Rover at the time.'

'You didn't return to the Range Rover after setting the body on fire and say something about "letting the foxes have a roast dinner"?'

Harrby's eyes narrowed. That question reached him.

'I did not,' he said.

'You didn't then turn your Range Rover in a wide circle and return to the road, driving down the mud track between two fields of maize?'

'I didn't; between two fields of maize or any other crop.'

'The track marks left by that vehicle have been photographed, the tread matches your vehicle's tyre tread exactly.'

'I don't doubt it. The brand of tyre I use is widely available and fitted to many Range Rovers.'

Menninot paused. 'Sir Nigel, you have attended the police station willingly, I am now arresting you and detaining you for further questioning in connection with the murder of the as yet unidentified boy whose body was found on Marston Moor seventy-two hours ago. You are not obliged to say anything but anything you do say will be taken down and may be used in evidence. Do you understand?'

'They can do this?' Harrby appealed to Cohen.

'Yes.'

'Do you understand, Sir Nigel?' Menninot persisted.

'What? Yes, yes.'

'If you haven't been charged within twenty-four hours from now' – Cohen spoke to Harrby and glanced at his watch – 'that is, by five minutes to four in the afternoon on the seventh of May, they must release you.' He stood. 'Don't talk unless I am present. You know where to contact me.'

Menninot reached for the off switch. 'This interview is concluded at fifteen fifty-five.' He pressed the off switch and then the eject button. He took one cassette, placed it in the perspex cover and handed it to Harrby, who took hold of it and then handed it, without speaking, to Cohen.

Cohen nodded to Vossian and Menninot and left the room.

Ken Menninot and Leif Vossian sat in the rest room drinking coffee in plastic cups purchased from a vending machine. Two constables threw darts, two women police officers sat and smoked and chatted. A television on the wall broadcast a black-and-white film. The window looked out on to the river and a townscape of modern buildings nestling against medieval walls.

'What have we got to go to court on?' Vossian sipped his coffee. 'Precious little if you ask me,' he continued before Menninot could reply. 'We've got photographs of tyre tracks which could have been made by any Range Rover, and the damage to the parked car was caused by Harrby's vehicle but it was an incident clearly lacking in criminal intent and there were no injuries caused, which makes it a civil matter and so nothing to do with the police and no witness to say that it was Harrby driving it. And there's no direct link between the murder and the road traffic accident. We can't charge him and force the CPS to run with it, not on that. If your witness was still kicking then, yes, that might have made the difference, but he isn't, he's on a slab. Anything else from Wetherby on the inside of the vehicle?'

'As a new pin.' Menninot shook his head. 'It's pretty well impossible to lay a dead body on a car seat without leaving some trace, some seepage of body fluid, a hair, a drop of blood, so he must have laid the lad on plastic sheeting or something.'

'Which he would have burned. Frankly, I'm surprised you've charged him.'

'I wanted him to sweat. I'll ask the custody sergeant to release him at ten minutes short of the twenty-four hours. Then he can collect his Range Rover. But I want him to sweat.'

'That's not, strictly speaking, approved procedure.' Vossian spoke with determination. 'He's guilty. He's as guilty as sin. I'd like to turn his house over, but we won't find anything, talk about squeaky-clean . . . but without Robert McGregor's evidence we haven't got enough grounds for a warrant.'

A pause. The thud of three darts impacting cork. The soft hum of the conversation of the female officers.

'The file, boss,' Menninot said. 'I did lock it away.'

'I know you did, Ken.' Vossian shook his head. 'By which I mean I have every confidence that you did.'

'Who are these people? What are we up against?'

'Ken, if only I knew. You liked the lad, didn't you?'

'Aye, he was a good lad, he was following his dad down the wrong path. You know, all he needed was a six-inch gap and he'd be in your house like a lubricated viper. But essentially he was all right. He could have been straightened out. Poor lad.'

He lay on the narrow bed on the thin red plastic mattress and gazed at the ceiling of the cell. He thought it strange that he no longer felt fear. He had read of this, of the tranquillity that comes over the condemned man.

He had seen it before, in the eyes of those who knew that

within two or three days they will begin to die, horribly, amid a circle of dancing, chanting adults and children. Sometimes though, there is terror in their eyes, but equally when the realization that all hope is gone sets in, there is then the look of peace in their expression.

He had occasioned it, that look, when he used to train the novices, and took them to witness and to take part in the murderous assaults and acid attacks on those who wanted to leave.

He thought of the novices. None of them knew what they were joining before it was too late. And when it was too late they subscribed to one of two attitudes. Either they remained in because they were too terrified to leave but made no secret of their fear or distaste, their contribution was never more than perfunctory and they were never more than foot soldiers. The other attitude seemed to be a full acceptance of the situation, realizing they were trapped they would embrace the coven and throw themselves into it, utterly committed, thriving on the frenzy of the rituals, novices like that were made of the right stuff and rose through the hierarchy.

He thought of his own recruitment. He and Cynthia had moved to the extreme end of 'the scene' in the Vale of York, and even that was becoming tame. They were young, energetically sexual and had been approached by a man whom they had met on occasions before. He asked them if they wanted to try something really heavy. It was heavy, the first death they had witnessed and they had been captured on film taking part. Then, from that point, they were captured in another sense. Their novice training began, they quickly learned that the only way out was feet first and they were told that Dolly would be moving in with them, nominally as their maid, but only nominally. They would learn much from Dolly and they must do her least bidding. And that had been, oh, thirty-plus years ago. He was thankful that they had had no children.

He and Cynthia had found themselves trapped and had remained willingly, lured by the sensuality, by the sexuality of extreme debasement and by the thrill of power that comes with the ritualizing of evil.

So now he had failed. He would die. Either by his hand, preferably, because that was better than disappearing and being kept until given up as a sacrifice. He had had the forensic commission and had done well until he had failed, and when he had failed as he had done, he had failed magnificently. He wondered if he was burnt out. He had heard that one of the symptoms of burn out is that the person believes he is doing his job but in reality is falling far short. But burn out would not be acceptable as an excuse for allowing the existence of the coven to become known because no excuse is acceptable. And Cynthia had been with him. She would have to pay some penalty for not ensuring he carried out his responsibilities. So what will happen to her? He'll invite her to take a final drive with him but she may elect to throw herself at the mercy of the High Priest and High Priestess. She would perhaps be reduced to novice status, be given many unpleasant commissions, and most likely have to sell the farm, hand over the proceeds and live out her life in poverty. She may prefer that to an early death.

In the cell Harrby smiled contentedly as he knew the peace of the condemned man.

Ken Menninot drove out to the Trafford Estate and parked outside a house where a number of cars were parked and the curtains of which were drawn shut. He walked up the pitted, cratered path, past the front door and knocked at the side door of the house. The door was opened by a young man who nodded in recognition of Ken Menninot but otherwise remained impassive. The young man closed the door almost, but not completely, shut. He returned a moment later and opened the door and stood aside. Menninot swept his hat off and stepped into a narrow kitchen and walked through the kitchen to the living room of the house. An ashen-faced woman sat in a chair by a gas fire, she clutched a glass as did other adults who stood or sat in the room. A bottle of Ballantines whisky stood on the table by the window. The woman looked up at Ken Menninot.

'It's not every policeman that would be welcome in this house, Mr Menninot.' Her voice shook with emotion.

Menninot bowed his head slightly at the implicit compliment.

'But my husband says you're a bandits' copper and Robert said the same.'

'Robert was a good lad, Mrs McGregor, he would have stopped being a bandit as soon as he found the right girl.' Menninot paused. 'I see it so often, as soon as I meet them, right at their first caution I can tell the ones that'll make a life of it and I can tell the good lads that are straying and need catching for their own good, and Robert was one of the good ones. I called to say how very sorry I was.'

'Aye, you can say that, but what are you doing about yon that killed him? What about catching him?'

'We'll do what we can, Mrs McGregor.'

'There's talk in the street.' A short man with long hair, too long for his age, in Menninot's eye, and with whisky on his breath turned to Menninot. 'They say the car drove right at our Robert, deliberate like . . .'

Menninot said yes, the police had heard that too.

'Who'd do that to our Robert?' The man appealed to Menninot. 'Robert had no enemies.'

'I'm sorry.' It was the only thing Menninot could think of to say. 'I really don't know who could have done it.'

'Or why?' Mrs McGregor appealed as the man with long hair replenished his glass generously. Only then did he lean forward and replenish Jeanie McGregor's glass.

'I don't know that, either, Mrs McGregor. I am truly sorry.'

'So why now?' Vossian leaned forward.

The chubby-faced man opened his mouth. Inside it was mostly gum. 'It's got to the point that I don't count the ones that I lost, it's got to the point that I've come to count the ones I've got left. Mind, they're right at the back, they won't get kicked out easily.'

'I wouldn't bank on it.'

'Sensitive, caring sort of man, aren't you, Mr Vossian?'

'No.'

'Honest at least.' The man was in his late forties, he gazed up wistfully at the sky through the thick frosted glass set high in the walls of the agent's room. He wore a blue-and-white striped shirt, rough denim jeans and soft-soled shoes.

'So you want out while you've still got one or two teeth left, that it?'

'I want out. You got me sent down for a long time, Mr Vossian . . .'

'You got yourself sent down for a long time, Gerald. Me, I just did my job. But I think you're where you ought to be.'

Gerald Peep screwed his forehead into the palm of his hands. 'We only get one bath a week in here,' he said.

'You're about due for it, I think.'

Peep shot a glance at Vossian. 'I have a gland problem. On the outside I had to have two baths a day, three in hot weather. That's why I get attacked, I'm not just a beast, I'm a smelly beast – that's my nickname in here, the "stinking beast".'

'Gerald, I enjoyed the drive to Wakefield, short as it was, I dare say I'll enjoy the drive back, but there has to be a reason for me to make the journey and it's not to talk about your health problems. Why did you want to see me?'

'Twenty years,' Peep moaned. 'Only done two. See, the things I miss: eating what I want when I want, choosing my own company – here I have twenty-four-hour human contact and I'm lonelier than I have ever been.'

'Some of the loneliest people live in families, don't tell me.'

'It's a stroll along the lane to the Bird in the Hand, especially in the summer, especially after a shower of rain, you can really smell the vegetation. Sometimes in here I close my eyes and think myself there, rewalking it, walking up to the landlord in the snug and ordering a pint of bitter, pulled from the wood. In the Bird, no music playing, just a few old boys talking and the rattle of dominoes, a log fire in the winter, not many pubs like the Bird in the Hand left out there . . . I miss that bit.'

'Gerald, police time is expensive time . . .'

'I want out, Mr Vossian.'

'Little I can say, Gerald, except that I can imagine you do. Some blokes like being in prison, they cope better inside than out, but I don't figure you for one of those.'

'First offence and I go down for twenty years.'

'You ruined a lot of lives, Gerald, a lot of your victims were children, you've given each of them a life sentence in a sense. Some would say that one twenty-year stretch in exchange for fifteen life sentences, fifteen lives ruined before they had begun, is not a bad deal. And those are only the fifteen we know about. I'm an old and jaded cop, Gerald, I know there must have been a lot more.'

Peep glanced up and nodded at Vossian. 'There were.'

'And this is what you want to talk about? Your conscience is plaguing you, is it? Gerald, you're the classic sex offender – did you know that sex offending is the only sort of offending that you grow into, all other offending you grow out of?'

'Didn't know that.'

'It's because the motive for it is lust, not easy money, or to get anger out of yourself, it becomes a way of life, you graduate through the layers. How did you start, voyeurism, flashing?'

'Watching children do sports in their PE kit.'

Vossian nodded. 'Be better for you if we'd have caught you then, nipped it in the bud, got you into some kind of therapy. Instead you avoided our attention until you were well in with a ring, swapping little people like other people swap railway memorabilia.'

'Would still be doing it if it wasn't for Galt, big mouth that he is.'

'You know the story there, caught him bang to rights with a car full of kiddie porn and he coughed fully and completely in exchange for a reduced charge and a word put in at the trial. But that's the way it goes, Gerald, paedophile rings will collapse like a house of cards once the police become interested.'

'So I found out. Galt was the last guy I thought would name names.'

'There's no honour among thieves with paedophiles, Gerald. You should know that, once the leaks on you'd shop your own grandmothers for a plea bargain. So all those other offences . . . ?'

'I don't want to give any information about them. You won't find out about them.'

'What is it, then?'

'That lad they found on Marston Moor.'

Vossian's eyes narrowed. 'Go on.'

'I might have information, if not about him then another murder, of an adult, a guy, tortured to death. I seen it . . .'

'All I can do is put a word in for you at the parole board, but you won't be up for parole for a day or two yet.'

'A day or two, you have some way of talking, Mr Vossian. Ten years, more like.'

'Could be shorter, work with the psychologist, ingratiate yourself with the chaplain, volunteer to clean the toilets, you'd get your first parole hearing soon enough: won't be released on the first parole but it's the first obstacle.'

'If I survive.'

'You can survive ten years, less maybe.'

'No, I mean survive, survive – these are very heavy people, Mr Vossian, you have no idea who you are up against, I'm not safe anywhere, not even in the VPU. If I give names, if I make statements . . . I want protection, not just in here, but for the rest of my puff.'

'It could be arranged, we have a witness protection system, fix you up with a new ID, transfer you to another nick, maybe in the south of England. But you need to have gold dust to trade for the red-carpet treatment. And I don't just mean gold dust, Gerald, I mean gold dust, capital G, capital D. Gold Dust.'

'I'll have to have a guarantee.'

'No.' Vossian looked steadily at Peep. He saw a frightened man. 'No, we hear what you have to offer, then if it's good we trade. So what do you have?'

Peep shook his head. 'I'll have to think about it.'

Vossian stood and tapped on the door. Outside in the corridor, a bunch of keys rattled, the lock turned. 'You know where I am, Gerald.'

*   *   *

At ten p.m., when their shift finished, Simon Markova asked Carmen Pharoah if she would care to go for an Indian. Carmen Pharoah pursed her lips and moved her head from side to side and then said yes, but it would not lead any-where, she said she would be spending the night in her house. Alone. He took her to the Last Viceroy on King's Staith where they sat in the window and looked out on to the waterfront bustle and irritated the staff by ordering a pitcher of chilled water with their meal rather than wine.

'This is nothing like the food you get in India.' Simon Markova forked chicken Masala into his mouth.

'You've been there? I saw brochures about Goa on the table in your kitchen.'

'I had a bit of an adventure there.' He sipped some water. 'I'm a bit of a railway buff; when I have the children for a weekend we invariably go to the Railway Museum and I'm always more enthralled than they are. Anyway, I had plans to do a transit across India, by rail, from Mumbai to Calcutta and then take a trip on the Darjeeling Himalayan Railway. That's ninety miles of narrow gauge-working in the foothills of the Himalayas. Built by the British in the nineteenth cen-tury, still with the original steam locomotives and original vehicles.'

'Oh yes?' Carmen Pharoah's attention was involuntarily drawn to a group of bikers growling along the Staith.

'Anyway, I called in on a friend who was living with her husband to be, an Indian guy, on –'

'She's white?'

'Yes. On a farm near Mumbai, well, about five hours by car, which is near in Indian terms. I called on them bringing much goodies. They'd given me a shopping list, you see. Anyway, I had every reason to believe I was calling on a couple who had a good and stable relationship.'

'And?'

'Nothing could be further from the case; it was highly stressed and at critical mass. On the second night he locked her in a room and spent six hours pulping her face.'

'You didn't stop it?'

Simon Markova shook his head. 'No, I didn't. You see, it's

126

when that happens that you know you're in the Third World. No cops to call, no ambulance crew to pick up the pieces, no convenient local hospital. I knew that there was a loaded gun in the room, it was their bedroom, because they have a bandit problem in Maharashtra State, by which I mean real bandits, not the sort of bandits we lock up. If I had gone in then it would have been two shallow graves at the edge of the farm, which was really only a smallholding by British standards. Intuitively, I knew the best thing to do was to let the violence run its course. If I had interfered it would have escalated. Anyway, the next day when we were travelling back to Mumbai to wait for a plane to London, Kathleen thanked me for having the good sense to stay out of the room. So I was right not to interfere.

'At least she saw that before she married him.'

'She married him?' Carmen Pharoah's jaw dropped.

'She returned only a matter of weeks later and married him. I saw a photograph of her garlanded with flowers in her wedding sari.'

Carmen Pharoah shook her head in disbelief. 'At least she went in with her eyes open.'

'Which is all you can say. A trip planned for six weeks, reduced to six days because of an incident which lasted for six hours.'

'The devil played the drums when you went to India.'

Simon Markova smiled. 'I hadn't thought of it like that. But anyway, that was ten years ago now. I've been married, become a parent, and divorced in that time and now I feel I'd like to return. I feel I want to make my peace with the place.'

'Have you the money?' She poured water into their tumblers.

'A distant relative of mine has died. She left me a modest sum. I'm not going to declare it to the CSA and I want to use it for something, buy something or travel. I don't want to dip into it now and again to ease the monthly budget, because if I do that it'll only evaporate and I'll have nothing to show for it, and I've always believed that you should do something with any money that you inherit. Earn your beer money but use your inheritance. So I think I'm going to revisit India, and lay a ghost or two.'

He drove her home. She asked him how he got on with Leif Vossian.

'Don't take his Iceman character personally.'

'No?'

'No.' Simon Markova turned into her street. 'He used to smile. His wife and children were killed in a head-on car crash. They were in a small Datsun, the other car was a Volvo estate.'

'Oh . . .'

'The other car was driven by a couple of joyriders. They walked from the crash and they walked from the court.'

'Didn't get custody?'

Simon Markova stopped outside Carmen Pharoah's door. 'No, they were both only thirteen. That's hard for anyone to accept, harder still for a cop. He sees them from time to time, they're accumulating track and they'll go down for something eventually, but that's small change for Leif.'

'I didn't realize . . . I thought . . .'

'You thought it was because you are black, or a woman, or both . . .' Simon Markova shook his head. 'Perish the thought. It happened about two years ago, but that's all. He used to live in Naburn then. Buried his wife and children locally in Fulford cemetery. Couldn't cope with the suddenly empty house so he sold up and bought in a quiet village north of the city. It'll be a long time before Leif smiles again.'

In her house, Carmen Pharoah sidestepped the bin liners and walked to the room where she had installed her answering machine. The light was flashing. Just the one message.

'Wesley here . . .' The voice sounded tinny. It was an old machine. 'It's nine . . . p.m., that is. Just phoning.'

She sank to her knees. The room was illuminated by the soft glow of a streetlamp. She picked up the phone and dialled his number. If he answered, she thought, if he answered she'd hang up, if it was his answering machine she'd say something. In the event she reached his machine. 'It's Carmen . . . I'm glad it's your machine. Look, Wesley, listen to me. I had a house in London, I was settled in my

128

job, I had a social life, I gave that up to come to York to be with you . . . then I got here, committed myself to a new mortgage, new job and then you tell me it's over . . . then you tell me it's over . . . then you phone me . . . it's not on, Wesley, it's not bloody on . . . if you don't want me then stick to that decision, and don't keep phoning me. Go back to your wife, but don't ask me to be a bit on the side . . . I'm thirty-two . . . if you know what that means for a woman . . . I'm beginning to panic. Don't phone me again. Not unless you're prepared to leave Selina.' She replaced the handset softly and stripped and showered. She laid the mattress on the floor and pulled the duvet over her and let her eyes rest on the soft glow of the streetlamp as it fell across her ceiling. Outside, a church bell chimed midnight.

Sleep overwhelmed her finally, one and a half hours later. It was Friday, 7th May, 01.30 hours.

Four Days in July

7

The July of that year was one of the hottest, if not the hottest and driest July, since climatic records had been kept. That made it the hottest and driest July for in excess of two hundred years, and of all England, Yorkshire was particularly badly affected, mains supplies of water were turned off to domestic users, standpipes were put up in the streets instead, Thruscross reservoir dried up and people journeyed there to walk the still discernible streets of the village of West End, which had been abandoned and submerged thirty years earlier when the reservoir was first created. That July, and well into the following month, it was already hot by eight thirty a.m., people strolled in shirt sleeves at midnight, tempers flared in traffic queues. Devers and Shapiro, dressed in lightweight cotton dresses, and now finding that they worked well with each other, called, as requested, on Mrs Fee.

'I can't say whether they're settled in or not.' Mrs Fee and Shapiro and Devers sat in Mrs Fee's living room, net curtains hung limp in front of windows which had been flung wide. 'They keep saying stranger and stranger things, it never seems to stop. They've got very confident as they realize that nothing's going to happen to them here, but I've never met children like them, something really dreadful's happened to these children, something really horrible. Are the others the same?'

'Pretty well,' Devers said. 'Fifteen children, in addition to the three children you have, have been in care for a couple of months now, similar tales are unfolding, and we've been careful not to allow the children from different homes to come into contact with each other.'

'So as not to contaminate each other's evidence,' Shapiro

explained. 'The parents are not saying much to us, they appear frightened for some reason, frightened of something other than the law, and more frightened of that than the law, but what "that" is we don't know.'

'Well, it's something weird.' Mrs Fee paused. 'I never knew fostering could be so difficult – you see, they've started making mud pies out of their excrement. I caught them, the three of them, putting their business into little mounds on the linoleum in the bathroom, doing it as natural as if they were playing at dolls' houses. But it's Kimberley now, the middle child, as she's been getting more confident she's been telling me things. I asked her if she'd speak to you two ladies like her big sister had done and she said that she would. So I asked you to call.'

'Thanks, well done.' Devers smiled.

'I think you'll get more out of Kimberley than you did Sadie, and they're still doing those drawings, figures mostly, but the girls won't draw mouths on the faces they draw; even when I've taught them how to draw a mouth they refuse to draw one, and they have strange ways of drawing eyelashes – they draw the eyelash in towards the eye, and sometimes don't stop at the eyelid, but continue the line representing the eyelash actually into the pupil that they have drawn. When my children were that age they drew lines outwards from the eyelid to represent the eyelash. Maybe it's just a quirk of theirs, nothing more than that. But I'll go and get Kimberley, let her tell you the things she's been telling me, she's a bright girl, but older than her years, it's as if she's missed out on her childhood . . . The children eat strangely, too, snatching at their food, their play is aggressive and they mimic the sex act with the animals.'

'The animals?'

'Play animals. They have a farmyard set and Sadie was working a cow against a dog, they're not to scale, the animals, working it in that way, but like two humans: you know, belly to belly, not like two animals, and Shane and Kimberley were looking on really intently as though they knew what was happening.'

'But we do know what's happened to them, remember.'

134

Devers spoke quietly. 'All three have been raped, they'll have a lot to work out of themselves, playing with animals like that is more easily explained than is the drawings they've done or making pies out of their body waste. Confess that concerns me more than mimicking the sex act with plastic models of animals.'

'I also found Kimberley stamping on a doll.' Mrs Fee spoke matter-of-factly. 'Just the other day. I said to her, "What on earth are you doing, pet?" and she said, "This is how they killed the baby," then she looked at me and colour drained from her face and she ran at me and buried her head in my skirt and I confess I never thought she'd stop crying. I logged it like you said I should.'

'Thanks.' Devers smiled. 'It all adds up to the body of evidence which we'll have to present when it comes to court when the day comes.'

'And on that day, or weeks' – Shapiro took out her tape recorder and began to set it up on the table – 'it'll be a matter of accumulation of evidence rather than one single act or piece of evidence.'

'I understand that. So would you like to see Kimberley now?'

Mrs Fee left the room and returned a moment later gently leading Kimberley Hampshire by the hand. Kimberley looked neat in a red dress and black shoes. She had clearly been dressed up to meet the police and the Social Services. She slid on to the vacant armchair and edged back until her back was pressed hard against the chair and her arms down either side of her, precisely as Devers and Shapiro remembered her elder sister Sadie had sat when they had talked with her a couple of months ago.

After she had introduced herself and Shapiro, Devers asked Kimberley how old she was.

'Six,' she answered, correctly.

'Mrs Fee tells us that you've been telling her about some things and that you'll tell us, Kimberley.'

Kimberley Hampshire shot a glance at Mrs Fee.

'About the bad things, Kimberley,' Mrs Fee prompted.

'About killing the baby?' Kimberley asked.

A silence descended on the room. Devers nodded.

'They killed the baby. Thems jumped on it and said, ''ha, ha!'' '

'Who jumped on it, Kimberley?'

'The big master, and some other men, thems had masks on. So I didn't see who but them people who live in Endon, I saw their cars.'

'When?'

'At a party, the last party.'

'At a party?'

'But not a party, not a nice party.'

'Where do the parties take place?'

'Different places, under a big house, in a big hole in the ground.'

'What happens at these parties, Kimberley?'

'Bad things.' Kimberley Hampshire glanced nervously at Mrs Fee.

'It's all right, pet.' Mrs Fee smiled. 'You can tell those ladies, they're friends of ours.'

'You tell . . .'

'No.' Mrs Fee was calm, warm, but firm. 'No, pet, you see, it's no good if it comes from me. It has to come from you.'

Kimberley Hampshire turned to Shapiro and Devers and bravely, both women thought, said, 'Thems dress up as clowns and animals, the children don't have no clothes under the house, but if it's in the hole in the ground the children have clothes. All the men had their willies . . . the willies are painted bright colours . . . I have to put them here.' She pointed to her mouth.

Shapiro sighed. Devers swallowed hard. Mrs Fee slowly moved her head from side to side.

'They killed the baby boy at the party.'

'How did you know it was a baby boy?'

'Him had no clothes on, seen his willy. Him crying bad and they jumped on it going, ''ha, ha, ha!'' till him stop crying. All us standing in a ring made to say words again and again.'

'What words, Kimberley, can you remember?'

'Domi Die, Domi Die, Domi Die,' she replied with practised ease, as if at home with the familiar.

'Thems burns the baby, bury it in the ground. Thems put a little girl on the table and cut her here.' Kimberley drew her hand upwards over her stomach. 'Thems pull all the bits out. Table had special cloth over it, dark colour, purple, with shiny bits sewn on.'

'What happened to the girl who was on the table?'

'Burnt. Chopped up. Buried in a hole, thems cover the hole up.'

'Do you know where this hole was Kimberley?'

'Near the hole in the ground.'

'How long did these parties last, Kimberley?' asked Shapiro, after a pause, allowing Kimberley Hampshire space.

'All night. We comes back at daytime, early daytime.'

'Do the parties happen during the day?'

She shook her head.

'How do you come back from the big hole in the ground?' Devers asked, again after a sensitive pause.

'In cars.'

'Whose cars do you know?'

'Mr McGuire's, and Mr Dovedale, and Mr Boot, and Mr Rivers.'

'Mr McGuire?' Shapiro repeated. 'The teacher?'

Kimberley Hampshire nodded.

'But don't tell him . . .' Kimberley Hampshire became frightened, clearly terrified. 'Don't want him to find me.'

'Don't worry, we won't tell him where you are. He won't find you . . . But tell us, Kimberley,' Shapiro asked, 'what do you think might happen if he did find out where you are?'

'Kill me, kill my mummy, kill my brother, my sister . . .'

'All right, he won't find out. Promise.'

'Like the animals at the parties, sheep bleeding from its neck and its bum, made to drink the blood, it was warm and salty and eating pooh made us sick.'

'Pooh?' Shapiro looked at Mrs Fee.

'It's the children's word for excrement,' Mrs Fee explained. 'They've spoken of "pooh pies".'

A pause. A welcome breeze ruffled the net curtains.

'Thems stick needles in us,' offered Kimberley Hampshire.
'Needles?' Shapiro repeated. 'Like big pins?'

'No, needles like at the hospital.' Kimberley made the unmistakable gesture of a syringe being plunged into her arm. 'Makes us feel funny, like being there but not there, sort of awake but can't speak no more. And drink yellow stuff, makes us sick. Can I go now?'

Devers smiled at her. 'Yes, of course, Kimberley, thank you, you've been very brave. Can we come and see you again?'

Kimberley Hampshire nodded and slipped off the chair and out of the room. She closed the door behind her as if observing training by Mrs Fee. In the room the three women could only sit in silence.

Claire Shapiro broke the silence: 'The drawing of the lash towards the eye and into the pupil, I've come across that before, it's done by children who have witnessed something really dreadful. And not drawing mouths on figures, that's a recognized symptom of a child who's been forced to perform oral sex. I think I now know what's going on here.'

'Tables with purple cloths, human sacrifices, Domi Die, Domi Die.' Devers nodded. 'I think I know as well.'

It was Monday, July 26th, 11.30 hours.

Monday, July 26th, 14.00 hours
John Sorenson, Carmen Pharoah and Tessie Cahill walked side by side on a wide pathway in the expansive grounds of Foss Dyke Hospital. The sun beat down, Sorenson wore a Panama and a white T-shirt, the women lightweight dresses, each half closed his or her eyes against the glare and watched as an ambulance shimmered through the heat haze rising off the roadway.

'Aye.' Tessie Cahill glanced at the hospital buildings away to her right, solid, stone built, confident. 'I do tend to use this place like Club Med. Book myself in, get fattened up and cleaned up. I was letting myself go again and the news of that lad on Marston Moor just tipped me over the edge. I was hitting on an empty stomach. No, I'm not mad. I do have a condition but it's not the schizophrenia that the white

coats think it is. Mind you, that's a change I've noticed –
when I was first admitted all those years ago the doctors all
wore white coats, now they don't, but I still call them white
coats. You ever come across multiple personality disorder
before, love?'

Carmen Pharoah confessed that she hadn't.

'There is a self-help group for MPD sufferers,' Sorenson
explained. 'They told me once that they believe only four
per cent of MPD sufferers are correctly diagnosed, the rest
are given labels such as "personality disorder", "psychotic"
or "schizophrenic", as Tessie here.'

'Aye,' Tessie Cahill echoed, 'as Tessie here.'

'It means what it suggests?' Carmen Pharoah turned to
Sorenson. 'More than one personality in the same body?'

'Yes, I've got to know Tessie quite well. We think she has
five, one of which is Ben, the keeper of the pain. You're only
aware of five, are you not, Tessie?'

'Just me and four others.' Tessie Cahill smiled. 'The me
you're speaking to now is the core personality.'

'Tell me about the keeper of the pain.'

Sorenson answered: 'The mechanism appears to be that,
if a child is constantly being exposed to horrific experiences
it will invent an older child, a pretend brother or sister or
friend who absorbs the pain. But as the core personality
grows older, the keeper of the pain remains the age at which
he or she first appeared. Tessie tells me she has recollections
of rituals from about the age of three . . .'

'Younger, I think,' Tessie Cahill said.

'If not younger. Ben, when we speak to him, appears to
be about nine years old.'

Carmen Pharoah shook her head. 'Five personalities?'

'Thirty or more are not uncommon. It manifests itself in
late teens or early adulthood, sufferers complaining that they
tend to feel they are arguing with themselves. If you think
thirty different personalities in one body is a little difficult
to believe,' said Sorenson, 'try to get your mind round the
concept of Poly Fragmented Personality Disorder.'

'What on earth is that?'

'Well, as the name implies, that is the condition wherein

each personality within an MPD sufferer has its own multiple personality disorder.'

Tessie Cahill smiled. 'I answer to the name of Lucky.'

'You're really beautiful, Tessie.' Sorenson rested his hand on her forearm. 'I mean that.'

Tessie Cahill beamed at him and Carmen Pharoah smiled approvingly, but her spine was chilled.

'It's when the keeper of the pain emerges that the person starts exhibiting age-inappropriate behaviour, strange speech, strange voice, that misdiagnosis occurs, which is what happened to Tessie, didn't it, love?'

'That's what got me banged up in here the first time. I was twenty-three years old. They found me in Askham Bogs.'

'I still don't know York too well.'

'It's by the Leeds Road, south of the city. They found me wandering in a daze, blood streaming down my legs – I'd pushed a broken bottle up there, right up, wedged it in . . . I don't remember doing it.'

'That's because it wasn't you, Tessie, that was Amy. I've spoken to Amy, she's about five or six and she did it to stop the rapes.'

'Amy' – Carmen Pharoah found her voice falling to a reverential whisper – 'is one of Tessie's personalities?'

Sorenson nodded. 'Tessie, the reason we are here to see you, I would have come anyway, but the reason myself and DC Pharoah are here is the same reason that you are here.'

'You talk in riddles, Mr John.'

'It's the little lad found on Marston Moor two months ago now. That upset you, started you drinking, and you ended up here, getting pampered in Club Med.'

'Gets me off the estate for a few weeks. Gets me fed. I'll start to wash in a week's time, that's why I hum a bit now, love, I don't want to appear too independent or too motivated or else they'll bump me out before I've had a proper holiday.' Tessie Cahill winked at Carmen Pharoah.

'DC Pharoah is investigating the murder of the little lad.'

'All alone?'

'Me and my colleagues.' Carmen Pharoah smiled.

'Pretty well all of the City of York Police force, methinks,'

140

added Sorenson. 'But I wonder if you'd be prepared to talk to DC Pharoah about your experiences, you know the things that you've told me about, the things that made you create Ben, and made Amy do what she did?'

'Yes,' Tessie Cahill said, 'if it helps the police investigate the murder.'

'It'll let us know what's going on,' Carmen Pharoah said.

'Of course I'll do what I can to help. But can we talk alone, just me and DC Pharoah?'

'Carmen. You can call me Carmen.'

'I'll go for a stroll.' Sorenson smiled. 'Plenty of grounds, and to think they're trying to close the Foss down and move the mental-health facilities back into the city.' He paused. 'It's just occurred to me, before I go for a wander, Tessie, do you think it would be a good idea for us to introduce Carmen to Ben?'

'If you like,' Tessie Cahill said. 'If it will help.'

'Can I speak to Ben?' Sorenson's manner was warm yet had an authoritative quality about it. 'Five, four, three, two, one, Ben are you there?'

Tessie Cahill's manner changed suddenly, within a period of a second, her eyes began to swim, seemed to lose focus and then refocused as if waking up and her facial expression became that of the ever alert child. It was the frozen watchfulness Carmen Pharoah had heard about during in-service training on child abuse. Tessie Cahill's body tensed, fear entered her eyes.

'Ben?' Sorenson prompted.

'Yes.' Tessie Cahill nodded urgently, anxious to please.

'How are you today?'

'All right.'

'Only all right? We aren't going to hurt you, Ben. This is Carmen, and you remember me. So only all right?'

'Want the bad things to stop. Good idea to stop the dance, stop the bad things, stop the master.'

'Tell Carmen about the master, Ben.'

Tessie Cahill turned obediently to Carmen Pharoah. 'He makes us hold hands and dance in a circle. Meakey takes us in his car and we go to a hole in the ground, and the master is there with his cloak and stick and we dance to music and he pulls us to him with his stick and does bad things.'

'Bad things?'

'Up the bum with his willy.'

Carmen Pharoah nodded. 'Go on, Ben.'

'He would be nasty but people have to like him. In a black coat down to his feet. The little girl said stop doing that but the master wouldn't and the grown-ups laughed. She wanted to run out of the dance but was scared to leave . . .'

'Why, Ben?' Carmen Pharoah pressed. 'Why was the little girl scared to leave the dance?'

'Good morning, Mr Magpie.'

Carmen Pharoah followed Tessie Cahill's gaze and saw a black-and-white bird hopping on the grass some yards away.

'One for sorrow,' Tessie Cahill chanted, 'two for joy, three for a girl and four for a boy, five for silver, six for gold and seven for a secret never to be told.' Tessie Cahill smiled at Carmen Pharoah. 'But if you see a single magpie, you say, "Good morning, Mr Magpie," then the sorrow doesn't get you.'

Carmen Pharoah turned and said, 'Good morning, Mr Magpie.'

'You say that even if it's morning or afternoon or evening.'

'I grew up in the West Indies, we don't have magpies there, so I didn't hear the rhyme until I came to England. But I've never heard about saying good morning to a single bird. I'll remember that, Ben. Thank you.'

Tessie Cahill looked intently at Carmen Pharoah. 'Did you have good grown-ups?'

Carmen Pharoah paused. John Sorenson saw that she was stung, but she smiled and said, 'Yes, Ben, I had good grown-ups.'

Tessie Cahill reached out and held Carmen Pharoah's hand. 'Black.'

Carmen Pharoah smiled. 'Yes, Ben, it's black skin – well, it's really a sort of chocolate-brown, I suppose.'

'Nice.'

'I think it's a nicer colour than pink.'

'Nice being black?'

'It really depends where I am, Ben. I confess I'm finding it difficult being black in York. Didn't mind being black in Stoke Newington, and when I go back to St Kitts to see my mum I wouldn't want to be any other colour. Why?'

Tessie Cahill didn't reply but began to run her hand up and down Carmen Pharoah's forearm. 'Girl wouldn't leave the dance because she saw the baby killed. Girl seen the children in cages. Girl kept underground for long time, girl seen children fighting in a pit, hitting each other with crosses . . . girl made to take stuff from adult's bum, made to make a pie with it and eat the pie. Girl too frightened to leave dance.' Tessie Cahill clutched Carmen Pharoah's arm.

'It's all right, Ben, it's all right,' Sorenson said. 'Can we talk to Tessie now? Five, four, three, two, one, Tessie are you there . . . ?'

Tessie Cahill's face flinched, her demeanour changed, again she appeared to be waking up. She once again became the woman who had sat on the bench a few minutes earlier. Carmen Pharoah shook her head slowly, not daring to believe what she had just seen and heard.

'We met Ben,' said Sorenson.

'How was he?'

'As ever. He began to get distressed so we let him go.'

'Thanks.'

'So, I'll go for a wander.' Sorenson turned away. 'I'll walk round the perimeter. See you back here.'

'Can we walk too?' Tessie Cahill turned to Carmen Pharoah. 'I think I'd like to.'

'I think I'd like to, too.'

The two women strolled away, in the opposite direction to John Sorenson.

'So what do you want me to tell you, love?'

'Well, I really don't know. I have to say that the things I've heard over the last couple of months have been a revelation, even to myself as a police officer. We are quite used to human horror stories, but even allowing for that my eyes have been opened and I have to say that there's still a part of me that doesn't believe it, though less than my colleague. You remember Simon Markova, he and I interviewed you

143

when you were brought in to the police station the other month?'

'Oh him, yes.'

'I think he's very sceptical, but I still have a part of me that doesn't believe it.'

'Or doesn't want to believe it.'

Carmen Pharoah glanced at Tessie Cahill with raised eyebrows. 'Probably that's it,' she said. 'Yes, probably that's it.'

'We couldn't ask for help in those days because nobody would believe us. In those days cruelty to kids meant neglect or battering and nothing else. And anyway, if you talked you'd be killed. Later on if you get known to the white coats you don't pose a threat and they leave you be. But when I left I had to keep moving. I left York, lived in the northern towns, kept moving my flat every few weeks. By the time I got back to York I was already known to the doctors for being a nutter, that time in Askham Bogs was the final breakdown. I'm safe but I couldn't identify anyone anyway, don't know where they are now.'

They walked off the concrete path on to grass, beside rusted railings that had been pushed over at an angle by expansive shrubbery.

'Could you tell me how it's organized?' Carmen Pharoah occasionally glanced up but for the most part she and Tessie Cahill walked with heads bowed. 'And as much as you want to tell me about yourself.'

'You believe me then?'

Carmen Pharoah smiled. 'I don't know, it's all very new. I think it also depends on what it is you tell me.'

'Well, looking back I think I was fostered for abuse. I don't know who my natural parents are. I had a foster sister, not a blood relative. She's younger than me and I remember shortly after she arrived I was sitting on top of the stairs and a group of the adults were talking in the living room and I heard my dad say, "Well, we had to have another girl, didn't we?" and then they all laughed. I believe that we were both fostered to be abused.

'We were cut, burned, stabbed, locked in cages, in the boots of cars . . . not fed for days, no one to talk to, no one

144

to listen, no one to hear us and the adults calling me a "good little devil". As I grew up I just saw the devil staring at me in the mirror, my mind sort of blanked out and the inside people like Ben and Amy came out. That's what I call them, the inside people.'

The two women walked on.

'It all starts in the home, with the mothers taking an active role, especially in getting the kids ready for sexual assault, like being got used to having your private parts touched by someone else, quite hard sometimes, and getting the kids used to eating and drinking body waste, it's the time that kids learn to fear birthdays and Christmas.'

'Why?'

'Because that's what it's like, love. Everything is done to insult Christianity, so Christmas Day is always a day for a sabbat, that's a holy day, sort of. Kids would be assaulted by men dressed as Father Christmas or as a clown, a "Christmas cake" would be made containing dead rodents and insects, and the kids would have to eat it. But not the adults, once you're part of it your life is dedicated to worship and your own pleasure, but if you break the rules you'd be in big trouble. You see, it's not kept down to a few ceremonies now and again, it's like a way of life, love. But members of the group won't socialize with each other, not like having the equivalent of a church social. They'll call on each other to discuss business and may stay for a chat and a drink, which is probably what was happening that time when I heard my dad say that they had to have another girl. When people from normal society called on us my dad would go up to the mantelpiece and brush his fingertips over the clock which was there and that was a sign to me and my sister to remain quiet, because this visitor was not one of the group. He or she might be a neighbour, for example, because the households had to appear normal, even churchgoing.

'We moved to Durham when I was about seven and lived on a council estate in the city and went to normal schools, and you'd recognize the other children who you had danced naked with, but we never spoke to each other, always avoided looking at each other, even if we were in the same class at school. If adult members met each other in the street they'd walk on without speaking, love, but they'd recognize each other.'

They walked in silence, skirted a stand of bramble, and then Carmen Pharoah asked what sort of people compose such groups?

'All sorts, love, all sorts of jobs – politicians, lawyers, police officers, probation officers, social workers, nurses, doctors, businessmen, top jobs . . .'

'Professional types then?'

'Aye, and a lot of old money. There was always money about it. Big houses, warehouses in docklands, once I was hung from an inverted cross for two days inside a church.'

'I find that difficult to believe, if not impossible – you'd have been found by one of the clergy or the laity.'

'I knew you'd say that, but you're thinking of your brick-built St Barnabus chapel in a housing estate. Try thinking of a private chapel in the grounds of a private estate in Scotland. That's what I mean by old money.'

Carmen Pharoah shook her head. 'We just won't have the resources for this . . .'

They walked on in silence.

'I've killed someone,' Tessie Cahill said suddenly.

Carmen Pharoah, the police officer, looked at her keenly. 'Yes, I did hear something about that. We'll have to talk about it in the future, Tessie, but not now.'

'I did, my hand was on the handle of the knife, an adult's hand over mine and we plunged the knife into this little lass. I remember the look in her eyes. Then I was told I was a murderer and if I didn't keep silent I'd go to prison. That's what I was told and I believed them. They're always finding things to control you with. And that last summer before we moved to Durham I took this four-year-old off the estate, brought him to a car and he was driven away. His parents still live in the same house, old now, but they keep his bedroom just as it was, and a light in the window for when he returns. But he won't return – weeks later I saw him murdered. You can't understand the self-hatred that brings. I have a drink problem because of that . . . the things I've done . . .'

'Tessie, we'll have to talk about things like that later, maybe in a few weeks' time. Not yet, but at some point soon we'll have to sit down together and I'll have to take a detailed statement from you.'

'All right, but will you tell those people what happened to their son thirty years ago?'

'It won't be my decision. Speaking personally, I can't see that it will serve any purpose. It'll distress them dreadfully and we're not likely to have proof.'

'Just a statement from a mad cow.'

'I didn't mean it like that, Tessie.' Carmen Pharoah smiled. 'A statement isn't sufficient by itself. We'd really have to have a body, or portion of identifiable remains in order to be able to break news like that to his parents.'

'You won't find the body, you never do, hardly ever. Which is what's not right about the body on Marston Moor. Somebody's for the chop for that.'

They continued to walk. An observer would observe two women, enjoying the summer, strolling side by side in the hospital grounds; a 'pastoral' visit perhaps.

'I think that you still find it all hard to believe.' Tessie Cahill broke the silence.

'I confess I do, the organization, the extent . . .'

'It has been going on for hundreds of years. I mean, has anything you've heard been impossible? I mean physically impossible?'

'No, no, I don't suppose it has.'

'So then it's possible, right? Got to be, if it's not impossible. Then it must be possible.'

Carmen Pharoah nodded. 'That's fair. Difficult to comprehend, but certainly possible in the simple physical sense.'

'That's your problem, love, you're not up against the impossible, be easy if you were, you're up against the improbable. You're up against the "don't want to believe it so I won't believe it" attitude. But explain the appearance of the body on Marston Moor and the date he was found, explain the children that go missing each year and whose bodies are never found. Explain the children's bodies found from time to time and nobody knows who they are. Explain that.'

'That's more uncomfortable, you're right, Tessie . . . when we were talking to Ben he told us of children kept underground. What do you know about that?'

'They exist, kept in cages, they don't know any other life. I saw them when I was put down there with them for six weeks as a punishment. They couldn't talk, just moaned a lot, drank their own urine and caked themselves with mud to keep warm. They were kept to be sacrificed.'

'I just don't want to believe it.'

'That's how it survives, by being unbelievable.'

They walked round the back of the hospital, parked vehicles, fire escapes, laundry baskets. In the middle distance was the figure of John Sorenson, in a white T-shirt, picking his way along the tree line. Eventually they formed a group of three.

'Productive talk?' asked Sorenson, warmly.

'Very.'

'Will you continue with your walk?'

Carmen Pharoah shook her head. 'No, I don't want to talk any more. I've really heard enough.'

'It's close to medication time anyway,' Tessie Cahill said. 'I'll go back to the ward, nip in the rear entrance.'

Walking to the car park, Sorenson said, 'And I used to think my dad was hard for stopping my pocket money and locking up my bike.'

Carmen Pharoah knew he was fishing and thought about being sent out by the nuns to bring a branch of a sapling from the grounds but said only, 'Yes, it puts it into perspective, that's for sure.'

Carmen Pharoah returned to Friargate Police Station and hurriedly ran up the stairs to the CID corridor. In front of her she noticed another female police officer also in plain clothes, also moving with urgency. Carmen Pharoah followed the other female officer along the CID corridor and watched her turn into Leif Vossian's office. Carmen

Pharoah caught up with her as she tapped on Vossian's open door.

'Sorry to disturb you, sir,' Claire Shapiro panted, 'but it's more than a sex ring, it's witchcraft.'

'It's not, you know.' Carmen Pharoah stood beside Claire Shapiro. 'It's Satanism. We've got a real problem here.'

Leif Vossian didn't react. Then he nodded slowly and indicated a middle-aged lady occupying a chair in the corner of his office whom neither Shapiro nor Pharoah had noticed in their haste and urgency. 'DC Pharoah and DC Shapiro, I'd like you to meet Mrs St John, Mrs Natalie St John.'

Natalie St John nodded and smiled at the two officers, who in turn acknowledged her.

'You see I haven't exactly been idle over the last few weeks. We've really got Bill Hatch to thank; he recalled a conversation he once had in the bar of a hotel in Aberdeen with another member of his profession and so he suggested that we contact the Leicester Police and compare notes. It was that which put us on the scent, and the three of us have clearly arrived at the same place at the same time. Mrs St John has travelled from Nottingham to help us. The Leicester police recommended her and she has travelled up at ridiculously short notice to talk to us. She is a national expert on Satanistic child abuse. You'll both find a note in your pigeonholes. Mrs St John will be speaking to us tomorrow in the conference room, nine a.m. sharp, it's a three-line whip to all CID officers and Child Protection Officers. No matter what shift you're on.'

'Yes, sir.'

'Yes, sir.'

'I'm reviewing the case with Mrs St John right now, you have both clearly got new information. You may as well join us, tell us what you've uncovered. Please, grab a pew.'

She'd had worse, she'd had much, much worse, she'd had the keep-me-informed merchants, she'd had the spineless, in her view, self-serving careerists who had placed their careers before the welfare of the children at risk, but Derek Wyatt she thought was OK as a principal social worker, next up in her line of management. Mirrium Devers thought Derek Wyatt to be OK. He sat back, dressed in cheesecloth shirt, shorts and sandals and listened as she recounted the interview with Kimberley Hampshire, and of Kimberley's disclosures therein. His colour paled but his attention didn't seem to waver. When she had finished he said, 'Right, I'm going to inform the director, and then both of us stay silent about it.'

Devers nodded. 'Walls have ears.'

'That's the ticket, these people are deeply entrenched. They may be in this building, in the police force, they'll have someone in a position to tip a group off, help them keep one step ahead. If you could write it up and ensure that the file is locked away. There's a tendency for workers to leave files on desks and cabinets unlocked, which I dare say is fair enough if they give us cardboard buildings to work in and if only twenty per cent of our cabinets are lockable, but this one stays under lock and key.'

'I'll keep it in my desk.' Devers stood. 'It has a drawer which can be locked.'

'Good, fortunate for us. Spare key?'

'I'll let you have it.'

'What are the police going to do, do you know?'

'Contact us, they said. And feed the information to something called CATCHEM.'

'What on earth is that?'

'A computer database, apparently. I only heard about it today, it stands for Central Analytical Team Collating Homicide Expertise Management. It's collating all information about child murders in Britain since 1960. So Claire Shapiro told me just now, just before I left her to come here.'

Devers drove home to Wistow. The village looked the same, the house she and Sandy rented looked the same, the countryside basked in a hot airless day. She parked her car in the driveway and her eye was immediately caught by a black object on the front doorstep. She saw immediately what it was.

It was a cat. Dead, of course. That did not in itself alarm her, what did cause a chill of horror to shoot down her spine was its posture. It hadn't died there of natural causes, it hadn't been flung there by a callous owner or a heartless motorist, it had been propped up in a grotesque, half-human sitting position, its eyes wide, frozen in terror.

It was Monday, 26th July, 18.30 hours.

8

Tuesday 27th July, 10.00 hours–12.00 hours

'We don't use the term.' Natalie St John was seen by the officers in the conference room to be a lady of early middle years who could perhaps carry more fashionable clothing than she chose to wear, not really needing the calf-length skirt, but clearly she pursued a policy of preferring grace and elegance rather than clinging to the last vestiges of youth. She wore neat shoulder-length hair, and pale lipstick. A watch, a wedding ring and an engagement ring were the only decoration. She responded to Ken Menninot's question about Satanistic child abuse. 'I don't doubt for a second that the practice is ritualistic and also Satanistic, but the point being that the crime is the issue not the belief system which lays behind the crime. I would defend people's right to worship Satan, it's the crimes they commit which is opposed. The preferred term is Generational Sadistic Abuse – GSA for short.'

'GSA,' Menninot echoed. A wall-mounted clock ticked loudly.

'I'm a social worker, I've developed an interest in this issue, written on the subject, I give seminars and assist the police to obtain evidence by helping children to disclose. A long, slow and, for the children, a painful experience.' She sat back in her chair, holding her hands together in her lap, minimizing body movements as if observing a polished act designed to lend gravity to her words. 'Certainly, it seems that you have a group practising here in York which is quite in keeping with Satanistic practices, everything being done to defile Christianity, so ancient centres of Christianity will have active covens. We understand that Canterbury is particularly significant for Satanism, but don't quite know in what way. But York, as a seat of Christian worship, will certainly have a strong and powerful group. Confirmed, I think, by the discovery of the body of the boy on where . . . ?'

'Marston Moor,' Vossian answered.

'That's near the centre?'

'Quite near, ten minutes by car.'

'Bodies of children are found from time to time. Off the top of my head I can think of the girl of about eight found in the Brecon Beacons, dismembered and burnt, the body of the boy washed up upon a beach in Fife in the early 1970s.'

'On a beach?' Vossian asked.

'Yes, no damage to the body so he hadn't drifted across the North Sea from the continent. Confess that incident had me puzzled until the revelations about the Glamorgan case came to light. You may recall that case, practice centred on a barn but that group terrified children into compliance by taking them out into the Severn estuary at night and throwing them over the side of a small boat, one at a time, then circling them until they became exhausted and pulling them back into the boat just before they drowned. It may well be that a similar practice had taken place off the coast of Fife, but they didn't rescue the poor lad in time. The people of Fife built a cairn in his memory. He was never identified. None of these children are, their births are not registered and they are kept underground, literally and metaphorically.'

David de Larrabeitta's hand went up to his mouth.

'The cuts on the eyelids and hairline and groin virtually confirm that the boy was a victim of GSA, the practice of placing those cuts is part of the child's dedication to Diana, the Satanistic deity of sex, the cuts supposedly allow Diana into the body to control thought, sight and lust. That the boy was dedicated means that he was valued in some way and was being assumed further into the coven, that he was murdered means that he had transgressed in some way. Covens are unforgiving towards any member who comes to pose a threat or has transgressed. For that reason the person who failed to ensure the proper disposal of the corpse is in trouble.' Natalie St John paused. 'Adults are victims too – another reason for the GSA group to thrive in York is that

153

it is a university town and as such has a mobile, shifting population, not perhaps among students themselves, who are almost all well integrated with a network of friends and whose absence would be soon noticed, but rather there will be a fringe element of adults who have marginalized their lives and find acceptance only amongst the bohemian nature of the student café and pub culture. Such people make easy prey for GSA groups, being easily lured by the promise of friendship.

'The GSA group in York will have access to a large house or a remote farm, money, lots of it, is always involved but your chances of finding any forensic evidence will be slim to zero. We were once able to identify such a barn in Warwickshire from the drawings and verbal disclosure of children in a Birmingham case, and we visited it, myself and two police officers. The outstanding thing about it was just how clean it was inside, not even animal droppings which you'd expect in a barn, but this place hadn't even got that. Our problem was that we didn't know what we were looking for. If we had known we might just have been able to pick up some evidence, even in a sanitized crime scene.'

'But even so . . .' Vossian said.

'As you suggest, an ultra-squeaky-clean barn in the middle of the countryside is significant in itself, but as evidence . . . ?' Natalie St John gave a slight shrug and a smile as if in exasperation. 'What is nothing evidence of?'

'I take your point,' Vossian growled.

'Each group will have at its head three leaders. Sometimes two, being a High Priest and High Priestess. Others appear to have three leaders because a triad is the strongest of all human bonds. With two, one is likely to betray the other, four will split into two groups of two, but three will remain loyal to each other. Below that there is a second echelon of seven members, or second-in-commands, still very revered, and each of these seven will have a specific commission and one will have the forensic commission.'

'Forensic? As in pertaining to criminal investigation?'

'Yes. Although antiforensic might be a better description. Because this person's job is to cleanse the scene of crime, and the person that cleansed the barn near Birmingham clearly did a thorough job. Less so the man or woman in the York group and that person, I can assure you, is in the soup.'

'Oh?'

'The body of that little boy should have been burned, thoroughly incinerated and chopped into bits and buried or fed to pigs, which is why so few sacrificed victims are found. The person with the forensic commission in the York group has clearly blotted his copybook. He'll either be sacrificed himself *pour encourager les autres*, and his body disposed of, or, and this is the preferred option because the group know that you're involved, they'll feed him to you in some way, either the culprit himself or a stand-in culprit, as an apparent suicide or death by misadventure and with some evidence linking him to the murder, a lock of hair from the deceased, and an apparent suicide note. Anticipate that, because they'll be desperate to buy off your attention. It's akin to the old practice of separating out an old and sickly cow and ham-stringing her for the wolves to find, so as to allow the rest of the herd to escape. The other thing that might happen is that your violent-crime rate might rise.'

'Tell me.' Markova was alarmed.

'If a GSA group believes itself to be under investigation it will attempt to divert attention from itself and stretch your resources.'

'That will not be difficult.'

'They know that. So you may find happening a series of violent, even murderous, muggings, or violent and murderous random attacks, a number of arson attacks, maybe even a serial killer will appear ... anything to stretch your resources and divert your attention from the group. Satanists dislike attention, they'll slip into a church at night, perform a ritual and slip away and not leave a trace of their being there. It isn't at all in their interest to advertise their existence, it's all part of the buzz. Only they know what has happened. As in the practice of leaving a child in the bottom of a newly dug grave all night, clutching animal entrails, and removing the child and all traces just before dawn. A few hours later a Christian funeral will take place, but only the

GSA group will know the coffin has been laid in a defiled grave. Or they might perhaps slip into a cemetery at night and lay on the grave of a newly buried person, remaining there until they feel they have absorbed the spirit of the deceased. All such things and similar things happen without a trace being left and if I were a betting lady, I would lay good money that the case of the Marston Moor murder will be wrapped up very soon by your being offered the culprit. The person with the forensic commission may well take his own life on his own initiative in preference to giving himself up to the group for sacrifice. I know I would.' She paused. 'I think in passing I'd like to point out that in fairness Satanism, like Christianity, is a broad church; it has its levels, its mainstream and its offshoots. We believe some Satanists never commit any form of crime in the observance of their belief. But only some.'

Gerald Peep walked up to the prison officer. 'I want to see the police officer I saw the other month, back in May, it was, DI Vossian, Friargate, York. I want to make a statement.'

The prison officer nodded. 'All right, Gerald. I'll ask the governor to phone him, DI Vossian of Friargate nick in York.'

'That's it. Thanks.'

Nigel Harrby carried the suitcases out of the house towards the Fiat.

'Not the Mercedes?' His blonde wife stopped walking and stood questioningly.

'Too conspicuous.' Harrby flung the suitcase into the Fiat's boot. He turned to her. 'You don't have to come.'

'I know.' Cynthia Harrby smiled, shielding her eyes against the sun.

'They'll spare you.'

'I know that too, but there'll be some penalty to pay.'

'You know what I'm going to do?'

'And I know that too. Let's quit while we're ahead.'

'Well, you've time to change your mind. I've got enough cash to keep going for a few weeks. I thought I'd visit a few places in the UK I've always intended to visit, Wales, for instance. Never been to Wales.'

'Well, let's go. They'll be here soon. I overheard Dolly on the phone. We don't have any time to spare, they've given us longer than I thought they would as it is.'

'You mentioned other commissions?' Markova prompted.

'There'll be a Thane, who obtains the paraphernalia, the equipment, the animals, and human victims. He also ensures correct procedure is observed. There'll be a scribe who keeps a written record.'

'Gold dust if we can get hold of that.'

'If you can, though nobody outside the group has ever, to my knowledge, seen one and even then I assume they're written in code or symbols.' Natalie St John paused, searching her memory. 'There will be a head disciple who supervises the training of the children and adult novices. A policy maker, or Commanders, and a medical person who obtains drugs and attends to pregnant children, especially at the birth. And others whose commissions are not known.'

'What about funding for this sort of thing?' Pharoah asked.

'That's a good question. In the first place, any GSA group will be of monied people, especially at the core, but it will raise money by drug trafficking or child pornography. If you're able to trace a child-pornography distribution network to its source, you'll possibly also be close to the centre of a GSA group.'

'Some chance of that.' Markova settled back in his chair. 'In our own force the Vice Squad once wanted surveillance equipment, especially long-lensed binoculars to observe a known child-pornography dealer and were told they couldn't have them because they were needed to watch the house of a suspected burglar.'

'So now it's my turn to express disbelief. Frustrating, isn't it?'

'Very, they could have pulled that guy if they could have watched from a distance, couldn't, so did it from a parked car and he saw them and had a bonfire in his back garden, all the evidence went up in smoke.'

'I meant, actually, that it's frustrating when nobody believes you. The big problem is that GSA groups have such an appearance of normality, they live in nuclear families, the children can be taken to church, which gives a good impression, but the motive is to transmit the message to the children that, "Here we are in the house of God and nothing's happening to us, so Satan is the stronger." Or children can be sent to church twice on Sundays, which again gives a good impression, but the real reason is to increase their value as objects of defilement.'

'A whole different way of life.' Shapiro shook her head.

'GSA groups,' Natalie St John continued, now well into her stride, 'will employ everyday names for their own practices so that children will be given books with titles like *Treasure Island* or *Black Beauty*, but the story within the covers is unlike anything Robert Louis Stevenson or Anna Sewell wrote. All the children will be forced to play hunt the thimble or musical chairs, which sounds harmless, except that the "thimble" is not a thimble but a body part from one of the sacrificial victims, one of the eyes appears to be popular. Musical chairs involves the adults of the group sitting naked in a line, with the children also naked dancing round them, and when the music stops the children have to rush to the nearest adult and initiate sexual play. If a child is seen to copy another child then that child is punished in some way. So that not only do the children have to initiate sexual play, but they have to be inventive, they have to demonstrate the ability to be sexually experimental.'

'Excuse me.' Vossian leaned forwards and rested his elbows on the table. 'Where does this information come from?'

'From children who have disclosed over the years, from adult survivors who have overcome fear and have spoken out. The significant thing is that people and children not known to each other, from different and distant parts of the country, all report the same rituals and practices, and the fear in the adult survivors is real, it's all too real. One woman tried to leave a group and was badly beaten up by her uncle for doing so. He was a policeman. Probably still is.'

The group stiffened with tension.

'I'm sorry' – Natalie St John smiled – 'but you have to face facts. These people are everywhere. And what better place than in the local police force? They're in a position to tip off the local group about any investigation and to frustrate the investigation or even derail it completely. That particular woman feigned mental illness and the group no longer saw her as a threat because she had no credibility and the more she rambled on about being made to skin cats and dogs alive, about being made to torture and kill other children, about children kept in cages, the more she reinforced the diagnosis of mental ill health, but everything she was saying was true. So many other people report the same experiences.

'The other thing that happens,' she continued, 'is a process called loading the language. All groups and organizations do it, the armed services, for example, tend to load their language with initials and abbreviations which make it totally incomprehensible to someone in civvy street. The police force will have certain phrases its officers use when speaking among themselves.'

'That's true.' Menninot smiled.

'Loading of language within groups will happen naturally, but the armed services, for example, deliberately foster and encourage it because it serves to provide a sense of belonging and a sense of separateness. GSA groups do the same.' Natalie St John paused. 'You'll also find that the children most certainly will have been exposed to horror videos so that if it came to a court case the defence will be able to argue that the children are fantasizing, having watched a number of video nasties. Interestingly, children from GSA groups who've been taken into alternative accommodation do like watching video nasties: they feel comfortable with them, they're a source of the familiar in a strange environment.'

'That's asking an awful lot of foster parents,' Shapiro commented. 'I doubt if I'd be prepared to do it if I were a foster parent.'

'Some aren't, but some will cooperate. You see, children have to be introduced to GSA ritual, and they have to be weaned off it, and allowing them access to video nasties while in care is ethically fraught, but it's done hand in hand with therapy and eventually the child will say that he or she doesn't want to watch the video any more. Then you know they're beginning to recover.'

A pause. The clock ticked.

'The thing to remember' – Natalie St John relaxed, signalling the close of her delivery – 'is that a bizarre referral needs a calm, logical, step-by-step investigation. Don't get caught up in Hammer-film hysteria, you'll only lose credibility. In one case, I think it was Telford, which was the first successful prosecution of a GSA group, the Crown barrister opened by saying that, "there had been newspaper reports that Satanism has been involved in this case. I mention it now, and will not mention it again," and he didn't, building his case only on proven facts about child abuse. That case was won and a number of life sentences handed down; more importantly, full Care Orders were obtained on all the children involved and all were permanently fostered or adopted. Not all have that sort of happy ending. But I will be pleased to help you in this one as much as I can.'

It was midday, Tuesday, 27th July.

9

Wednesday, 28th July, 10.30 hours–21.30 hours
David de Larrabeitta thought Michael McGuire looked smug.
McGuire with his blue T-shirt, faded jeans and battered blue
trainers, his beard, sat back in the chair and looked smug in
de Larrabeitta's eyes.

'But you have consorted with the Hampshire children?'
de Larrabeitta pressed.

McGuire glanced at the police mutual calendar on the wall,
at the twin audio cassettes revolving in the machine. He said,
'Yes. I offered to tutor them, the girls anyway, they were a
bit slow at school.'

'How did you contact them?'

The question foxed him. He paused as if searching for an
answer, no longer looking smug. 'My children met them,
they were playing near the quarry at the edge of the estate.
One thing led to another, I met their mother and when she
found out that I was a teacher she told me that they were
slow at school and so I offered to tutor them, the youngest
girl in the main – Kimberley – but I also helped Sadie from
time to time.'

'I see.' De Larrabeitta paused. 'Mr McGuire, you will be
aware that Sadie and Kimberley and their younger brother
Shane have been received into the care of the local
authority?'

'I am aware of that. They're part of the Pyrrah family.'

'You're well informed, they were not mentioned by name
in the media. Their identity was, and still is, protected under
the reporting restrictions that were imposed.'

'It's local knowledge that it was the children of the wider
Pyrrah family. The word spread from the Trafford, yea even

unto the green fields of Endon.' McGuire once again began to look smug.

'Do you know why they were received into care?'

'There have been rumours.'

'All the children have been medically examined and all have injuries consistent with chronic penetrative sexual abuse, both vaginal and anal. That also includes Shane Hampshire, aged three years.'

'I am very sorry to hear that.'

'Kimberley has advised us that you were one of the men responsible for this.'

'Untrue!' McGuire leaned forwards. 'Nonsense. Absolutely untrue. I enjoy a good sex life with my wife. Children hold no sexual attraction for me.'

'So why would Kimberley allege that you assaulted her in this way?'

'Fantasizing, I assume.'

'Perhaps, but we are learning that children don't fantasize about matters of this nature.'

'I'm still unable to help you.'

'I see . . .' De Larrabeitta paused. 'Mr McGuire, you have children of your own?'

'I do.'

'Boy and a girl, twelve and fourteen respectively?'

'Been doing your homework.'

'We like to look at the wider circumstances. But we'll come back to them.'

'What do you mean, you'll come back to them!' McGuire's face flushed with anger. 'You leave my kids out of this.'

'Mr McGuire, I'm afraid your children are very much a part of this until we, the police, are satisfied that they are safe and well.'

'Safe and well . . .'

'Mr McGuire, you own a car and a trailer?'

'I do.' Spoken icily.

'If I were to tell you that Kimberley has drawn a picture of herself and other children in a car, pulling a trailer which seems full of portable hi-fi equipment and lighting equipment on their way to "the quarry" or "the hole in the ground'' where they dance round a cloaked figure among other things, would you have any idea what they were talking about?'

'I would not.'

'Or about children, infant children, being murdered and their remains burned and buried near the ''hole in the ground''.'

'Preposterous.'

'Sexual play with children.'

'Stuff and nonsense.'

'Terrifying children with snakes, making them eat faeces and insects?'

'You're off your head.'

'Do you know anyone called Meakey?'

'No.'

'You wouldn't be known as Meakey, perchance?'

'Perchance I would not.'

'But you are the only person in Kimberley Hampshire's circle of human contact who owns a car and trailer, and Kimberley told us the drawing she made was of her and other children going to ''the quarry'' or ''the hole in the ground'' and I quote ''Meakey's car''.'

'I still can't help you.'

'Why did you come to Endon?'

'To settle, to get out of the rat race.'

'Why Endon?'

'Saw the place advertised in Dalton's weekly. Right size, right location, right price. Jumped at it.'

'A lot of newcomers in Endon?'

'One or two from various places, South Africa, New Zealand.'

'You know each other, the newcomers, I mean?'

'I've said before, the locals won't talk to us so we talk to each other.'

'The minister's new too, the Reverend Seers?'

'So I believe.'

'Talk to him?'

'In passing.'

'He has a cloak, does he not?'

'What man of the cloth doesn't?'

De Larrabeitta paused. 'This interview is concluded at ten forty a.m. on the 28th July.' He switched the machine off and pressed the eject button. He handed one tape to McGuire and placed the second on his notepad.

'That's it?' McGuire stood.

'For the moment.' De Larrabeitta also stood. 'Thank you for coming in, Mr McGuire.'

It was Wednesday, 28th July, 10.45 hours.

Wednesday, 28th July, 11.45 hours
'Kimberley' – Mirrium Devers sat on the floor with Kimberley Hampshire, and had watched as Kimberley had placed the smaller plastic figures in a circle round a larger robot figure – 'do you know the names of the other children who go to the bad parties?'

Kimberley Hampshire nodded.

Claire Shapiro, sitting on the settee, leaned forwards, eager to hear everything the child might say.

Kimberley Hampshire placed a figure from the circle next to the robot. 'Bad man,' she said.

'Why is he a bad man, Kimberley?'

'Does bad things, but the girl would have to like him or he'll hurt her.'

'How will he hurt her, Kimberley?'

'Make the girl cry.'

'Kimberley, all these people in the circle, are they all children?'

Kimberley Hampshire nodded. 'Bad man in the middle. Grown ups stand outside the circle going, "ha, ha, ha!"'

'And the children don't like the dance.'

'Be good to stop the dance. Merrylegs says dance to go on.'

'Merrylegs? Who's Merrylegs, Kimberley?'

'Grown-up. Just here.' She pointed to a place on the carpet outside the circle of figures.

'Merrylegs is one of the adults?'

Kimberley Hampshire nodded.

'Which one of these children is you, Kimberley?'

164

Kimberley Hampshire pointed to the figure next to the model robot in the centre of the circle.

'He's doing bad things to you.'

'Yes.'

'So who is this, this figure here?'

'Michael McGuire.'

Mirrium Devers nodded matter-of-factly, showing no reaction, but her heart missed a beat. She knew that this was how the information comes out, nothing, nothing, then a flood, and she also knew that any overreaction, any startled expression would block the flow. Even a 'good girl' expression of encouragement would be seen as suspicious by Kimberley Hampshire and children like her. Mirrium Devers was aware of Claire Shapiro leaning further forwards on the settee and said calmly, 'And this, who is this?'

'Gillian McGuire.'

'And this?'

'Susan Rivers, and this is Catherine Rivers.'

'And him?'

'It's a her. It's Nancy Dovedale. This is a he, this is Simon Dovedale.'

'And this one?'

'Robert Boot, and this is Edward Boot.'

'And here?'

'My cousin, Paul Pyrrah, all the others are my cousins. The really bad things only happen to my cousins and my brother and sister, but the other children have to dance and watch the bad things. Watch us dance round the master till he hooks us with his stick.'

'This happens in the hole in the ground?'

'Yes. At night, light shines over the master.'

'How long does the party go on?'

'All night. Stop now.'

Driving away from the Fee household Devers said, 'Merrylegs?'

'Name of a horse, isn't it?' Shapiro allowed her eyes to stray from the road ahead so that she could enjoy the sight of the sun causing the Minster on the skyline to glow warmly.

'In *Black Beauty*, as I recall from schooldays – you know the children's book? Black Beauty and Merrylegs run away together. That's the only Merrylegs I know.'

'Really? I never read the book. And the names she mentioned, did you get a note of them?'

'McGuire, Dovedale, Rivers, Boot . . . Yes, I did.'

'Who are they?'

'They're the newcomers, they're the families who settled in Endon over the last few years, as if drawn by the same magnet. They give our community constable the impression of knowing each other prior to coming to the Vale of York.'

Devers shook her head. 'Can of worms is just not the expression for all this.'

'What Kimberley said about the really bad things happening only to the children in the Pyrrah family network worries me.'

'Oh?' Devers glanced at her.

'It may mean that we won't have the concrete physical evidence of sexual abuse with the newcomers' children that we have with the Pyrrahs'.'

It was Wednesday, 28th July, 12.30 hours.

Wednesday, 28th July, 14.00 hours
David de Larrabeitta held the phone to his ear and listened as the receiver on the other end of the line was placed on a hard surface and a man's voice shouted down an echoey corridor. 'Alison, it's the police, for you . . .'

'The police?' The answering voice was high pitched and alarmed. 'What do they want?'

'Didn't say,' the man answered and de Larrabeitta heard hard-soled sensible shoes marching towards the phone and pictured the man being elbowed aside.

'Alison Goodenough,' snapped a female voice.

'Mrs Goodenough, this is DC de Larrabeitta speaking, of the Child Protection Unit at Friargate Police Station.'

'Yes?' A note of caution was held in Alison Goodenough's voice, but also a note of relief. De Larrabeitta's designation meant work, not a personal issue.

166

'I'm sorry to phone you at home, and on school holidays . . .'

'Yes, yes.'

'We're investigating a suspected child-abuse situation involving a number of children who attend your school.'

'The children of the Pyrrah family, yes, it was me who referred them to the Social Services back in May.'

'And others.'

'Oh?'

'The McGuires, the Riverses, the Dovedales and the Boots.'

'Yes, they're all children who attend my school. I can't say that I've noticed anything particularly unusual about them but I'll phone their class teachers if I can get hold of them, though they're likely to be in Benidorm or some such dreadful place this time of year. I used to go abroad until I failed to see the attraction of anywhere outside England. Especially in the summer. What sort of things are you concerned about?'

De Larrabeitta paused. 'I'd rather not say at present, but if the class teachers have noticed anything unusual I'd like to know about it.'

'Very well.' Alison Goodenough spoke in a huffy tone, as if, thought de Larrabeitta, as if she, the headmistress, had the right to know everything. 'I'll start phoning now.' She put the phone down heavily.

It was Wednesday, 28th July, 14.15 hours.

Wednesday, 28th July, 14.30 hours
The sun streamed in through the opaque glass window in the agent's room. Gerald Peep wrung his hands, sweat poured from his brow. 'The heat,' he said.

'Hottest and driest since records began.' Vossian eyed Peep cautiously. He found Peep's body odour overwhelming, but didn't remark on it. 'But you didn't ask to see me so we could talk about the weather.'

'No, no, I didn't.' Peep wiped his brow and flicked the sweat on to the industrial-grade linoleum. So profusely was he sweating that drops of perspiration were heard to splatter on the floor.

'I've been thinking about what you said the other month.'

'You want to give information?'

Peep nodded. 'Yes. Anything to get me out of here, it's driving me out of my head . . . sex offenders . . . we're just not part of the criminal fraternity. Being on rule forty-three is no joke, the screws can't watch you all the time, you're always watching your back.' Peep clenched both fists and put them to his forehead.

'I can't pretend I'm sympathetic, Gerald, what about your victims? You've given them life sentences, they'll take it to their graves, what you did to them, their lives are permanently blighted. But let's hear what you've got.'

'I'll need all the witness protection you can offer, changed identity, move to a prison in the south of England or Scotland – prefer the south of England.'

'I'll see what I can do. The more you do for us, the more we'll do for you.' Vossian remained calm, unemotional, aloof even. 'But remember, a statement by itself is not enough. You'll have to agree to testify.'

Peep nodded. 'I'll agree. I have to get out of here, didn't realize I'd miss my liberty so much . . .'

'Understand that this will not obtain your liberty for you?'

Peep glanced at him.

'I told you last time, this will count in your favour at your parole hearings, that's all. How heavily it will count will depend on what information you can give. You'll still be looking at a good few years in the slammer.'

'A good few years . . .' Peep echoed.

'You ruined a lot of lives, Gerald, you betrayed a position of trust to do it, that made it much worse.'

Peep paused. 'Would you be interested in a guy called Harrby? Local worthy type, has a farm out Knaresborough way.'

Vossian leaned forward. 'Yes. Yes, indeed, we would be interested muchly in Harrby, the Honourable Sir, or whatever his title is.'

'I saw him kill a guy. I didn't know what I was getting into . . .' Peep was close to tears.

'How did it happen?'

Peep paused again, then he said, 'Harrby's into witchcraft. He's a witch.'

'No, he's not,' Vossian replied quickly. 'A lot of witches would be upset to hear you say that.'

'Oh . . .' Peep paled. He caught his breath. 'You're not one of them!'

'How would you know? But no, I'm not. Gerald, we know a little about Harrby, he's not a witch, he's a Satanist.'

'Satanist,' Peep repeated.

'We believe so, there's a two-pronged investigation under way at the moment, one of the prongs is driving towards Harrby, but we're a tad short of E for evidence: in fact, it's ground to a halt.'

'I can believe that. He's clever.'

'So what happened?'

'He had something over me. He still has.'

'Oh.'

'A film. A video . . . he picked me up at a scene party in the Vale . . . you know, S & M . . . asked me if I wanted something "heavy", and I said yes, like you would.'

'Like *you* would, Gerald.'

'It was a way of speaking. Went to his house the following week, and oh . . . talk about chickens, tender, ripe . . .'

Peep's eyes filled with pleasure. Vossian wanted to retch.

'Both about six or seven . . . really compliant . . . didn't speak, just sort of grunted . . . I didn't see him move to the corner and start filming me with a camcorder.' Peep buried his head in his hands. 'I didn't know I'd been filmed until he came by my house and dropped off a copy. He told me the other copy would be with the police unless I was at his house at midnight that night.'

'Go on' – Vossian made eye contact – 'this is good stuff, Gerald.'

'So that was me, a pressed man, getting initiated, standing round chanting . . . I got taken along with a carload of heavies to beat this guy up, work him over with pickaxe handles. He was a pressed man like me, they said, this is what happens if you try to leave. The first time I had to watch, months later they attacked a woman who wanted out, worked her

169

over good they did, hurt her bad, then they gave me a phial of acid, told me to pour it on her face.'

'And you did, you left her on Harrogate Stray, she was found by an early-morning jogger. I remember the case.'

'That's the one.'

'You did that?' Vossian's voice hardened.

'I was scared not to, by then I was rigid with fear. They said, "You've done that, the only place you're safe now is with us." They didn't need to tell me what would happen if I left. That woman, she attended a few meetings, after that, wearing one of those plastic face masks, she was too scared not to attend, then she threw herself under a train.'

'I remember.'

'The coroner recorded suicide which was brought on because she was depressed by the disfigurement caused by the acid. But it wasn't that, it was the only way out of the group. This is why I need protection, Mr Vossian. I'm not safe anywhere, not even in prison.'

'Was Harrby present at either assault?'

'No, but somebody else was, another guy, the one that taught me and the other pressed men about the symbols and the ceremonies.'

'His identity?'

But Peep just shook his head.

'I only knew Harrby and his wife. They were not the group leaders either, some other man and woman were the High Priest and Priestess.'

'So what happened when he murdered someone.'

'Jesus, that was horrible, made the assaults and the acid attack look like a Sunday School picnic. This guy, youngish fellow, a dosser, I think, pulled him off the streets somehow, kept him down with the children . . .'

'What!'

'I was going to tell you, I was coming to that . . . Underneath Harrby's house, in the cellar, he's got children in cages.'

Vossian's jaw sagged. 'Gerald, if . . .'

'I'm telling the truth . . . I'm not bothered about parole, I'll be safer in here than out there, but only safer, not safe. I want this off my chest. I saw about six children, kept like animals, but more than six cages, kids just moaned all the time, just infants . . . about two or three years old.'

'When did you see this, Gerald?'

'When . . . ? Three, four years ago.'

'Go on.'

'This guy was down there, kept there for weeks, they dried the poor sod out, made sure he knew what was happening to him, strung him up. They were standing round him in their robes, some children were there, not the kids from the cages but other children, older children who knew what to do in the ceremony. Then Harrby held his knife, the guy was screaming in terror . . . he cut him deeply on his arms and legs and then plunged the knife into this guy's chest, and while all this was going on the group and the kids were chanting and working themselves up into a kind of frenzy which sort of peaked just as the knife was plunged into this guy's chest.'

'Harrby did that?'

'Yes. About three or four years ago, about the time I first saw the children in the cages.'

'The children in the cages, they were not kept to take part in ceremonies?'

'Oh no, no, the children who stood in the group and joined in the ceremonies were the natural children of the adults, plus some children belonging to outsiders, but I don't know where they came from. The children in the cages were kept for sacrifice, that's why they couldn't speak, no reason to educate them, see?'

'See?' Vossian shook his head. 'No, I don't "see", frankly.'

'You think I'm stringing you along, Mr Vossian?'

'I don't know what I think, Gerald. I really don't.'

'Well, take a trip out there, why don't you? See if Meakey . . .'

'What did you call him!'

'Meakey, it's a nickname he's known by. Don't know where it comes from. Anyway, if Meakey knows you're on his scent he'll have cleared out the cages, but he won't get rid of the cages so easily, they're set in concrete. And that guy, that poor guy that Meakey or Harrby murdered . . . I

171

was made to burn his body and then chop it up, someone watching me, you know, supervising. I rolled the bones into some old sacking and buried them on his land. They'll still be there.'

'Could you take us to where you buried them?'

'Could but I won't. Don't want to be seen cooperating, I'll tell you exactly, I took some bearings. At the back of his farmhouse there's a wood, not right at the back, across a field.'

'Yes.'

'On the facing treeline of the wood there's a dead tree, you know, a hollow trunk, dead wood.'

'Yes.'

'I buried the sacking containing the bones behind the dead tree, about three feet down, covered it with rubble and rocks as I was ordered to do, then put six inches of soil on the rubble and planted a sprig of ivy on the soil.

'You know, the way they told me to carry the bones over the wood, no hesitation – "take them over to the wood" – sort of gave me the impression that that was where they buried all their victims. The wood's just one big burial ground.'

'Gerald, if this checks out, if we get a conviction, I think we could make a case for an early parole. Even from your life sentences. But I think you'll need your new ID.' Vossian stood and tapped on the door of the room. Outside keys rattled.

'Oh, by the way, Harrby's maid – Dolly, I think she's called – she's part of it. Quite high up in the group.'

'Thanks, Gerald. Thanks a lot.'

In his car, Vossian picked up the mobile phone and dialled Friargate. He asked to be put through to Ken Menninot. 'Ken,' he said when Menninot answered, 'we've got what we need to move on Harrby.'

'We have?' Menninot's voice crackled.

'We have. You get warrants for the arrest of him, his wife and the maid, suspicion of murder.'

'And the maid?'

'Yes, I'll explain when I get in. And we want a warrant to search the premises.'

'It's as good as done, boss.'

It was Wednesday, 28th July, 15.00 hours.

Wednesday, 28th July, 15.00 hours

Alison Goodenough phoned David de Larrabeitta one hour after he had phoned her.

'I have,' she said with a voice of controlled indignation, 'managed to speak to three of my staff about the children you mentioned . . .'

'Yes.' De Larrabeitta found his own sense of indignation rising. 'Perhaps I didn't make myself clear, I'd rather have spoken to them directly.'

'I will know what is going on in my school.'

'If anything.' De Larrabeitta found his own voice getting hard. 'We don't yet know if anything is going on. But perhaps you could let me know what your staff have said, and I'll talk to them directly at a later time.'

'Only if I am present, Mr de Larrabeitta. Only if I am present.'

De Larrabeitta paused. 'I'm sorry, Mrs Goodenough, but we will speak to whoever we please, we don't need your permission, or your presence.'

'I don't know whether I should help you at all given your attitude.'

'We'll charge you with obstructing the police in the course of their enquiries if you don't.'

Silence. De Larrabeitta thought that Alison Goodenough had probably been a head teacher for too long, having everything her way, including her household, judging by her meek-sounding husband.

'Very well,' she said at length, 'but I may take your attitude up with your superior.'

'That's your prerogative.'

'Well, the class teachers I have spoken to each had something to say about the children you mentioned. And I too have an observation.'

'Good.'

'Well, my observation first then.'

'If you like.' De Larrabeitta thought that it just had to be her observation first. But no matter, it doesn't matter what order it goes into the pot, so long as it all goes in.

'Well, the children of the families you mentioned, the McGuires, the Riverses, the Dovedales and the Boots all live in the same area, in Endon, at the edge of our catchment area. I've noticed the adults, the parents of those families, talking with each other at the gates of the school at the end of the school day, and seeming to carry themselves as apart from the other families who live locally, but their children don't associate with each other, which appears strange; the adults of those families seem to need each other, the children of those same families avoid each other. I mention it because it seems strange.'

'I'll make a note of it.'

'Well, the staff member who teaches one of the Boot children had to reprimand him for producing some very sexually explicit drawings.'

'What! How long ago was that?'

'How long? In the Easter term. Some months ago now.'

De Larrabeitta groaned. 'Months?'

'Yes.'

'And you left it at that? Months! Don't you see the significance of those drawings?'

'Mr de Larrabeitta, I saw the significance of nothing. The staff member concerned has only just informed me, just now on the phone. I dare say it's something I'll have to take up with her next term. But she's a spinster lady, very close to retirement, these are things she has difficulty coping with, she is not well versed in modern interpretations of sexually explicit drawings.'

'And the drawings themselves?'

'Oh, destroyed. Now, another staff member has children from the Dovedale and the Rivers families. She reports those two children showing great fear of an ants' nest which was brought into the class, in a display case, but with live ants scurrying about; not just squirming, but real terror, so much so that Mrs Chambers, the class teacher, believed that she detected a phobia in both children and referred them to the educational psychologist. That referral is still pending, the Department of Psychology moves with a slowness which is passing graceful.

'Mrs French also has children from two families, the McGuires and the other Boot child. In free art lessons when the children can draw what they want, both children have drawn what appear to be a circle of figures, standing round a larger figure, and both have displayed sexually inappropriate knowledge beyond their years.'

'Which is?'

'Eight. I assume that we will be conferencing this, I have already had all the children of the Pyrrah family received into care.'

'That's up to the Social Services Department. The police don't convene conferences in pursuance of concept of care. We attend and comment on the likelihood of charges being brought, but that's all. Good day.'

It was Wednesday, 28th July, 15.30 hours.

Wednesday, 28th July, 17.00 hours
Vossian, Menninot, Pharoah and Markova drove out to Scythe Farm in two cars. They were followed by a van containing half a dozen constables and a sergeant, and behind the van were two dog vans each containing two sniffer dogs and handlers. The vehicles turned up the driveway to Scythe Farm and crunched the gravel outside the front of the farmhouse as they drew to a stop. The officers got out of the vehicles, the dog handlers let the dogs out of the vans and slipped the leashes around their necks. They surveyed the house. It had an empty look about it. There was no movement, nothing stirred. Menninot strode up to the front door and banged on it with the flat of his hand.

'They're gone!'

The police officers turned to their right, towards the direction of the voice. A middle-aged man with a ruddy complexion, stripped to the waist yet still wearing a cloth cap despite the sun, walked towards them. He wiped his hands on an oily rag. 'They've been away for a day or so now. Took her Fiat, left his Mercedes, as you see.'

'And you are?'

'Cawtheray, Tom Cawtheray. I'm the farm manager. I'm the only one left, the crew didn't get their wages so they've gone elsewhere, the maid's left too, she left one night. She reckoned she didn't know where they'd gone, but they owed her money, so she left. She was here late one night, the next morning she was away. All happened very recently. They owe me money too, but I'm sixty-three, no work for me anywhere, I'm under my wife's feet at home, so I come here, find something to do. I'd rather do something for nothing than nothing for nothing.'

'Where do you live, Mr Cawtheray?'

Tom Cawtheray gave an address in Knaresborough.

'I see,' Vossian said. 'Could we ask you to vacate the farm?'

'Now?'

'If you don't mind. And not to return. We don't know what, if anything, has happened, but it may be that the entire farm is a crime scene. We have to keep the violation of it to a minimum. We know where to contact you if we need to chat to you. You haven't noticed anything untoward going on in the farm or in the house?'

'Can't say I have. Sir Nigel left me to get on with running the farm, never interfered, it was like he was never there most of the time.'

'Thanks.'

'I'll just get my shirt.' Cawtheray turned and walked away and then turned back and said, 'None of my business, but if you want to get in the house you'll break your shoulders before you open that door. Try the door at the rear.'

Vossian nodded his thanks. 'Right, lads, rear of the house, take the dogs to the wood across the field from the back of the house. You know where to start.'

'Behind the dead tree – yes, sir,' answered the senior dog handler.

'That's it. Then let the dogs loose in the wood. I'll be in the house if you need me.'

Once again Menninot noticed the chill inside the house

at Scythe Farm, the everything-in-its-place perfection. The police officers went as a group from room to room, gaining the overriding impression that the Harrbys had left in a hurry. There was no sign of anything having been removed from the house, the wardrobes and drawers were full of clothing, jewellery remained on the dressing table.

The door to the cellar was found in the scullery. It was unlocked and opened easily. Instantly, the smell was overpowering, hitting the police officers as it were in the middle of their foreheads. It wasn't the smell of decay, or corruption; it was the smell of bleach.

In the cellar the police found a stone-built table, they found a purple cloth covered in silver shapes which had been stitched on to the purple, shapes of half-moons, of pentagrams, of stars. They found ornamental knives, a silver chalice, a goat's head. They found a larger pentagram painted on the flagstones of the cellar and they found the cages, a row of twelve cages, set in a raised concrete plinth which ran the length of one wall of the cellar. All were empty, and all, like the cellar as a whole, had been scrubbed with bleach. 'Like Mrs St John's barn in Warwickshire,' Vossian said. 'This is a completely sanitized crime scene. We'll get Forensics in here, but I'll lay a year's salary that they'll find nothing. We can only imagine what went on down here.'

The group of police officers stood in silence. Eventually Leif Vossian turned and spoke softly to Menninot: 'Carry on here in the house, Ken, room by room, anything you may think to be significant. I haven't been this way before, I don't know what to look for any more than you do. I'm going to the wood.'

Menninot smiled with clenched lips. 'Very good, sir,' he said.

Vossian left the cellar and stepped out into the sunlight. Through the open kitchen door, which had given easily, as Tom Cawtheray had suggested, he saw a dog handler striding through the grass towards him. He walked forward, meeting the man halfway. 'Found something?'

'Yes, sir,' the man replied earnestly, in an agitated manner. 'Right where you said, behind the dead tree.'

'Come along. Show me.'

Vossian and the dog handler returned to the wood. Stepping out of the glare of the sun, the shade of the trees brought the nuisance of flies. Vossian initially brushed them away from his face and then gave up, rapidly learning to tolerate them. The dog handlers had dug away the topsoil, pulled up an ivy plant and removed rubble. They had found a sack cloth, peeled it back and exposed a bundle of bones. 'Didn't take it any further, sir. Saw that and came to get you. The dogs have shown interest in a few other places in the wood, too, sir. We've marked them all.'

Vossian knelt by the hole in the ground. He stood. 'Better get Bill Hatch here,' he said.

Bill Hatch turned his Land Rover into the driveway of Scythe Farm. He drove slowly up to the front of the house and parked between a green Mercedes Benz and a police-dog van. He stepped on to the gravel and screwed a battered Panama on to his head as protection against the sun. Bill Hatch knew from bitter experience that there is no more uncomfortable place on the human body on which to be sunburned than the scalp. Leif Vossian, who with thick golden hair had no need of a hat, strode towards him, tall and slim, striking in the blue suit Hatch noticed he seemed to favour.

'Thanks for coming so promptly, Dr Hatch.' Vossian smiled.

'Not at all. What's the flap about?'

'If you'd like to step this way, I'll put you in the picture.'

Vossian walked side by side with Hatch across the meadow towards the wood. Hatch listened in silence as Vossian put him in the picture. As they approached the wood, close enough to fall under the welcoming shade of the foliage, Vossian said, 'We've located sixteen separate burial pits, all contain bones, little flesh that we can see, not all human though.'

'Oh?'

'No, even we can tell a dog's skull from a human skull, least we think it's a dog's skull. But we haven't excavated anything, thought we'd better bring you in first.'

'Let's have a look at them, then.'

Hatch went from burial pit to burial pit, each marked by blue-and-white police tape tied to nearby trees, each appeared circular, each about two feet down. 'Same pattern in each case.' Vossian knelt beside Hatch as he examined the first pit. 'Each as deep as this, eighteen inches to three feet below the surface. All covered in about a foot or two of rubble, then a soil layer, then a plant placed on the soil layer, usually ivy. Seems like an attempt to prevent the bones being dug up by foxes and to camouflage the burial pit.'

'Seems likely.' Hatch picked up a length of bone. 'Femur,' he said, 'from a child of about three, perhaps four, perhaps two.' He replaced the bone with a reverence that reached Vossian. He walked to the next burial pit, and the next and the next and pronounced on the bones. 'Adult, femur, severed roughly as if by an axe.' 'Child's skull, as you see, about three years, possibly female going by the width of the orbits, but at this age it's not possible to sex accurately having access only to the skull. I'll have to look at the other bones.' 'Dog, as you say. Alsatian, I'd say, distinctive elongated snout, or possibly a collie.' At the sixteenth pit he turned to Vossian. 'Sure this is all?'

'No, frankly. It's all we've found in this wood. There's a thick stand of bramble there which the dogs can't get into, we'll have to clear that before we're certain there's nothing more buried in this wood. It's a huge farm, with two more areas of woodland. They'll have to be searched. We'll do that tomorrow, running out of natural light now, and there's no hurry. They've been down there some years, another night in the clay isn't going to make a deal of difference.'

'That's true. From my point of view, you can begin to excavate the bones. The important thing, the vital thing, is to keep the bones from each pit separate, that is to say, the contents of each pit go into the one production bag, that bag is then sealed and labelled. Don't let the bones from one pit contaminate the bones from another. That would make things difficult for me.'

'Understood.'

'You may also like to draw up a map of the wood, plot

179

the positions of the graves, there may be a pattern that can't be discerned on the ground. But that's really your department.'

'It would have been done anyway.' Vossian felt confused by Hatch's comment. It wasn't at all like the Bill Hatch he knew to tell him his job, but he let the matter ride, deciding to remark upon it only if there was a recurrence.

'I'd be interested to see the cellar.' Hatch and Vossian walked out of the wood, back towards the house.

'If you like.'

'The cages interest me, definitely child-size, you say?'

'Yes, very small, two feet square, something like that.'

'It's professional rather than morbid interest,' Hatch explained. 'You see, if the skeletal remains of those children show age-inappropriate development, malformation, and severe malnutrition, being kept in cages in that manner would go some way to explain that.'

'Well, there's the door.' Vossian nodded to the kitchen door of the Scythe Farmhouse, at which a constable stood. 'The cellar door is in the kitchen. I'm not going in again, not unless I have to, and I know I'll have to at some point.'

Bill Hatch said nothing but walked slowly towards the door, acknowledging the constable in the crisp white shirt who stepped aside to let him pass. Vossian watched him enter the house.

Some moments elapsed. It was a still evening, silent, a sombre mood had settled on the area. The sun was still to sink below the skyline when Hatch reappeared, pale and visibly shaken. He looked at Vossian, held eye contact over the thirty-foot gap which separated them, turned and walked to where he'd parked his Land Rover.

It was Wednesday, 28th July, 21.30 hours.

10

Thursday, 29th July, 18.00 hours – Friday, 30th July, 14.30 hours
Mirrium Devers drove to Wistow. In her head she felt
intense, a sense of being more real than usual, in her stomach
she felt sick. She turned into the drive of the house and was
unconcerned by the disapproving looks of her neighbour.
She left the car and entered the house. Sandy greeted her,
the two women embraced and kissed. Mirrium Devers
looked keenly into her lover's eyes and then pushed the
woman away from her, but kept a grip on her forearm.

'I want space tonight,' Devers told the larger, heavier
woman, 'a meal then space. Understand?'

Sandy Neef made to protest but Devers twisted the skin
of Neef's forearm between her thumb and forefinger. Neef
gasped but Devers continued to twist until Neef said, 'Yes,
Mirrium.'

Ken Menninot drove home to Beverley. He turned into the
ever neat and trim Molescroft Park and halted his car at the
kerb beside his house. His children welcomed him, his wife
kissed him, warmly. He gave his children a little time and
then went to the kitchen, where his wife was stirring the
sauce for the spaghetti bolognese. He took a can of chilled
lager from the fridge.

'Trouble?' asked his wife.

'No!' Menninot snapped. 'It's hot. Do we need spaghetti
on a day . . .' He shook his head. 'Sorry.'

'Problems at work?' His wife laid the wooden spoon on
the work surface and rested her hand on his forearm.

'Yes, in a way of speaking.'

'You're in trouble?'

'No, no. Nothing like that.' He drank deeply from the can.

'It's just that tomorrow we've got a job on. Won't be pleasant. In fact, it'll be sheer bloody awful. Makes me sick to think about it.'

'Oh?'

'Look, it's best I'm out of the way this evening. I don't feel hungry. I'll just walk about. Maybe I'll go down to the Monk's Walk for a pint. I'll get back after the kids will be in bed. Perhaps I'll be hungry by then, if you could put something on one side for me.'

'Yes.' She squeezed his arm. 'You do that, Ken, you take some time out.'

He smiled. He had a lovely wife, even if she didn't understand police work. He knew that. He didn't tell her often enough, he knew that too. Have to rectify that. But right now he'd finish the lager then slip away.

Carmen Pharoah sat against the wall. She was naked, the room basked in the glow of the streetlamp adjacent to her house. She cradled a glass of chilled wine in her hands. 'It's cool against the wall,' she said. 'You should try it.'

'It's OK over here.' Simon Markova stood against the window looking out over Pharoah's back garden, watching a cat move in the shadows. 'The shower was good. You should try that.' He wiped his face and head with the towel Pharoah had provided for him. 'Your garden needs digging.'

'Oh yes? Know the right man for the job, do you?'

The phone rang.

'Let it ring,' said Pharoah. 'The answering machine will get it. See who it is first. If it's bloody Wesley I'll ignore –'

'DI Vossian here,' said a stern metallic-sounding voice after Pharoah's taped answer had played. 'Can you phone me?'

Markova and Pharoah glanced at each other.

'He sounds agitated.' Pharoah reached for the phone. 'This is DC Pharoah speaking.'

'Hate people who do that.'

'Do what?'

'Interrupt messages once they know who's phoning them. Anyway, I need you in tomorrow, six a.m. sharp.'

'Oh.'

'And Markova too. Do you know where he is?'

'Haven't a clue.' Pharoah looked at Markova, glistening in the moonlight, and winked at him.

'Well, we've got Emergency Protection Orders in respect of the children of the Endon families. Principally it's DC Shapiro's case but you'll be aware of it.'

'Yes, sir, I am.'

'It's a joint operation with Social Services. We're lifting the children at seven a.m. Suggest you get a good sleep. It'll be a long day tomorrow.

'And if you should see Markova . . .'

'Of course.' She replaced the receiver and lay on her side on the carpet. 'Clearly some developments on our day off.'

'Oh?'

'Dawn raid on the Endon families. You know, Claire Shapiro's case . . . and Leif says that if by any chance I should see you . . .'

'That guy doesn't miss a lot.'

'You should buy yourself an answering machine. Save a lot of embarrassment.'

Derek Wyatt sat at the table opposite his son. His wife sat in the chair reading. His son moved a chess piece. Wyatt captured it with his knight and slapped his hand on the table. 'Halfwit!'

'Derek . . .' his wife protested.

'I told you, always check every piece on the board before you move. You gave that to me!' Wyatt stood, left the room. Behind him he heard his wife say hurriedly, 'It's all right, Samuel.' Wyatt walked out of the back door and to the far corner of his garden. His wife joined him. '. . . So it's a seven o'clock snatch, a joint with the police. EPOs taken because of the Pyrrah and Hampshire children's disclosures and a statement given by a sex offender in Wakefield trying to get an early parole, but the police think he's genuine. We've had to tee up foster places in Sheffield and Leeds, we have no places left . . . I dreaded ever having to be involved in anything like this. But it's come my way.'

A bat twisted and turned in the evening sky and an owl hooted.

Mirrium Devers couldn't sleep. She slipped out from under the duvet, away from the heavily slumbering Sandy Neef. She pulled on a short towelling bath robe, stole Neef's cigarettes and dainty lighter and left the house, walked barefoot to the road and studied the shapes of the houses in the glow from the streetlamps, clearly visible in the summer's evening. She let the bath robe fall open, it was cooler that way and why not? Three a.m., no one to see her. She then smoked her first cigarette for ten years.

Carmen Pharoah too couldn't sleep. She rose from the bed without waking Markova, dressed and slipped out of the house and walked the streets of York, finding herself at the Minster, walked underneath the towering mass as it loomed in the gloom. She had come to learn the strange Jekyll and Hyde nature of this small city, a place for tourists and families during the day, but violent at night when the colliers and agricultural workers come to the town for their beer. Now, at three a.m., it was slumbering. She walked along St Leonard's. As she walked in front of the Theatre Royal, a police patrol car slowed and crawled beside her, the constable in the passenger seat wound down the window as Carmen Pharoah reached into her handbag and showed her ID. She and the constable smiled to each other and the patrol car drove on without a word being exchanged.

As Carmen Pharoah walked she again noticed how fond the people of York seem to be of flowers arranged in hanging baskets. And as she walked her mind drifted from incidental thing to incidental thing; how the bell-ringers of the Minster always appear to practise on Tuesday evening, how folk-music purists who sing holding their right ear and tell of hardships in the field, or in the factory or at sea, all seem to be computer scientists or teach in a university. She pondered how shamefully wrong it had been that down the centuries many, many young men had died because a handful of their elders hadn't been able to find a solution. And she thought of the nuns who had taught her, of how in those days York had just been a place on the map of England, about halfway up and a bit to the right and now fate had brought her here. What would they think to see her now, the warm and kindly Sister Mary, the terrifying Sister Agnes, walking these silent, grey, twisting, narrow streets as a dreadful day was dawning? What would they think?

Ken Menninot didn't attempt to sleep. He had returned home at eleven p.m., eaten the meal that had been left in a warm oven for him and, knowing that he wouldn't sleep didn't attempt to, but sat in the kitchen, drinking coffee, wondering if he'd done all right in life.

The conference room at Friargate Police Station began to fill as people filed in, some in uniform, some in plain clothes. They settled naturally in two distinct groups, each preferring the company of their own group. The police officers looked with distaste at the social workers, the social workers looked without expression at the police officers. Those holding the Emergency Protection Orders took them out of the envelope, checked them over and returned them to the envelopes. No one spoke. The Minster bells chimed seven. All eyes turned to Leif Vossian. 'All right,' he said, 'you know which teams you're in, you know which teams go to which houses, you know what you've got to do. Right. Let's do it. Go, go, go, go.'

Friday, 30th July, 12.00 hours
The police officers and the social workers sat again in the conference room of Friargate Police Station. Now, unlike five hours previously, they sat as a single group, as if welded by common experience. Many smoked. Many had a faraway look in their eyes. Each relived the events of distraught children, of sometimes, strangely only sometimes, desperate parents.

'There was a ring there. Dare say still is.' Mirrium Devers broke the silence, and also broke a taboo of being a social worker speaking first in a mixed group of police and social workers in a police station, especially when she addressed no one in particular. 'I mean, I went to the Boots' house, the woman opened the door, up and dressed, and you know what she said? She said, "We thought you'd come." ' Devers shook her head. 'She knew we were coming, we hadn't even interviewed her but she knew we were coming to snatch her children.'

'I know what you mean.' Claire Shapiro addressed the group as much as she addressed Devers, and glanced out of the window, flung open in the oppressive heat. 'We had a difficult time in the Riverses' household, trying to get two hysterical children out of the bathroom. They'd locked themselves in and we had to force the door. Then their fingers had to be prised from the radiators, that was messy, but while all that was going on upstairs – you can imagine the commotion – the phone rang. I was standing next to it, without thinking I picked it up and said, "Hello," and the voice on the other end of the line said, "They've got ours, have they got yours yet?" I said, "This is the police," and the person, whoever it was, put the phone down. You're right, Mirrium, the families are linked and they were expecting us.'

'Got tipped off,' said de Larrabeitta. 'Not enough time for them to evacuate, or maybe they want it like this, maybe they want to be martyrs.'

Claire Shapiro ran her fingers through her hair. 'If that's the case, they're going to have a few tricks up their sleeve.'

'I had an easy time,' Carmen Pharoah said. 'We went to the McGuire household and Mrs McGuire told her children to "go with dignity". Those were her very words. At the time we were so grateful that they cooperated, the children came without a struggle, no display of emotion at all. But, you know, by mid-morning I started to think about that. I mean, no parent, especially no mother, no matter how self-possessed, no matter how reserved in her Englishness could compose herself so rapidly, so completely, so as to enable her to tell her children to "go with dignity" the minute her house was invaded by a posse of social workers and police at seven thirty in the morning. It just wouldn't be said in sincerity.'

'It had a rehearsed quality about it.' Markova nodded. 'I was there, same snatch. It was as if it was intended for the media, not her children.'

'Which is a good place for me to come in.' Vossian spoke, silencing the room, but only after he had allowed the group to unload.

'You did an excellent job, you all did a distasteful but necessary job. But see what you did as being in the best interests of the children, the grounds for the EPOs were strong. As people here have just said, there appears to have been a network among those families and they appear to have been waiting for us. That's worrying, so take care who you talk to.' He paused. 'I'm no child psychologist, haven't got a paper qualification to my name, but those children are badly damaged. I saw them put on the coach to take them to their foster homes, they were swearing like troopers . . . a little girl . . . I've heard drunken coal miners who couldn't use bad language the way she was using it. Made the hairs on my head stand on end. Anyway, again, well done.' Vossian paused. He held the pause, then continued. 'Somebody has already mentioned the media. As we speak, a press release is being prepared and after its release I can imagine that newshounds from all over the Western world will be descending on the most fair city of York. Be careful who you speak to. If a journalist approaches you upfront, that's easy, refer him or her to the police or local authority press officer. But newspaper people are as fly as a barrel load of monkeys, so remember, never drop your guard. The great bloke you got into a conversation with in the pub may well be a reporter keen to ply you with alcohol to loosen your tongue; the pretty young thing in a miniskirt who lets you chat her up in the wine bar and gives you the glad eye all the while is probably of the same vocation. So be strict with yourself. If you have to talk about it, talk about it to a colleague. Don't even share it with your partner if you can help it. Chatty husbands and wives have proved a fertile field of information for a resourceful reporter before now. Careless talk could blow this case before it gets to court. So for a third time, well done, please now return to normal duties. To those who've been asked to come in on a day off, thank you. I hope you can rescue something of it.'

It was Friday, 30th July, 12.30 hours.

Friday, 30th July, 13.30 hours
Bill Hatch read over his report on his postmortem findings on the bones which had been excavated from the wood behind Scythe Farm. He had been able to identify twelve infant corpses, the bones of which showed signs of malnutrition, and the teeth of one infant had an unusual eruption pattern leading to pronounced buck teeth which could have been easily corrected had the child come to the attention of the National Health Service. The only inference that Hatch could draw from this was that the child's existence had been a guarded secret. The remains of two adults had also been disinterred, one male, one female. The bones had been hacked, possibly after death, possibly to allow the bones to be buried in a smaller space. In the cases of the adults, the skulls were absent, thus preventing any possible identification by means of dental records. The remaining groups of disinterred bones had belonged to animals, dogs and cats, and a goat. Tantalizingly, intriguingly, harrowingly, a femur, possibly from an adult male, had been found amongst the goat's bones. Hatch picked up the phone on his desk and dialled Friargate Police Station. As he did so his eye was caught by a pale-blue open-topped sports car cruising out of York along Wigginton Road; a driver and his slender passenger enjoying life. 'DI Vossian, please,' he said when his call connected.

'Vossian.' Said in a growl.

'Bill Hatch. I've got my report here of my findings of the examination of the bones found in the wood on the farm. Thought you might want to hear the gist of it before it's faxed. Not able to identify the cause of deaths in any of the cases, though.'

'No matter. What did you find?'

Bill Hatch told him.

*   *   *

Simon Markova returned home at two fifteen p.m., picked up his mail from his hall carpet: two bills, a letter from his bank reminding him about his overdraft and two unsolicited envelopes of junk mail. He went into the front room of his house and flung the curtains wide, sunlight streamed blindingly through the net curtains, flies trapped between the net curtains and the glass buzzed angrily. He glanced out over the playing fields and watched a group of boys stripped to the waist playing soccer. He wondered at their ability to run at all in the heat, let alone play soccer. At a greater distance but still on the playing fields a second group of boys played cricket. More sensible, he thought, turning to the settee and lying on it, intending only half an hour's nap. In the event, sleep overwhelmed him and he had a dream about being charged by a bull elephant which burst out of a thicket and came at him demon-like. So real, so vivid was the dream that when he awoke he recalled with clarity the lines furrowing the animal's brow as it came on, and the blue sky behind the beast, and so real was the dream that for some minutes after he woke he still felt the actual and sudden fear caused by it and his hands were still trembling as he made a cup of coffee. He drank the coffee in his kitchen, sitting at the breakfast bar leafing through the previous day's edition of the *Yorkshire Post* and gradually the sense of fear gave way to anger that he'd slumbered so long, waking at five thirty. The whole afternoon gone. He'd be in good form in the pub that night if he went, but his sleep pattern had been confused, he knew he'd have difficulty waking at five a.m. to be at Friargate for six for the start of the early shift. Mug of coffee in hand, he returned to the front room and sat in front of his modestly sized television. Hating Australian soap operas more than he thought it possible for a man to hate anything, he waited until six p.m. before switching on the set. The Endon snatch hadn't merely made the six o'clock national news, it was the lead story.

'Children from four separate families living in the Endon district to the east of the City of York were taken from their homes in a dawn raid by police and social workers, it was confirmed today,' said the seriously countenanced schoolmaster-like newsreader. 'Neither the police nor the Social Services would say why the children were removed nor would they confirm rumours that Satanic practices were involved. Phil Box has this report.'

The report then cut to a white-shirted reporter standing, microphone in hand, in front of the quarry at the edge of the Trafford Estate. 'This,' said the reporter in earnest, indignant tones, 'is the quarry where children are alleged to have been abused by their parents . . .'

Simon Markova's jaw opened in disbelief.

'. . . it is here in this shallow quarry, dry at present due to the drought conditions, but normally half full of water, at the edge of a housing estate that children as young as five have allegedly been made to dance round a cloaked figure who would hook them with a shepherd's crook and pull them towards him in order to commit acts of a sexual nature . . . the parents have been denied access to their children and have not been told where they are being held. This is Phil Box for television news.'

The newscaster said, 'And we'll bring you more of that story as it develops. Now today's other news . . .'

Simon Markova's phone rang. He leaned to one side and picked it up.

'It's Carmen.' She spoke before he could answer.

'Yes, I've just seen it.' He guessed easily why she had phoned.

'The parents have been talking to the press. Clever. Oh, so clever.'

'I know.'

'We never pointed a finger at that quarry, not to my knowledge.'

'We didn't, Claire Shapiro just believes it's a quarry somewhere. But can't identify it from the children's drawings, except that it's a car ride from Endon, but not a distant car ride because the car always appears crammed full. No more than fifteen or twenty minutes' drive, she thinks – the quarry that the media's been shown is five minutes' walk from Endon.'

'Apart from the fact it's full of water and strewn with

rubble, if you tried to dance there you'd break your ankles. And it's so easily overlooked.'

'But they've done what they set out to do, the media's swallowed it, and we and Social Services have been discredited at the outset. The parents have manipulated the media.'

Carmen Pharoah gasped down the phone. 'Makes me want to pick up the phone and put the press right.'

'Well, don't.' Markova spoke sternly. 'Remember what Leif said, and he's right to have said it. If you speak to the press, even anonymously, you'll contaminate the evidence and blow the case when it comes to be heard. It also occurs to me that that's what the parents are trying to goad us into doing.'

'Of course, of course . . .' Pharoah paused, collecting herself. 'Yes, I can see that now, if they can bring on a trial by media the Crown's case will be shot. I'm glad I phoned you, I might have destroyed everything in my anger . . . heavens, what I nearly did . . .'

'Got to be like Dad,' said Markova, allowing his smile to be heard down the phone. 'Keep mum. That's the ticket.'

'I want to get drunk tonight.' Carmen Pharoah spoke calmly, matter-of-factly.

'Aye, I think there'll be a few people on both sides of the case getting ratted tonight. You coming here, or am I going there? Lady's choice.'

'I'll come to yours. I'm fed up of these walls.'

Ken Menninot walked down the narrow corridor to Leif Vossian's office. He tapped on the open door.

'Hello, Ken.' Leif glanced up and then returned his attention to the report he was reading. 'The fax of Bill Hatch's report has come through, says everything he said on the phone. Bones of very young children in the main, two adults and a few small animals. He points out that one child had badly protruding teeth which could have been easily attended to. He speculates from this that that particular child's existence wasn't known to the health services.'

'More children out there than we know about indeed.'

191

'He's also not able to determine cause of death.' Vossian laid the report down.

'Poor wee snappers. Anyway, I thought you might like to know that the Cardiff Police have phoned us. They impounded a car that had been left outside Cardiff Central Railway Station . . .'

'Not a Fiat, perchance?'

'That's it. Registered to one Lady Cynthia Harrby . . . probably been there for a few days. The Welsh boys took it into their pound, did the checks, found out about the warrants.'

'So they're in Wales?'

'They were, could be anywhere in Europe by now. I think the only safe thing we can assume is that they're travelling on public transport.'

'How the mighty have fallen. Imagine the Right Hon and his Lady actually having to queue for a sandwich.' Vossian gave one of his rare smiles. 'Do them the power of good.'

'Boss . . .'

'Yes, Ken?'

'The file. I did put it away.'

'I know you did, Ken. It's strange it wasn't replaced by whoever accessed it.'

'You do have a heavy footfall you know, boss, there's plenty of blind corners in this old building. If whoever it was heard you coming and hotfooted it . . .'

'Possibly, we'll never know, but let's keep that incident between you and me; if it should get out that there's a Satanist in the nick morale will plummet. I've already asked Wakefield to keep a special watch on Peep. A prosecution's going to hinge on his evidence, a statement of a dead man won't be allowed.'

'Can't be challenged by the defence.'

'That's it. Sometimes I wonder whether it's all worth it, Ken, such is the Law's fear of unsafe prosecutions that our job is made virtually impossible at times.'

It was Friday, 30th July, 18.30 hours.

One Day in December

11

9.00–9.15 hours, Tuesday, 17th December
Leif Vossian knelt by the grave in Fulford cemetery and plucked weeds from the gravel. The wind tugged at his hair, an easterly, a biter, it seeped into his clothes, chillingly, and caused dried leaves and discarded plastic bags to fly, a few feet from the ground, over the cemetery. He could not help addressing the headstone. 'This is the worst bit for me,' he said, and forced a smile. 'But I'll get through, coming up for Christmas. I mean I miss you all, all of the time, a second doesn't pass without me missing you, each day, all day, every day, I miss you, but Christmas is the worst. You know, no matter how much I try and pretend that Christmas Day is just another day with bells on, it never really works. The worst is staying in. I'm not working this Christmas either, my turn to be off for the two days, Christmas Day and Boxing Day at home for me. I mean, I can't go up the Fleece for a beer on Christmas lunchtime because I'd just stand by myself while everyone else is in family groups wearing their new clothes that they bought each other. The whole pub will smell like a clothes shop on Christmas Day lunch, and I'll be there announcing to the world that I'm alone at Christmas, so no thanks. But I don't care about myself, don't get me wrong, it's you I care about. You should be at home at Christmas, we didn't have enough Christmases together, not nearly enough . . . I don't know where you are. I'm not a Christian, not really, but I've heard enough about ghosts and paranormal happenings to believe that there's something else after this mess . . . I mean, there's got to be, this can't be all there is to it.' He ran his fingers through his golden hair. 'I suppose I could really talk to you anywhere but I come here for some reason . . . So do you know the answer now? The secret of

life . . . What do you see from where you are? Anyway, that's the trial over, suppose you know that, I suppose you saw it. I know now what they mean by media circus, and the papers this morning "Home for Christmas" after the defence tore the prosecution apart. Made them look ridiculous, made the prosecution case look like a wild fairy story. Mind you, I confess I was surprised they went ahead with the trial after Peep got it in the neck.' Vossian stopped plucking the weeds and rested his elbows on his knees. 'Aye . . . something strange happened there all right and no mistake. We'll never know the truth, but then that's been the feeling of this case all along. It's been like groping in a fog for something tangible. It's as though we could smell it, taste it, hear it, whatever "it" was, but we couldn't get hold of it. It's been like looking down a dark street and seeing figures moving in the shadows. But Peep, getting it like that, two other lags in the VPU did him in, kicked the life out of him, really making sure. They said he was a beast, but I mean, so were they, they're all beasts on the VPU. But what got me is that as soon as Peep was cold their families moved out of their council high-rise and into the suburbs, and would they say where the money came from? And those two guys that filled Peep in, they want to put their hands up to involuntary manslaughter and the CPS will buy it, I reckon. One very inexpensive conviction and it does wrap it up. Those lags will get about seven years for that and being as they're near the beginning of a fifteen-year stretch anyway . . . well, it's one way of getting away with murder, if you ask me . . .' He glanced up at the rooftops of the houses of Fulford, a dark cloud threatened rain. 'I'll be away now, love, but I'll be back.' He stood. 'They should've dropped the charges when Peep died. I mean, he was our star witness to all sorts of goings-on . . . Peep would have clinched it. Maybe they felt that they had to go to trial after all the publicity which surrounded the snatch. Couldn't do that then, not go to trial, couldn't do that, keep the kids incommunicado from their parents and then return them without so much as a by your leave . . . no, couldn't do that, I suppose, had to go to trial with or without Peep.' Rain began to fall, heavily, vertically.

'Well, that's it. I'll be back before Christmas, in fact, yes, aye, that's what I'll do, and I'll call back on the day itself. I wonder will you wait for me, wherever you are.' He turned his collar against the rain. 'But we could have done it with Peep.'

Sandy Neef stood in the kitchen of their house and looked out of the window at the windswept garden, a garden of massive proportions in comparison to the size of the gardens that belonged to houses in the city. But that in a sense, she reflected, was why she and Mirrium had come out to Wistow, out to the sticks, for space, emotional as well as physical. They hadn't bargained for the local hostility towards two women such as they, but they had kept themselves to themselves and had in turn been left alone as if disapproved of from a distance. At the foot of the garden looking small was the black coated figure of Mirrium Devers, with her back to the house, blending with the winter landscape. She was angry. Sandy Neef could tell she was angry. She had returned home yesterday angry, spent the night fuming, had phoned her work that morning feigning sickness and had gone out, stood at the bottom of the garden looking out over ploughed fields on a flat landscape under a dark and foreboding sky. Neef watched as Devers snatched a cigarette from her mouth and held it beside her in a stiffly extended arm, and then put it to her mouth again in jerky, fast movements. Yes, she was angry, she'd be angry for days and Neef knew better than to crowd her. At times like this Mirrium Devers needed much space, if peace was to be maintained.

Neef had known Devers would be angry as soon as she had heard the news of the not-guilty verdict and saw footage of the victorious parents giving impromptu press conferences on the pavement outside the County Court, promising to sue the City of York Social Services, and doubtless negotiating the price for their stories with the tabloids. She knew that the intimidation of her personally hadn't distressed Mirrium – Mirrium was strong enough to withstand being followed by well-dressed men driving Range Rovers and Rolls Royces, who spoke on vodaphones while she stopped her little car and made a call from a public call box. That had not upset Mirrium, nor had the ringing of their phone at three a.m., nor the dead cat on their doorstep. Those were challenges that Mirrium Devers could rise to and take in her stride, she could blow them from the palm of her hand. Maybe 'they' knew, thought Neef, pouring boiling water on to the coffee granules and glancing again at the statue-still figure of Mirrium Devers as the rain began to fall. Maybe that's why 'they' turned on the foster homes. God only knows how 'they' found out where the children had been accommodated, but they did. As in the foster parents in Sheffield who, assured that the parents didn't know where the children were, had taken them to a supermarket where they were approached by a man who said, 'Hello, children,' and who had then turned and walked away. The children, delighted to see him, identified him as 'Uncle David from Exeter'. Enough, Neef thought, lifting the coffee to her lips, for any foster parent. More frightening perhaps was the story, which had shaken Devers, of the foster mother raising her household in the morning, noticing a draught from the attic. She investigated, found the dormer window open, the musk of a man in the room, and the indentation of a prostrate body on the spare bed. 'They' not only knew where the children were accommodated, but could actually penetrate the foster homes. That was more than enough for any foster parent. The foster placements collapsed one after the other and the children had to be accommodated together in children's homes, where, according to the defence, they had talked with each other and so had contaminated each other's evidence. The children's testimony was neatly discredited. Mirrium said it at the time, 'they've' got what they wanted, made it so the children's statements couldn't be relied on. Mirrium had seen it coming, as soon as the foster placements broke down she had realized what 'their' game was. And she'd been proven correct. Now she needed space. Lots of space.

David Sant had often wondered how Simon Markova could cope with it and then he had found that, after living in a failing relationship, to then live alone is sheer bliss. He reclined on the settee and sipped at the mug of coffee. It was just such little things that he appreciated. Throughout his marriage, Carla had insisted that they should drink beverages out of dainty cups; now he could clutch a mug in his meaty palm as he was able to do at work. Even now, after all these weeks, going into months, he still felt the sensation of a weight slipping off his shoulders. So, he had been right, Carla had left him and she had taken Christopher and the two of them had moved in with her mother. Her mother lived locally and so he had been able to see Christopher often and had noticed that since the separation his son had seemed calmer and more alert, clearly benefiting from being removed from a highly stressed household. Those couples, thought Sant, those couples who remain together 'for the sake of the children' couldn't be more wrong to do so. The divorce proceedings had commenced and he had reverted to being David Sant, to the delight of his father, and to his own delight, for now the Sant line may perhaps continue after all. The name de Larrabeitta had come to make him cringe and feel contaminated.

He pondered Gerald Peep getting it in the neck like he did. Even being on the Vulnerable Prisoners Unit hadn't saved him. Strange how that had happened, he thought, strange indeed. And he thought too of how distressed the children had been when they were told that they would be returning home. The only compensation being that those weeks in local authority care had given them a different message about themselves, about their worth and their importance. He was left with the feeling that the game wasn't over yet.

'The sheer enormity of it.' Bill Hatch curled his fingers round Sam's ears as the Labrador jumped up on to the settee and nestled beside him. 'If you ask me.'

'Well, I did ask you.' Veronica came back at him, quickly, smugly, alert despite the early hour. He had noticed that she had developed such an attitude since she had commenced university. He didn't like it and he felt frustrated that he couldn't do anything about it; the years when she could be sent to her room until her attitude improved were long gone. 'The enormity? What do you mean?'

'The jury just didn't want to believe it and as the defence scorned and undermined the prosecution case it became easier and easier and more comfortable not to believe it and so they acquitted the parents. It didn't mean, though, that the prosecution was wrong. It meant the prosecution wasn't believed.' He didn't look at Veronica as he replied to her, here now for the Christmas and New Year vacation, and no plans to go anywhere, no plans even to visit Nadine in Staffordshire. It was going to be a long few weeks until the Easter term began. 'It's the phenomena of human beings disbelieving what is outside their comprehension, like the Aborigines who were fishing in the shallows of the northern coast of what is now called Australia as Captain Cook's ship . . .'

'*The Endeavour*.'

'That's it, as it approached and dropped anchor just off-shore. They glanced at it and went on fishing. They had no comprehension of a ship so large and so they ignored it, but when the crew of *The Endeavour* launched a long boat, and commenced an activity on a smaller scale that the Aborigines could understand, then they attacked the long boat. It's a bit like that, if you ask me.'

'Oh.' Veronica Hatch reached for her copy of *Cosmopolitan*. 'I think I know what you mean.' She opened the magazine and hid behind it.

Bill Hatch sighed and stood. He went outside, with Sam at his heels. He walked in his garden in the fresh morning rain. One man and his dog, and two contented pigs in an orchard.

Carmen Pharoah also walked in the rain, and decided to remain in York, at least, she thought, at least for the time being. Then she realized that she hadn't made a decision at all, rather a decision had been made for her. She had just spent an exhausting hour trying to comfort Claire Shapiro, who was distressed at the thought of what the children were returning to, and had then walked out into the rain-soaked greasy streets. It was then that she had realized that she had not made a decision. There was no decision to be made. There was no option but to stay, because to leave now would be running away. It might, just might have been different if they had won the case, then she could have left York leaving a victory behind her. She glanced at the Christmas lights hung across the streets, flashing in the shop windows even in the mornings, and felt how hollow they were, how meaningless. To leave York now would mean that she would not be leaving on her terms. When the time came for her to leave this small, feudal, quaint and violent town she would leave on her terms and her terms alone. So she would stay, turn her little house into a home, with the decorative, one-wing-down Simon Markova for company. He would, she thought, do very nicely. She walked from Friargate into the bustle of Coppergate and as she did so her thoughts once again returned unbidden to the trial. She wondered when it had begun to go wrong? Each person to whom she had spoken seemed to have had their own idea about the point that the case began to falter, but for Carmen Pharoah it all began to go wrong when the fifteen-year-old girl of the Dovedales retracted her statement, given weeks earlier and in tears as relief flooded into her. She was to have been a key witness but when she climbed into the witness box she said she had told the social workers what she had thought they wanted to hear and then said she'd obtained video nasties and shown them to the younger children, 'and that's how we all got to know about devils and stuff'. And she had spoken in the state of rigid terror of the classic intimidated witness. Carmen Pharoah also thought of Sam Meadows cycling his round in Endon and upon returning to Friargate reporting how the houses of all the families in the circle had suddenly sprouted 'for sale' signs, and that at the commencement of the trial, as though they were certain of the outcome, of the return of their children. Strange, she thought, they came apparently already known to each other, now they were leaving as a distinct group. Very, very strange.

It was when the guest had not come down for breakfast that

Gwen Davies first became concerned. Normally the woman came down at eight thirty sharp as she had done with her husband when he too was in the hotel. So punctual that Gwen Davies felt that she could set her watch by her. An English couple, soft spoken, quiet, they had always seemed preoccupied. They had been in the habit of leaving the hotel soon after breakfast and returning in the mid-evening. Gwen Davies had seen them once or twice, walking, just walking arm in arm, not talking, but always with that look of constant preoccupation. But this is Rhyll, off season, when any guest is welcome, and quiet, well-mannered, hard-cash-in-advance guests like the Coopers were especially welcome. Preoccupied or not, Mrs Davies had on more than one occasion found herself wishing she had a hotel full of the likes of Mr and Mrs Cooper.

Then Mr Cooper had left. Mrs Davies sat in the kitchen of the hotel waiting for Mrs Cooper to come down to breakfast and as she waited she pondered Mr Cooper's leaving. Ten, eleven days ago, she thought, he had left in the company of three men, quietly and without fuss, or so she had observed from her seat behind the reception desk, but there was something in the manner of his leaving, following one of the three men, with the other two walking side by side behind him, that gave her the impression that he was being escorted away. She had observed the men get into a car, a huge gleaming black vehicle which had driven away slowly, unhurriedly, as if the occupants had all the time in the world to reach their destination. After Mr Cooper had left, Mrs Cooper seemed to Gwen Davies to have become withdrawn. She still came down for breakfast at eight thirty, but if she went out at all she would only go out for about thirty minutes. Most of the time she remained in her room, vacating it only to allow it to be cleaned. Nonetheless, she remained in the hotel, kept the same double room she had occupied with her husband and continued to pay for her accommodation in advance, in cash.

At nine fifteen Gwen Davies went up to Mrs Cooper's room and tapped reverentially on the door. 'Only ten minutes left for breakfast, Mrs Cooper.'

No reply.

Gwen Davies knocked again.

No reply.

Gwen Davies tried the door. It opened.

Mrs Cooper lay on the bed. Fully clothed, quite still, with a plastic bag over her head. Gwen Davies caught her breath and stared at the body and then at the bedside cabinet on which lay cash in coins and notes, a bunch of car keys and two driving licences, both in the name of Harrby. Cynthia and Nigel Harrby. 'Harrby,' Gwen Davies spoke to herself. 'No, never mind, never mind that.' She closed the door. 'Call the police, got to call the police, let them sort it out.' She hurried towards the stairs. 'They'll know what to do.'

She wondered if there would be a ghost?

It was 09.15 hours, Tuesday, 17th December.